Trouble
in
Nirvana

by

Elisabeth Rose

Trouble in Nirvana

Cover Art by *Kim Mendoza*

The Wild Rose Press, Inc.
PO Box 708
Adams Basin, NY 14410-0708
Visit us at www.thewildrosepress.com

Publishing History
First Champagne Rose Edition, 2013
Print ISBN 978-1-61217-774-8
Digital ISBN 978-1-61217-775-5

Published in the United States of America

"You from the city?" His eyes flashed over her bare shoulders and neck.

"Yes. Why?" Awkward under his scrutiny, Primrose slid in to the car and clicked her seatbelt. Sexy? Definitely. Friendly? No.

"What are you going there for?"

"Visiting my brother." No response. He just stood there waiting, looking at her assets as though she were a piece of livestock until she felt compelled to add, "And I need a break from...things."

For the first time he smiled but it was really more of a scoffing little snort. "Hope you've got other shoes."

Her jaw clenched, relaxed. She licked her lips and took her sunglasses from the ledge in the dashboard. "Is it the next driveway on this side of the road?"

"Yes. About three k's. Called Nirvana." This time his lips tightened as though trying to stifle a laugh. "There's a peace sign on the gate post." He made peace sign sound synonymous with swastika.

"Thank you. I'm sorry I bothered you. Goodbye." She started the engine. He closed the door and stepped back as she swung the Golf in a circle. Her sweaty hands slid on the wheel so she nearly ran over the dog. It put on a little spurt of speed to get out of range.

When she looked in the rearview mirror he was staring after her, hands on hips, partially obscured by whirling white dust. No way would she show her face here again. He'd laugh that mocking, scornful laugh. Attractive he may be and if he smiled and wasn't so patronising she might well melt at his feet. But! Didn't think a city girl could manage on a farm? Dismissed her as useless based on her shoes? Country yokel!

Praise for Elisabeth Rose

Dedication

To Colin, Carla, Nick, and Paige

Chapter One

A plume of dust curled behind the car in an elegant tail as Primrose drove, scanning the paddocks on the left for a communal looking property. Danny hadn't given proper directions in his scrawled response to her letter, just "*ask for Danny's place at the Kullanurra pub*" and the woman there had said, "*it's about eight or nine kilometres from the Majura Road turn-off. On the left.*"

She glanced at the odometer. Seven point eight. Nearly there. A neat white signboard on a gate announced *Fairview*. More prosaic name than she'd expected but it looked perfect. The narrow driveway led to a well-shaded house with wide verandas, rainwater tanks, sheds, a barn and further on what looked like fruit trees and a large green patch of vegetable garden. Solar panels glinted on the roof and a wind turbine revolved briskly in the hot breeze.

Surprisingly impressive. The place had an inviting air of refuge and peace. Just what her battered heart and severely bruised ego needed. Big brother Danny had always been the spiritual one in their shambles of a family. The one who wanted life to be simple, based on need rather than want, in search of happiness while she was intent on perfection, her career. Perhaps he would be the guru she needed. Maybe, despite all prior signs to the contrary, he'd had it right all along.

Primrose parked under one of three large gumtrees by the house yard fence and got out of the car. Cicadas roared from the branches. She wiped grit from her mouth as a swirl of dust surrounded her. Sandy grains caught in the toe of her sandal and lodged uncomfortably under her foot. Already the shiny red leather was coated, and the soles were too thin to prevent the uneven stony ground from digging into her feet. She lifted the hatchback, dragged out her suitcase, slung her flute carry case over her shoulder and struggled across to the house.

A grey cattle dog came out from under the verandah to bark lazily, tail wagging. Primrose scanned the sheds and house for signs of life. Not much activity. How many people lived here at the moment? Two at least—Danny and Nirupam. Her image of the commune had been an enthusiastic group of five or six all working in peaceful harmony, hoeing the fields or picking fruit, making goat's milk cheese or potting honey from the hives.

Maybe Nirupam was in the house. She lugged the case through a sweet smelling arch of honeysuckle which covered the gate, using both hands to heave the suitcase up the wide wooden steps. Big, overflowing terracotta pots of parsley and herbs lined the verandah edge, lending a Tuscan villa air.

The dog sniffed her ankles. She risked a quick pat on its head. The tail wagged faster.

Primrose peered in through the screen door. The interior of the house beckoned cool, dark and inviting in stark contrast to the harsh glare outside. She rapped on the doorframe. Nothing. Again. Silence. The dog panted by her side for a moment then wandered away and collapsed in a heap.

"Hello?" She tried the door handle tentatively. The door swung open.

"Danny? Nirupam?" Primrose dragged her case through, blinking in the reduced light, and exhaled with relief as the cooler air caressed her overheated skin.

To the left through open frosted glass double doors was a living room. To the right lay a room with a desk and surprisingly, a computer. She could have emailed Danny instead of using snail mail. Why didn't he say? The answer brought a wry smile—because he would be anti technology. But there sat a computer. His?

"Anyone home?" She stepped tentatively along the corridor, peeped into an open door. A bedroom. Where was everyone? She needed a wash and the loo. Surely they wouldn't mind if she used the bathroom. They might not return to the house for hours. The front door was open—a welcoming sign which gave credence to the belief she was expected.

A little passage opened to the right with a door ajar. The bathroom—large and old fashioned with a shower over the tub and a black and white tiled chessboard floor.

She must look like something from a horror movie. A quick shower would be the go. Before the others came in and got the fright of their lives. Primrose stripped off shorts, sweaty T-shirt and underwear and stuffed them into a plastic bag brought expressly for the purpose, stepped carefully over the high side of the tub, and turned on the taps.

Wonderful! Very tempting to linger but no. A scrub with the cake of plain, yellow soap, rinse off and out. Primrose congratulated herself as she wielded her towel. Conserving water. She was already doing her bit as a responsible member of the commune.

Clean and fresh in a blue cotton sundress she turned her attention to her face. Moisturiser with built in sunscreen. Crucial in these conditions. The sun was vicious, not to mention the horrible dust. Deodorant, also crucial. Teeth cleaned using a bare minimum of water, a mouthful at most. Tasted different, soft and slightly metallic. A quick application of lipgloss. Spritz of perfume. Done. Now she was fit to meet her new companions. External body clean, internal ready to be scrubbed.

Primrose zipped up her case and opened the bathroom door. She'd move her things to the living room until someone came in and showed her to her room. She stepped into the hallway.

"Good afternoon," said a masculine voice from the other side of the screen door.

She turned toward the voice, her suitcase thumped into her legs and her flute and handbag swung awkwardly from her shoulder. She squinted at the man's dark outline against the glare of the yard outside. Not Danny. Too tall. Another of the communalists? He opened the screen and stepped inside, immediately filling the little foyer with his presence.

The collision with the suitcase must have disabled her legs because they suddenly weren't holding her up too well and something had affected her breathing. Who knew they hid hunks like this out in the country? He wasn't what she'd expected here. He wasn't what she'd expect anywhere. Dream of, maybe.

Average height, dark-haired, narrow angular face creased around the eyes by wind and glare. Plain, dirt smudged beige shirt hanging loose from broad shoulders over khaki shorts, well-shaped tanned legs ending in dusty work boots. Something indefinably sexy about the whole package.

"Who are you?" Dark eyes examined her from the feet up, stopped at her face, waited for an answer. No hint of a welcome.

She inhaled and air reached her lungs again. A friendly smile should help. "Primrose Pretty. I'm Danny's sister. Is he here?"

"No."

As he continued to stare, a thought formed and grew in her mind like an over enthusiastic fungus. A most embarrassing thought. One of the most unimaginably humiliating thoughts she'd ever thought. Had she invited herself into a total stranger's house for a shower?

He said, "This is a proper farm. Nirvana is next door."

Nirvana? Was that some kind of sarcastic joke? But he wasn't laughing. That stare signified annoyance. Primrose returned it with cool aplomb, masking, with any luck, her total, heart pounding embarrassment. Thank goodness she hadn't washed her hair. He need never know the full extent of her invasion.

"I'm sorry. No-one answered my knock so I came in and called out. I made a mistake. I'll go." As fast as she darn well could.

She hitched up the shoulder bags, charged around him, pushed the screen door open with her elbow, dragged her suitcase through. The man strode forward, took it from her and swung the deadweight down the steps as though the bag were empty. He marched across to her car, little puffs of dust punctuating each decisive footfall. The dog jogged across, wagging its tail and smiling, red tongue lolling.

Primrose followed, edging around the dog which had stopped right in her path.

"She won't bite you." He popped the hatch and lifted her bag inside then closed the door with a firm click.

"Thanks." Primrose opened the driver's door. Her clean feet were dusty already. "I'm sorry, Mr...."

"Tom Fairbrother." Still not the hint of a smile and no extended hand to shake. Fairbrother—explained Fairview. He needed a haircut. A flop of brown hair dropped across his forehead softening the angles of his face. Her heart did a little tango all by itself. He pushed the hair back with an irritated gesture. "Are you joining the commune?"

"For a while."

He stared down at her, brow wrinkled then smoothed as the information passed into his brain and was processed. "You from the city?" His eyes flashed over her bare shoulders and neck.

"Yes. Why?" Awkward under his scrutiny, Primrose slid in to the car and clicked her seatbelt. Sexy? Definitely. Friendly? No.

"What are you going there for?"

"Visiting my brother." No response. He just stood there waiting, looking at her assets as though she were a piece of livestock until she felt compelled to add, "And I need a break from...things."

For the first time he smiled but it was really more of a scoffing little snort. "Hope you've got other shoes."

Her jaw clenched, relaxed. She licked her lips and took her sunglasses from the ledge in the dashboard. "Is it the next driveway on this side of the road?"

"Yes. About three k's. Called Nirvana." This time his lips tightened as though trying to stifle a laugh. "There's a peace sign on the gate post." He made peace sign sound synonymous with swastika.

"Thank you. I'm sorry I bothered you. Goodbye." She started the engine. He closed the door and stepped back as she swung the Golf in a circle. Her sweaty hands slid on the wheel so she nearly ran over the dog. It put on a little spurt of speed to get out of range.

When she looked in the rearview mirror he was staring after her, hands on hips, partially obscured by whirling white dust. No way would she show her face here again. He'd laugh that mocking, scornful laugh. Attractive he may be and if he smiled and wasn't so patronising she might well melt at his feet. But! Didn't think a city girl could manage on a farm? Dismissed her as useless based on her shoes? Country yokel!

She was almost glad she'd used his shower. Weren't country people supposed to be friendly and open? Welcoming visitors? Tom Fairbrother looked at her as though she were a plague carrier. The pox of the city. Might infect him with some civilised behaviour.

By the time Primrose reached the road and turned left for Nirvana she was so angry she accelerated too fast and nearly spun out on the next corner. The shock of a giant, fast approaching gumtree calmed her into a more sensible speed until minutes later the peace symbol, weather worn and faded, announced she'd arrived. The name Nirvana was almost invisible on a board propped upside down against the fence.

7

Danny's driveway was two narrow tracks just wide enough for the wheels and with a strip of dry tussocky grass in between which scraped alarmingly at the undercarriage. The two threads wound away through the trees, over a little rise and then up a steeper rocky hill. The car clawed its way to the top then the house and accompanying sheds spread before her.

Derelict. The only word which sprang to mind. Squatting amongst gum trees the house was a plain rectangle of silver grey weatherboard so beaten by wind and rain and dust the walls were bare of paint except for another peace symbol wonky and misshapen sprayed on the front door. An ancient mud coloured couch sat on the verandah along with a couple of old wooden straight back chairs. The corrugated iron roof had been red once. The paint job probably dated from the time Mum's eccentric old stepfather lived here in his isolated lunacy.

A falling down fence with an open gate enclosed the house and the remains of a garden, now overgrown with weeds save for one lusty white climbing rose hanging over the verandah railing and some straggling pink geraniums against the wall. Bits and pieces of unidentifiable machinery parts lay about, propped against the shed or neglected to rust on the ground under the trees.

Heart sagging, Primrose drove down the slope. Stones and tree litter created an obstacle course and a gaping pothole set her jolting, breath held. Away to the side was a cultivated patch of cleared land with green things growing. Someone stooped over some kind of agricultural machine in the middle of the plot. Hens wandering about, scratching in the dry dusty ground in front of the house yard, scattered in a flurry of white and brown when the car appeared in their midst. She parked in the shade and turned off the engine. Sat for a moment staring. Disappointment clagged in her belly. Wind chimes tinkled gently amidst the roar of cicadas. Delicate and pretty, as out of place here as she was.

Rough wood and corrugated iron structures huddled amongst the trees. Two black goats peered at her through a rickety stretch of post and rail fencing attached to the nearest shed which housed a beaten up old white Kombi van and a nondescript yellow ute. A cute little sheep strutted out from behind the shed and stared. Round and woolly with little ears sticking up from the tight curls on its head. "Baaaaa," it said.

Primrose got out of the car. The person in the garden straightened up and stared her way. Too far to see if it was Danny but he was too broad shouldered and big. She walked toward the house swatting at the hovering flies. An engine roared from the patch of garden.

The sheep trotted toward her. Primrose smiled. Sweet. A pet sheep.

"Baaaa." The trot turned into a gallop. A charge. It lowered its head. An attack sheep. The realisation came too late. She made a dash for the gate in the fence around the house. If she could shut that the sheep would be thwarted. Heart pounding, legs fuelled by a burst of adrenalin she scrambled through the gap and grabbed hold of the wooden gate. Choked with grass it wouldn't budge.

The sheep galloped through and rammed its hard bony skull into her knees.

"Get away!" she shrieked. "Help!"

The sheep butted again. She lifted a foot, braced herself against the gate and pushed at the solid little body but her attacker jammed its feet into the ground and shoved back with lowered head. It stank. A rank greasy wool odour mixed with manure. Flies buzzed around them both.

Primrose ran for the verandah steps yelling, "Danny! Help!"

The sheep scampered after her, sprang up the steps and whacked into her legs again before she could open the screen door.

Scuffling footsteps sounded from inside. A dim shape appeared through the ripped flyscreen. "Sammy won't hurt you," said a tired female voice. "He likes to play."

She held the door open for Primrose to dart through. The sheep stood on the verandah glaring in at her and tossing its head, stamped a hoof in annoyance.

Panting, Primrose took proper stock of her rescuer. Long brown hair hanging limply straight on either side of a thin freckled face. Pale blue eyes dark shadowed with weariness, crooked toothed smile.

"Nirupam!"

"Hello, Rosie."

"How are you?" Primrose hugged her sister-in-law, feeling narrow angular shoulders and...what? She stepped back and looked. The faded pink Indian cotton dress which revealed scrawny pale arms and bony collarbones, draped over an unmistakable bulge. "Pregnant?" She bit back the surge of envy.

She and Martin had planned on babies. The idea had grown and blossomed in her mind the closer the wedding came. A soft, sweet-smelling child of her own

10

to cuddle and love and protect. Now the possibility of motherhood had disintegrated to dust along with her engagement. But not the desire.

"Yes. Eight months."

"I didn't know. Danny didn't say anything in his letter. Congratulations."

"Thanks." Nirupam turned and shuffled along the bare boards of the corridor with one hand supporting her lower back. She didn't seem particularly surprised or pleased to see her. Maybe being pregnant had affected her in some way—drained away her emotions and energy. Not that she'd ever been a very effusive girl. Quietly ethereal, other worldly, had always been her impression of Nirupam.

"Nirupam, is it all right if I stay?"

"Sure. We have two spare rooms at the moment."

"Thanks." One weight let loose. She'd have a bed tonight. She must be open minded. She was here to make changes in her life and she wouldn't change if she didn't open her mind—that's what the books said.

The house was larger than it looked from the front. Nirupam led her along the corridor down a step through an open living room type area furnished with two ancient couches and an assortment of easy chairs sitting in an old-fashioned carpeted pink and green sea of roses, then along another short corridor down two steps to the large kitchen at the rear. Obviously the communal room, it was the width of the house with the cooking and food preparation area at one end and a large wooden table at the other surrounded by wooden benches and a motley collection of kitchen chairs.

"Would you like tea?" Nirupam sagged down on a bench at the table with a sigh.

"No, thanks, I had a drink in town on the way through." Primrose sat on a chair which wobbled alarmingly but held up. "Are you well?" She didn't look it. She looked pale and exhausted.

"I get really tired." She closed her eyes as if in proof.

Primrose glanced about. Dirty dishes stacked in the sink. Dust and leaves on the floor. A couple of flies buzzing lazily against the window. A cardboard box with two tired looking lettuces and several cucumbers on the floor by the door. Various items of clothing, papers and books strewn on chairs and the table.

"How many people live here?"

The eyes opened briefly. "Six."

"Where are they? Where's Danny?" Six people who did nothing in the house except make a mess.

"Danny's gone to Braidwood. The others are away."

"There was a man in the garden."

"Kurt." Nirupam levered herself to her feet, pressing her hands on the table for support. Her big baby belly threatened to overbalance her, way out of proportion to the rest of the frail body. "I need a sleep."

"Of course. You must take care of yourself and the bub." Primrose leapt to her feet ready to offer an arm but Nirupam was already on her way, shuffling toward the door with hand pressed against her lower back again. "Which room will I have?"

"I'll show you."

Nirupam led her back the way they'd come. She opened a door near the front entrance. "This was Anne's. She was an artist." Her lips flickered with the ghost of a smile as she turned away. "Sorry, Rosie. I really have to sleep."

"Thanks." An artist. That was a good sign. Perhaps some of the others were artists of some sort too.

Anne must have enjoyed burning incense because the intense musky smell permeated the room, accentuated by the hot still air. Anne must also have been a prolific artist because she'd decorated the walls with great enthusiasm. Nudes were her forte. Full colour but fortunately not full frontal. The men peeped with bizarre coyness over their shoulders, oddly misshapen, the perspective all askew. The two women sat with grotesque legs and arms at strategic angles. She appeared to have been exploring the human form.

An old wooden wardrobe stood in one corner, its doors hanging open. A speckled mirror on the right hand door reflected Primrose's hesitant stance and dismayed expression. She shifted her focus to the bed. A single bare mattress on a sagging wire frame. The type of bed she'd slept in at school camps. The camps where you provided your own bedding. Her doona and linen was packed away in boxes with the rest of her meagre possessions under a friend's house in Sydney. But she'd brought her own ergonomic contour pillow. And two towels and two pillowslips.

She walked across and pulled the flimsy floral cotton curtains aside. This room faced the front but to the right she could see the garden where Kurt had stopped working and was busily relieving himself against a tree. He finished and turned back to the rows of plants. Primrose let the curtain fall into place. Then she had second thoughts and opened the dilapidated screen to push the window wide. Even hot air was better than this cloying pong.

She sat on the bed. It sagged under her weight. Is this why Tom Fairbrother laughed? He knew what she was in for and thought it served her right for some perverse reason? Punishment for being from the city? He thought she'd hightail it out of here seeking creature comforts. He probably knew about the sheep and didn't warn her.

The commune—she couldn't think of it as Nirvana, way too much of a stretch—deserved more of a chance than the ten minutes she'd been here. Nirupam would lend her sheets until she could buy her own. Wouldn't need more yet, too hot. Should bring in her things. She stood up and strode to the door. Stopped.

The sheep.

Nirupam said it liked to play. War games. Primrose examined her legs. Big red marks with greasy smudges. Definite bruising. How would she collect her bag? No way could she fend off that animal while struggling with her suitcase. Have to ask someone to bring it in. Kurt? Where were the other inhabitants? Who were they?

She could explore the house at least. First stop, the bathroom. The bath hadn't been cleaned for ages. A shower recess had worn tiles and blackened grouting with soap scum marking the glass sides and door in random white streaks. A dying fern hung suspended in the corner.

No toilet. Must be separate. Please not an outside hole in the ground with redback spiders on the seat. Primrose opened the next door and peeped in. Someone's very messy bedroom. She tried the room opposite and exhaled with relief. The toilet. Cleaner than the bath but still stained a nasty brown. A quarter roll of unbleached, coarse looking paper. She'd have to buy her own supply or risk a sandpapered bum. A cobweb draped from the ceiling.

Nose wrinkled, she backed out to stand uncertainly in the corridor before heading for the front door. Have to brave the sheep some time. The damned thing wasn't keeping her prisoner in the house. She pushed the screen door open as quietly as possible. A couple of hens scratched about nearby, intent on foraging.

She made it halfway across the yard then the thud of hooves on gravel sent a surge of adrenalin to her legs.

"Baaa." A screech like a banshee.

Primrose sprinted for the car and flung the door open. Safe. The sheep prowled about outside sniffing at the air, tossing its head and scowling. Lamb chops, that's what it deserved to be. She grabbed her bottle of water and took a long deep swallow.

All she had to do was sit tight until someone came or the sheep lost interest and wandered off to harass someone else.

It didn't wander off. The wretched thing strolled across to the house fence and began nibbling at the grass jamming the gate open. She lowered the window and rested her head against the headrest, eyes closed.

Ten minutes later a car engine sounded, joining the roar from the garden. Danny back from Braidwood? A white ute bounded down the rough track and pulled up right next to the Golf in a swirl of dust so Primrose couldn't see who was at the wheel. The driver got out and slammed the door. Tom Fairbrother.

She slipped lower in her seat, holding her breath. By peeping over the dashboard she could see him from the waist up as he walked away from the car. Broad back. Broad brimmed, battered hat. Then his tanned muscular legs came into view. He had a green plastic bag in his hand. Her dirty clothes. She'd left them in his bathroom! A mortified groan escaped. She clamped both hands to her mouth in horror as she stared at his retreating rear, registering with some vague part of her brain how neatly the shorts fitted.

The sheep spotted him and let out its war cry. Little hooves stomped and the battering ram of a head lowered for the charge. Primrose sat up straight, waiting for the attack with eager, bated breath.

Tom waved his arms and ran a few paces toward it. "Get out of it."

To her intense disappointment the cowardly thing turned and scuttled away, but to her even greater dismay the bag spun from his hand spilling her dirty clothes and underwear in lacy black confusion at his feet. He bent to pick it up but must have caught her sudden shocked movement from the corner of his eye because he stood still, peering at the car. An unexpectedly huge grin split his face from one ear to the other. White teeth flashed, and for an instant a lava flow of desire melted her from the inside out, a shocking realisation which short-circuited her whole body.

But only an instant. Primrose grimaced and exhaled, firmed her mouth. She collected her handbag and drink bottles and opened the door.

The grin had disappeared completely. He stood with her knickers dangling from his fingers. The attraction must have been a momentary brain fade brought on by shock.

"G'day."

"Hello."

"These yours?"

"Yes."

"Thought they must be. Knew they weren't mine." He held the lacy fragment up to study thoughtfully. "Couldn't figure out how they got into my bathroom. And I don't use perfume." The eyes swung to her face and stopped, boring uncomfortably through her bravado.

"Thank you." Primrose snatched the knickers and bundled them with her T-shirt and drink bottles into the bag he handed her.

"Did you get lost again?" The infuriating smirk was back on his face.

"No." The word held all the disdain she could muster. "Why?"

"I thought you'd have been inside by now."

"I have been inside."

"Car more comfortable, is it?"

"I was getting my things. Seeing as you're here you can help me with my suitcase."

"Okay."

She could have sworn he laughed but he'd walked past her to the back of the car. Primrose opened the hatch. She stuffed the plastic bag under her arm, pulled her handbag and flute case over her shoulder, picked up the music bag and waited for him to grab the suitcase.

"You a musician?"

"Yes. Flute."

He gave a snorting laugh he didn't bother hiding. "That'll come in handy. You'll fit right in."

"I'm a professional," she snapped. The sheep

peeked around the corner of the shed. Primrose eyed it warily and stepped so Tom was between her and it.

"Sammy got you, did he?"

No point denying it. "He's mad."

"He thinks he's a dog."

"I think he'd be better as dinner." She scowled in the direction of the sheep.

Tom glanced at her. "That wouldn't go down too well around here. They're vegetarians."

"I know." She didn't but she guessed. Danny and Nirupam always had been.

"I like a good steak myself. And roast lamb with my veggies." He met her eye. No hint of laughter but was there a twinkle in those grey eyes? Was he pulling her leg? Primrose opened the screen door and he charged through, hefting the case with ease. "Which room is yours?"

"On the left. The door's open, but you don't need to take it in," she called in a belated attempt to prevent him viewing her murals.

"Geez it stinks in here." Too late. "Crikey!"

He dumped the bag and stood staring at the walls. Primrose edged around him and dropped her music bag and the dirty washing on the bare mattress. She avoided eye contact by carefully placing her flute with unnecessary care next to the music case.

"I reckon that's Danny." He walked across and studied the man next to the wardrobe. The one with the extra large head and the extra short hairy legs. "Yeah, definitely Danny. Whose room was this?"

"Anne's." Primrose stared in shock at the grotesque replication of her brother. Was it Danny? She hadn't seen him in years.

"Aah." He nodded as if she'd explained everything. "What *about* Anne?"

He shrugged. "She liked to paint." At least he didn't call her an artist.

"Obviously." Primrose gestured at the walls and waited for more information, but Tom, remaining silent, had moved on to stare at the next image.

"Did she do anything else here?"

He bent over to study something at knee level. The shorts tightened over neat muscular buttocks. Her breath caught. She looked away.

"She'd wander about with her easel and paint trees. I didn't know she did this stuff as well. I always thought she was a bit odd. But most of them are odd who come here. Nuts." He straightened and turned to face her. "How are you going to sleep with this mob looking at you all night?"

"It'll be dark. They won't be able to see me." How indeed? Especially now one of them had been identified as her brother. What was he doing posing naked? What goes on here? She studied the distorted faces in alarm. No sign of Nirupam. "Do you know them? The other people?"

"At the moment I do but it's hard to keep up, they come and go so much. I know Danny and Nirupam pretty well, they're all right, just not very organised and too easy going with all the nutters who come through. Fern and Jason and their son have been here a few months. And there's Kurt. He's a bloody maniac."

"Do you think I'm another nutter?" Kurt was a maniac? What sort of maniac? She wasn't going to ask this man, though, with his sceptical cynicism.

Tom raised an eyebrow. His gaze started at her

silver painted toenails and strappy, mid-heeled, red, dust covered sandals, passed over her bare legs and above knee hemline, reached the low neck and thin straps of her dress, her silver earrings, stopped at her expensive, newly styled layer cut burgundy hair with the copper highlights. "I think you've got no idea about life on the land—just like the rest of the city people who come out here—and you'll last a week tops."

The blatant, slow appraisal left a hot tingling trail of nerve endings. She iced her voice and kept her gaze away from his. "I intend to stay longer than a week."

He said with infuriatingly casual scorn, "You might intend to. I'm saying you *won't* last that long."

"We'll see. Thank you for bringing in my suitcase."

He looked pointedly at the bag spilling dirty clothes onto the bare mattress. A tiny smile, quirky lopsided and dangerously appealing lurked on his lips.

"And for returning those."

"No worries." If he thought she was going to own up to using his shower he had another think coming. Primrose followed him outside and stood on the top step. "I'll leave you to it," he said.

"Hey you!"

Tom groaned. He turned hands on hips, to face the furious red bearded figure pounding toward them from the garden, weaving in and out between the trees like a runaway locomotive.

"Meet Kurt. The maniac."

"What you doing here, Fairbrudder?" roared the man in a strong German accent. The Terminator in baggy shorts and a filthy T-shirt. "Haven't I told you, clear off from this place? You're not welcome here."

Tom relaxed his arms but stood his ground while Primrose retreated to the shelter of the verandah ready to run inside and find Nirupam for protection. The hens clucked in concern and scattered from Kurt's path. The straw hat flew from his head revealing wild blonde hair. Up close he resembled a Viking—a berserk Viking intent on murder.

"G'day Kurt," said Tom when the maniac was close enough, red-faced and panting.

"You clear off, Fairbrudder." The gasping words were punctuated by great wheezing, heaving breaths.

"You want to be careful, mate, running in this heat. Might have a heart attack." Tom turned to Primrose with a slow, intimate smile which had her pulse matching Kurt's. "Goodbye. Have fun."

He strolled across to his vehicle, climbed in and started the engine. She gasped. Deserting her! How could he?

Kurt glowered, with grimy big sausage fingers clamped on equally dirty shorts-clad hips. "Clear off!" he yelled.

Primrose clutched the verandah railing too terrified to move in case his attention and rage shifted to her. When Tom's ute had disappeared over the hill he turned. To her astonishment he smiled. A gap-toothed grin in a dust-streaked, sweat stained face.

"Danny's little sister Rosie. Welcome to our commune."

"Yes. Hello, Kurt. I hope I'm not intruding. Nirupam said..."

"Everybody's welcome here." An expansive sweep of an arm. A wave of foul body odour hit her like a sledge hammer. "Except that Fairbrudder barshted." A

21

quick return of the glower.

"Why isn't he welcome?"

"He's a cheat. Cheated Danny of land. He hates us, he's jealous of our freedom and our lifestyle. Always complaining to the council." He waved dismissively. "Crazy man. That's why he lives over there. All alone." He gave a bark of raucous laughter. "No-body wants to live with him. He makes bad vibes there. Hahaha."

Danny was cheated by Tom Fairbrother? How? No sense asking Kurt. He seemed seriously unhinged.

"I wasn't sure you were expecting me." The closer he came the more convinced she was that he featured on her wall, facing the bed. The first thing she'd see when she woke every morning. Massive buttocks and meaty hams beneath a too thin and tall back topped by a red bearded face leering over its shoulder with a haystack of yellow hair and alarming purple eyes.

"Ja, sure ting. Danny said Rosie was coming."

He came to the bottom step, grinning. Manic eyes. Tom was right. So was Anne. She'd nailed them exactly. Flies buzzed about them both. Another wave of hot, fetid male body odour made her eyes water and her lungs seize.

"Gosh it's hot." She summoned up a cheery, bright voice. "I should get myself unpacked." She spun about and almost ran to the door, gulping clean, untainted air.

"You can help Nirupam in the kitchen. And care for the hens." His voice lumbered after her. "She's lazy lately. Shleeping all the time. Never works anymore."

Primrose turned with an indignant frown. "She's pregnant!"

He flung an arm in the air, scowling. "Pregnant is natural. No problem. Those native women, they have babies all the time. Easy. They don't shleep. They just keep working and when it's their time they squat down and out it pops. Natural, see?"

Primrose opened her mouth to object, saw the mulish expression and closed it again. He stared at her with unnerving intensity. No telling where an argument with this lunatic would finish. Humour him.

"What do I have to do with the chooks?" she blurted.

"Lock them in the shed at night. Let them out early in the morning. Collect the eggs. Check they have water. We have freelance eggs here. No chemical rubbish."

Freelance eggs? She nearly laughed. "All right." Sounded easy enough. Freelance hens wouldn't need much care by definition. "I'll unpack, then clean up in the kitchen." She escaped indoors before the rising bubble of laughter burst out.

"Don't use too much water," he yelled as the screen door closed. "Can't waste it like city people."

"All right."

Kurt must save water by not bathing.

Chapter Two

She tackled the pile of dirty dishes first. A search of the grimy cupboards under the sink revealed a scourer, an almost empty bottle of detergent and rubber gloves which proved to have a hole in the left index finger.

It took over an hour. Plenty of time in which to inspect Kurt's furious accusation. Tom Fairbrother is a cheat—making his name a contradiction in terms. He'd cheated her own brother. How? Danny wasn't a fool despite his vagueness and airy fairy attitude to life. He could be taken advantage of fairly easily, though. Too trusting. Too willing to see the best in people. Unwilling to argue and confront. Unlike his cynical sister. Even more cynical now, post Martin.

If Tom Fairbrother had cheated Danny she'd find out exactly how and why. Then she'd set about righting the wrong. This land belonged to both of them. If Fairbrother had cheated Danny he'd cheated her, too. She yanked the plug on the greasy, lukewarm water.

Two saucepans had to be left to soak with a scrupulous centimetre of soapy, dirty dishwater in each. Primrose dried the plates and cutlery and stacked them on the shelves. She went to her room for the bottle of spring water and unopened iced tea bought at the store on the way through town. Better they go in the elderly fridge which rumbled away in the corner of the kitchen.

While they chilled in the ice clogged freezer section she set to with a broom and cleared the ageing lino of a layer of tramped-in dirt and leaves. Then she wiped down the table and collapsed on one of the rickety chairs to catch her breath. Nearly five thirty and still oppressively hot.

Primrose dragged herself up and went to stand on the back step. Cicadas whirred and buzzed like a million tiny chainsaws. From here she could look away down the slope to the right to more sheds and a collection of fruit trees. Peaches? They were the main crop in this valley. She'd driven past several orchards on the way into Kullanurra. A flock of pink and grey galahs rose squawking into the sky, swirling and wheeling before heading for the distant hills.

Two water tanks nestled against the wall of the house. She wandered across the rough grass under the trees, one of which supported a car tyre swing, toward a washing line strung between two posts.

Someone had left various large pieces of sculpture lying about propped against tree trunks or standing in lopsided, drunken groups. Indiscernible white plaster shapes expressing something known only to the artist. Did Anne's talent extend to sculpture or were these the fruits of another creative soul? The wind chimes danced with a constant, delicate tinkling. A couple of faded multi-coloured wind catchers flapped from the boughs overhead.

A footworn path led away through the trees angling downhill and to the left. Primrose breathed in deep lungfuls of the clear fresh air. Still hot, but the sun was lower now and would go behind the far hills soon, those rough peaks she'd driven over. So calm, so peaceful.

Just what she needed. Clear her head of memories, forget a lying, devious man called Martin. Move to a higher plane. Leave him behind with his new, married girlfriend and her two year old child. What a mess he was in for—divorce, bitterness. Forget it. Not her problem. Served him right!

Was Tom a cheat? And what about those other accusations? He didn't strike her as a man who would rouse himself to hate anything—scoff, yes, have a private chuckle at the nuts next door, but hate was a very strong word, an extreme emotion and he seemed too...what? Laid-back. Jealous? Attractive? Primrose compared the neat, clean, comfortable house and the well-maintained grounds with this place. Jealous of what? Maybe it wasn't Tom who was the problem at all. Maybe he was right and Kurt really was a maniac. He'd certainly given a good impression of one. The question was—just how mad was he?

And had Danny gone the same way? Had they all gone feral out here?

****

Tom laughed all the way home from Nirvana. What a bunch of loonies. Kurt was always good entertainment, or would be if he wasn't so violent-tempered, and was more willing to take agricultural advice from a proper farmer. He'd bet pretty little Primrose hadn't come across anyone like him before.

He himself had never come cross anyone like her before. When he opened the screen door and saw her...The last time he'd been as stunned was when the horse tossed her head and caught him under the chin with a blow that brought stars to his eyes. Couldn't think straight for a good ten minutes afterward. Same thing happened without the pain. But he couldn't string many words together, too busy staring at such a vision appearing in his house.

She was different to the usual blow-ins they got over there. More refined, civilised and downright sexy. Very self assured and confident. Didn't seem to have the earth mother thing going. She was clean for starters, drove a good car and wore stylish store bought clothes as opposed to garments she'd woven, knitted, stitched together herself or bought at the Salvos. Played the flute. Professional, she'd insisted, so she must have a brain and talent beneath the packaging.

Funny—Danny had never mentioned a sister. He never talked about his family at all. Nirupam hardly talked about anything, poor girl. If ever there was a case for women's lib she was it. Her place appeared to be in the kitchen if she wasn't making her beautiful silver jewellery which as far as he could gather was their sole source of income. Apart from the peach crop. Not much profit there this season for anyone. So much for division of labour, equality of the sexes and everyone sharing the tasks in their brave new world.

How would Primrose, with her painted nails, French perfume and lacy underwear take to her role? Kitchen drudge. A week and she'd be out of there. She didn't belong in a place like that anymore than he did.

He parked in the shed. Delilah waddled across wagging her tail. He roughed her ears then looked up at the sky. Still hot but a few clouds were building up to the south so with any luck there'd be a bit of rain later. He headed off toward the workshop and the pump engine he'd been dismantling when Primrose arrived. The radio had been on with the cricket so she'd managed to get in and take a shower without his knowing. And he wouldn't have if she hadn't used perfume and left dirty clothes lying about. What cheek! He laughed. She wasn't going to own up, too proud. Too pretty to yell at. Much too pretty.

Last a week in that dump? He lifted the cover off the engine and peered in. Something was blocking the fuel line. He picked up a spanner. They were all crazy. And he'd had another tirade from Kurt. What a tiresome man he was. Why on earth did Danny put up with him? Why did Danny put up with any of them? They hardly contributed anything and he was always short of money, hence the sale of chunks of his land. The way Danny was going he'd end up with just the few acres surrounding the house.

Whatever the reason it wasn't his worry and he was a ready purchaser of as much land as Danny wanted to sell. Chances were he'd own the thirty acre Back Block soon. He whistled "Uptown Girl" as he removed the fuel line. Primrose was one very attractive female.

****

Primrose sat on the front verandah on the old couch. This side of the house was cooler now with the sun setting behind the hills on the far side. A ball of golden light, it hovered on the lip of the horizon, just visible between the trees by the sheds.

Kurt was still down in the garden. Nirupam hadn't reappeared. Neither had the other residents. Where were they and what did they do here? Although by the state of the place, no-body did anything much.

Was this a mistake?

Primrose stared unseeing across the paddocks. She knew her new life on the commune wouldn't be easy, but she'd expected a modicum of organisation and efficiency. Not whatever this was. The local joke? Tom Fairbrother made it obvious he thought so.

Danny had been here six years. Doing what? He'd never been good at organising himself. He'd never been interested in agriculture as far as she could remember. That's why becoming a self sufficient farmer had seemed such a ridiculous and hopeless venture.

The alternative would be going somewhere completely new and trying to restart a career. Very difficult, and she'd already done those calculations. Finding work as a flute player was tough. Not many fulltime positions were available and she really didn't want the freelance life anymore. That was one reason why marriage and motherhood was so appealing and why now, with that prospect smashed to smithereens, she was adrift.

No. Too early to panic. She needed to slow down, adjust. Accept change as a positive thing. And the last thing she wanted was to prove Mr. Smart Arse Fairbrother right. She could stick it out for a few weeks before making any decisions about leaving. The reality was she didn't have much choice. Her stomach gurgled.

Was dinner a communal meal the way she'd envisaged or was it every man for himself the way some of her student share houses had operated? Whichever way it worked it was close to seven and she was running on empty.

An engine roared in the distance. A motorbike. She stood up. The bike burst into view on the top of the hill. Danny? A cloud of dust trailed like a banner in his wake. The bike decelerated and ran into the shed next to the Kombi. Primrose waited for the dust to settle then walked down the steps. She crossed the yard, stopping as the rider got off the big blue bike and removed the helmet. He took grocery bags from the rear container.

"Danny!"

He turned, bearded, brow creased as he studied her. "Hello, Rosie."

The expanse of dusty ground between them stretched into a vast no man's land. Primrose paused, licked her lips, with a tentative smile hovering. Was he pleased to see her? A sudden and unexpected groundswell of emotion flooded her eyes with moisture, made her voice catch in her throat. "Hello."

He put the groceries down. "Been a long time."

"Yes." She moved forward uncertainly, but the frown had gone. He smiled and she ran the last few steps into his open arms, sniffing back tears. She'd forgotten being a sister. Those shared memories and experiences didn't go away, however neglected they may be. She and this man, her brother, were linked by invisible, cobweb thin bonds spun in childhood. Stronger than she'd thought.

"You're looking good," he mumbled into her shoulder.

She stepped back, ran a hand over her cheeks, grinning, wiping away tears. The clear green eyes hadn't changed, but the hair was lighter and he'd lost weight. A lot of weight. His frame was wiry thin, bony, beneath her hug. "I'm fine. You look good, too."

"How long have you been here?" He bent and scooped up the grocery bags and started walking toward the house.

"A few hours. I saw Nirupam. She's asleep at the moment. Hey!" Primrose grabbed his arm.

"Congratulations. You're going to be a Dad."

"A better one than ours, I hope."

"You will be, and Nirupam will be a terrific mother." Danny smiled briefly but said nothing. He stepped aside for her to go through the gate. Primrose said, "Is she well? She looks a bit pale, and you're both very thin."

"She tired, but it's natural according to Kurt and Fern."

"I haven't met Fern. I've met Kurt, and he doesn't strike me as knowing anything about pregnancy." Or women or probably anything else.

"Fern and Jason live here too with their son Mojo. He's seven."

Mojo!? What were they thinking? "What does her doctor say?" Primrose pulled the door open.

"She hasn't seen a doctor. No need. Fern's here."

"What?! What does Fern know about it? Is she a midwife?"

"No, but she's had a child."

"Has Kurt had any medical training?" Primrose squawked, unable to conceal the horror.

"No but—"

"But what? She needs to see a doctor, Danny. Where's she going to have the baby? Here?"

He nodded. "It's a perfectly natural thing, childbirth."

"Maybe, but women and babies still die. What if something goes wrong?"

He wandered off along the corridor toward the bathroom. "I don't know. It won't happen. Fern's predicted a perfectly healthy birth with her Tarot cards." He left the grocery bags on the floor outside the bathroom and closed the door.

Primrose stared after him, hands on hips. He hadn't changed. Still hopelessly vague, expecting things to take care of themselves. Well he had to do a darn sight better than vague with his wife in her condition. Fancy relying on the word of that maniac Kurt! And Tarot cards? What else did they have to offer poor Nirupam? Good vibes? Crystals?

"It's a good thing I'm here," she called after him.

"Take the groceries to the kitchen," he said through the closed door.

Primrose picked up the bags and peered inside. "Do we all eat together?"

"Yes."

"Who cooks?"

"Usually Nirupam or Fern, but she's away. Can't you wait until I come out?"

Nirupam? What's wrong with the rest of them? Primrose strode to the newly cleaned kitchen, the plastic bags swinging in her hand. Why were they using plastic bags? Even she had Green reusable bags. As she stacked away, she investigated the food situation. The fridge housed a tub of margarine; left over something red with mould on it; a hunk of cheese; jars of jam, honey, peanut butter, yoghurt and various bottles of sauce and mustard. Nothing home made. She removed her beautifully iced tea from the freezer and swigged most of it in one gulp.

The vegetable drawer revealed a lettuce, cucumbers and a couple of bendy carrots which she tossed out and replaced with the fresh batch. A big platter of tomatoes ripened on the shelf over the sink by the window. They were home grown. Maybe she could cobble together some sort of pasta thing with the tomatoes and onions.

Canola oil hid in a cramped cupboard under the bench. It would do. Too much to hope they had olives and parmesan cheese. Primrose took out two of the saucepans she'd washed earlier and filled one with water. The old gas stove gamely resisted her efforts with a match, but she won in the end and set the pan on top to boil.

The toilet flushed. A door opened. Closed. Footsteps sounded in the passage. Another door opened and closed. Checking on Nirupam. No wonder the poor girl was exhausted. They should be looking after her not the other way around.

A heavy tread came from the back entrance. Kurt appeared, bare chested, in a clean pair of shorts, with a faded threadbare towel slung over his shoulder. His wild blonde hair and rust coloured beard hung damply around his red, shining face.

"Hello," he boomed as if Primrose were on the far side of a paddock.

"Hi. Have you been swimming?"

"Ja. In the creek. Natural. Wash in the creek the way natives do. Only trouble, not much water now. Just one pool with leeches in it. But they don't bother me."

No doubt they knew better. If they survived the toxic run-off.

He surveyed her dinner preparations. "You cook tonight? What you making?"

"Pasta."

"You go on. Have you shut in the chooks?"

Hadn't given them a thought. "I'll get this started first. Can I use those tomatoes? Home grown ones taste so much better."

A series of furrows appeared in his brow. "Fairbrudder brought them. Said he had too many. Hah!"

"I thought you'd grown them." Primrose turned to hide the smile. "What's in your garden?"

"Lettuce, cucumbers, capsicums, chillies, herbs and tomatoes."

"Are yours ripe?"

"No." He picked up her half drunk bottle of iced tea and drained it in one greedy swallow. "Bad year for tomatoes. The root stock was rubbish. Just got two, three little ones coming. Fairbrudder tells the supplier not to give me the best. See? What can you do?" He crushed the drink bottle in one massive fist and tossed it toward the bin in the corner. "Hard to grow vegetables here."

"But his grew."

"Because he bought up all the good stock first. He didn't need so many. Just took everything to stop us."

"Would he do that?"

"Sure. Cheaters never change. Fairbrudder is the wrong name for him. He's Unfairbrudder." He grinned at his witticism.

"What's your other name?" Hitler perhaps? Goebbels?

"O'Malley."

"Really?" She nearly dropped the tomato. "I thought you'd have a German name."

"I changed it. O'Malley is a good name. Easy to spell for Aussies."

"What was your name before?"

"Schmidt."

"Why didn't you change it to Smith?"

"Too many Smiths. Too common like weeds. Nah, O'Malley is a good name."

Primrose concentrated on peeling an onion. Insane laughter bubbled in her throat making her shoulders shake. Danny and Nirupam came in and sat at the table. She forced the laughter down and turned. Nirupam was still pale with dark purple rings under her eyes even after her sleep. Danny held her hand in both his. Loving and protecting each other. Primrose swallowed the little surge of envy.

"Rosie is cooking dinner," announced Kurt.

"Thanks, Rosie." Nirupam offered a feeble smile. "You shouldn't have to cook on your first night."

"It's all right. I'll take my turn now and someone else can do it tomorrow."

"I don't cook," said Kurt. "I work outside."

"What about the others? Are they eating here tonight?"

Kurt said, "They're in Narooma doing a psychic healing workshop."

Primrose sliced the onions. "Do we have garlic?"

Nirupam pointed. "In that cupboard."

"The water's boiling." Kurt made no move to add the pasta.

Primrose jammed spaghetti into the pot. "Perhaps you could wash a lettuce." She held her breath. He may have washed in the creek, wherever that was, but the walk up the paddocks had raised another pungent sweat.

"I have to put on a clean shirt." He left the kitchen.

"How long has Kurt been here?"

"About eight months," said Danny.

"I thought the idea was to share the chores."

"We started out that way, but Kurt thinks everyone should stick to what they do best," said Nirupam.

"Aren't you the boss, Danny?" What on earth did Kurt do best? Bully people? It wasn't grow vegetables.

"We have a weekly council to decide what should be done."

"His way?" Primrose raised an eyebrow at Danny. He looked away. Typical. "Danny, it's our land not his. Why should he tell you what to do?"

"He doesn't. We discuss things."

Primrose stirred her sizzling onions. Someone had to stand up to Kurt. It sure wasn't going to be Danny. "So who pays for the groceries and the rates and everything? Do you have a kitty?"

"People contribute what they can," said Nirupam in a vague other worldly tone.

"Money creates problems," said Danny. "Possessions make people unhappy. The less you have the happier you are."

"Right. Especially if someone else can pay for everything."

"You don't understand." A very familiar tone from their childhood. Long suffering, irritatingly patronising but now with a hint of sadness. "You never have, Rosie."

"I'm trying to. That's why I'm here." She chopped up a pile of tomatoes and dumped them into the pan. She hadn't ever understood Danny. But he'd never understood her, either, it cut both ways, his accusation. Perhaps neither of them had bothered to try.

"Why *are* you here? We were really surprised to get your letter," said Nirupam. "We haven't seen you for years. Since your Mum's funeral, I think. Or our wedding."

Danny's fault, not hers. He was the one who turned his back on society and went bush.

"No. I know. I've had a...I needed to get away from everything. I thought here was the best place."

"What happened?" Nirupam's expression was gentle, uncritical.

"I was engaged. You didn't know, same as I didn't know about your baby." She turned the heat down under the tomatoes, checked the pasta and sat down at the table opposite Danny. She blinked rapidly as more unaccustomed tears threatened. "We're not very good at family things, are we?"

He tilted his head briefly. A half smile flicked on and off. "We didn't have a very good example."

"We should be better, Danny, we're all we've got. I think that's part of why I'm here."

"You're welcome, Rosie." Nirupam stretched out a thin arm and squeezed Primrose's hand. "For however long you want to stay."

"Thanks." She bit at her lower lip. "Martin decided I wasn't what he wanted after all. He preferred a woman with a child, who was already married to someone else."

"Idiot."

She looked at Danny, surprised at the comfort the single word gave her. Surprised at his unquestioning support of her as an attractive and valuable person. A desirable woman.

"I'm over him now." If she said it often enough it may become fact. "It's nearly two months ago. It wasn't him alone that made me decide to change my life. I didn't have anywhere to live. He moved out and I couldn't afford the place on my own. I've been staying with friends." She hesitated but the sympathetic expressions and silence made her continue. "I had some tough gigs. They ran for seven months in total. I hated going to work. It made me wonder if I'm cut out to be a professional player. And on top of Martin I just couldn't stand it anymore. I was hoping if I came here I could sort myself out."

Danny nodded. "Same reason we came here. To escape that sort of stress."

"You need to find your centre, your essence." Nirupam sat back with a beatific expression. Like the Buddha. "Fern can do some psychic healing techniques with you."

"What exactly is psychic healing?"

"She channels spirit guides who help solve people's problems. There are other techniques, too—like crystals and past life regressions, Tarot, angel cards, primal screaming, rebirthing. She chooses, depending on the client."

"I'll think about it." How on earth did you choose which method to use? Especially if you were a born cynic. And did they work regardless? Her mind was trying hard to be open but she'd already been born once and with Nirupam about to pop, another birth decidedly unnecessary. And she had enough problems with her current life without going back and adding more from whatever character in the past she may have been.

"She's helping me," said Nirupam. "I feel so tired all the time. Fern says my energy fields aren't aligned correctly and I need the right crystals in my room."

"Do you think maybe you could be deficient in iron? Anaemic?" Judging by what was in the food department malnutrition was a distinct possibility. "Wouldn't hurt to see a doctor. Just to be sure. You don't want the baby's health to suffer."

"Doctors are all quacks." Kurt stomped in and pulled a chair out with a thud. "They don't know anything. Nothing wrong with Nirupam. It's the parasite baby sucking all the goodness from her body. It's natural."

Primrose clenched her teeth and averted her eyes from his hulking frame. "What do you think, Danny?"

"The nearest doctor is in Braidwood." As if travelling sixty kilometres was an insurmountable barrier. "And they cost a fortune."

"You can claim it back through Medicare if they don't bulk bill. But if it's a money thing I'll pay. I don't want Nirupam and the precious baby to be in any danger."

Danny looked at Nirupam. "Maybe a check-up?"

"All right." Poor Nirupam hardly had the energy to open her mouth, let alone argue. No wonder she let these people make decisions for her.

"Waste of money," muttered Kurt.

"I'll take the risk," said Primrose crisply. "I'll phone in the morning and make an appointment."

Kurt grinned. "We don't have a telephone."

"I have a mobile."

"It won't work out here," said Danny. "We use Tom's next door if we need to call anyone."

"Does he mind?" Primrose stood up hastily to check on her cooking. What would he say when she appeared asking to use his phone, having already helped herself to his bathroom? But she had no choice. Nirupam's health was more important than her own pride. The baby must be given priority.

"No, but we don't use it much," said Nirupam.

"We don't need any help from that bastard," growled Kurt. Primal screaming aimed at that crazy man was suddenly very appealing.

"What's your problem with him?" Primrose turned to Danny. "Kurt said he cheated you." If they shared everything then this topic must be open for public discussion as well.

Danny shifted uneasily in his chair and looked to Nirupam for assistance. Typical! The furtiveness of the action caused a familiar rush of annoyance at her brother the evader of confrontation. He'd never stood up to their father, even when he was big enough, always disappeared when things became nasty and left home as soon as he was able. Not that he didn't keep in touch with her and Mum—but it was from a distance.

"Fairbrother," began Kurt but Primrose cut in swiftly with, "I'd rather hear it from Danny, thanks."

Danny said, "I don't have any problem with Tom. A few years ago we were in a bit of financial trouble so I sold him fifty acres of land." He glanced at her then away. Furtive? Guilty? "I didn't think you'd mind. You never cared anything about this place and you're earning money."

Primrose eyed her brother with sudden fury, then remembered Kurt. No way was she washing family dirty linen in front of him, no matter how estranged she was from Danny.

"He'd only take the river land and he named his own price. Paid virtually nothing," roared Kurt.

"Cheated Danny of the best land."

She kept her gaze on her brother, ignoring the smelly, wild-eyed German huffing and puffing on her right. "But why did you sell to him?"

"Didn't have any other offers. I wanted to sell the stretch along the road." Danny hesitated, looked away. "Tom didn't want it because it wasn't adjacent to his property."

"Did he pay the market price?"

"He made an offer and I accepted." Danny's feeble defiance. "The amount doesn't matter, Rosie. We made enough to get ourselves out of debt so that was that. I can't pay you your share if that's what's bothering you. You were the one who said one signature was enough," he added with an almost petulant, childish expression.

"No. It's not the money, if you needed it." Primrose sighed, glanced at Kurt who was taking in the details with a greedy expression. "I wouldn't have objected but it would have been nice to know."

Danny all over. Take the easy option. Let Tom Fairbrother walk away with the best piece of land, no matter he could have hung out for twice as much. But what did the deal say about Tom's moral standards? Not a lot.

Chapter Three

Tom heard the car coming this time. He strolled across the yard to meet Primrose, the casual stride hiding a sudden, unexpected surge of anticipation.

She wore denim shorts today with a sleeveless pink T-shirt. He indulged himself in a long look at her legs and nicely rounded bottom as she got out of the car.

"Morning." He flicked his eyes quickly to her face as she turned to greet him.

"Good morning." She removed her dark glasses and wiped her palm across her brow. Tired. Her eyes had dark smudges under them.

"Sleep well?"

To his surprise she laughed. She had dimples. Beautiful dimples which gave her a cheeky, girlish look and chased the weariness from her face. Sexy as all get out. "No. Terrible. Possums use the roof as a midnight racetrack and as well as lumps in the mattress, mozzies, and the heat, I had nightmares about Kurt. He's on my wall, too."

Tom grinned. "I've got some leftover paint if you want to redecorate."

Her eyes lit up. Green with darker brown flecks shining in the sunlight. "Really? Thanks." The smile morphed into a grimace. "Think they'd mind?"

"Kurt's sure to."

"In that case I'll take you up on your offer, thank

you." The light danced in her eyes again, locking on his for a long, unsettling moment until he remembered she wanted paint. If she wasn't flirting with him now he'd be a walkover if she ever decided to. None of the local girls could match her. Smart and sexy. Dangerous.

"You'll need a roller and brush too." He headed for the store shed, focussing hard on the task, not the image in his mind of her smiling mouth. Lucky the leftover paint was white although any colour would be better than the catastrophe she had. Her voice stopped him. He turned.

"Actually, Tom, I came over to ask if I could use the phone, please. I'm worried about Nirupam. She's really tired all the time. Do you know she hasn't seen a doctor yet?"

He studied her face. Lips firm, eyes screwed up against the glare. Her tone implied he was somehow at fault. She replaced the sunglasses. All businesslike distance in a moment.

"I'm not involved. It's their business."

"But you're their friend, aren't you? You gave them those tomatoes." Her gaze bored into him. Was there some other agenda here? One he didn't know about?

"I had too many."

"Kurt thinks you deliberately stopped him getting decent plants. Did you?"

Was she serious? How dare she? Silly, interfering woman.

"What do you think I am? First you accuse me of neglecting Nirupam's health, now you accuse me of thwarting Kurt's inept attempts to grow tomatoes." He took a step closer and glared down at her. "Nirupam is

Danny's wife, not mine and the child is his, not mine. They, as do I and clearly you, prefer to run their lives their own way. Kurt won't take advice from anyone but is more than ready to blame anyone, usually me, when his crops fail. Which is most of the time."

Her cheeks grew pinker and pinker as he spoke but a determined frown creased her forehead beneath the wisps of multicoloured hair.

"I agree with you about Kurt but as an intelligent, concerned person surely you could see Nirupam isn't well. You can't just turn your back on something if it's obviously wrong and someone's health is involved. Two someone's in this case."

"I don't interfere in other people's affairs and I haven't seen enough pregnant women to know. Have you?"

"She's incredibly tired and very pale. They think someone called Fern will fix her up with crystals. I think she needs a steak and she certainly needs a doctor."

Tom drew a deep breath. Add stubborn to her faults. She was right but it wasn't any of his business. Why on earth did she think it was? He said curtly, "The phone's in the kitchen. Help yourself. You know the way. I'll get the paint."

"Thanks." Equally as terse.

Tom strode to the store shed and flung the door open. What was it about this girl that attracted him as much as irritated him? She was pretty in name and presence—more than pretty, she was downright irresistible with her dimples, neat figure and her sexy legs. But she was bossy and impertinent. The complete opposite of her brother. What sane man would get involved with her? Not him, and apart from everything else she was a city girl slumming it. She'd be bored within days by the monotony and discomfort of commune life.

But she'd give Kurt a run for his money which couldn't be a bad thing and anything she did to improve that place over there was worth encouraging.

He pulled two tins of white paint from under a tarpaulin. She'd need a tray, roller and brush. He lugged everything to the car. Primrose was still in the house. Was she taking advantage of his bathroom again? Chuckling, he pulled the screen door open and walked down the hallway. No sound of water running. Her voice startled him.

"N-I-R-U-P-A-M. Yes, I know. It is unusual. It's Indian." A pause. "She's Australian." She lolled against the kitchen bench with the phone against her ear and rolled her eyes when she spied him in the doorway. "Eight months." More silence. "Thank you. Good bye." She disconnected.

"Okay?"

"Ten o'clock tomorrow in Moruya. The Braidwood doctor suggested we go there instead because of the better maternity facilities. What do I owe you for the calls?"

"I've no idea. Don't worry about it."

Primrose opened her purse. "Two dollars should cover it."

"I said don't bother."

She clinked the coin on the bench. "I don't want to be a freeloader—or cheat you out of anything." She met his eye with fearless directness. The stolen shower hovered between them. He almost laughed. Her grim expression wasn't within cooee of laughing. No sexy overtones now.

"Like to use the facilities while you're here?"

Her jaw tightened. "No, thanks. I'll be going." She started for the front door.

"The paint's in the car." He followed her rapidly striding figure. Boy, she had an exceptional rear view. He curled and uncurled his tempted fingers. "Clean up in water."

"Thanks."

"If you need any help, give me a yell."

"I won't, but thanks."

"No worries." He walked across to the car with her. "Early in the morning's best to start painting otherwise the fumes'll knock you flat."

She grimaced. "Another night with the tribe."

"Last one. Then you'll only have possums, mozzies, and the lumpy mattress."

"And Kurt." She paused, obviously considering her next words. "He throws some wild accusations around."

"Most of them are about me."

"Why does he have it in for you?"

The switch from defiance to intimacy threw him for a moment. "I told you. He's mad."

"But I thought you were joking." A little frown appeared. Her teeth tugged at her lower lip. "He's not dangerously mad, is he?"

"He hasn't hurt anyone yet."

She shuddered. "Yet?"

Didn't look like she'd be lasting the week. Especially if she stirred things up the way she was going. Pity. She was entertaining and decorative to have around. Given time she might relax and drop the aggressive attitude. He said, "That's what these communal places are about, aren't they? What you're after? Equality. Everybody welcome."

She glanced at him suspiciously. "Yes. Sort of."

He kept a straight face and said with deliberate casualness, "You'll have to learn to be more tolerant."

"I'm *very* tolerant." Squeezed out through gritted teeth. About as tolerant as a cat in a sack.

"I couldn't stand it. I like doing things my way, not by committee."

"Is that why you live alone? By choice?"

He'd asked for that. Served him right. He stared out across the paddocks toward the river. Alison's face swam before his eyes momentarily—short blonde hair, sparkling blue eyes. Tell her? Might as well.

"I had a girlfriend but she couldn't take farm life. Too isolated, too hard."

Her mouth drooped. Sympathetic. "When did you break up?"

"Ages ago. It was mutual and amicable."

"My fiancé did a bunk two months ago." She met his eye and tilted her head, accompanied by a small shrug.

Startled by the personal frankness of her admission he said, "That's tough. How close to the wedding was it?" No wonder she was prickly.

"April."

"Better before than after."

"So everyone tells me."

"Doesn't help much?"

Primrose shook her head and looked away. "Thanks for the paint." She jammed sunglasses on, all business again. "How much do I owe you?"

"Nothing."

"Sure? I don't want to. . ."

He interrupted. "Positive. It was left over."

"Thank you. I'll be off then."

"See you later."

Tom watched the car disappear between the trees. Dumped by a fiancé. Tough. Explained a lot. Maybe if she was still here on Friday he'd invite her out to the pub. An evening with feisty, sexy Primrose would be very enjoyable. And safe. No complications would ensue because she clearly wasn't in the relationship market and although he was, in a general sense, she was so clearly wrong in every possible way he couldn't envisage a longterm affair. She wouldn't be around long enough for starters.

But a date with her would get right up Kurt's nose as well. Petty but satisfying. Had to take your fun where you could get it out here.

****

"Is it all right if I paint my room?" Primrose looked from Danny to Nirupam, ignoring Kurt who gobbled down a sandwich like a big hairy animal at the end of the table.

Danny said, "Yeah. We don't have any paint, though."

"Tom gave me some." No point responding to the food muffled snort of outrage from her right. She finished her own sandwich in one neat bite. No need to mention she had no idea how to go about painting anything. But how hard could it be? And no way was she letting Kurt, who was sure to be an expert, tell her what to do. Ask him for advice? Perish the thought!

"If there's enough we could do the baby's room,

too," said Nirupam with a rare show of enthusiasm. "I want the baby in the room next to us.'

"What about Mojo?" Kurt demanded with his mouth full. A piece of lettuce shot out but was trapped by his beard. "That's his room. He's got his own paintings on those walls. Very talented kid, Anne said. A genius."

And Anne would know. Primrose focussed on picking up crumbs on her fingertip. So would Kurt. She stuck her finger in her mouth to stop the laughter bubbling out but Nirupam's next remark was in such a helpless, pleading tone the laughter was swamped by a surge of anger at how that bully rode roughshod over her sweet, gentle sister-in-law.

"Fern said they'd be going up north soon. After the baby's born." Nirupam turned an anxious gaze on Danny for support. "Mojo could move to the other room."

"If this is your house you can do whatever you want, can't you?" Primrose offered in as innocent a tone as possible, the fury building like red hot lava deep inside. Danny wouldn't meet her eye.

"We make decisions as a community, otherwise the aura goes bad," said Kurt. "No-one has more rights than anyone else."

"Not even the person who owns the land and the house?" Could they see the steam coming out of her ears because her mouth was clamped shut? Aura? How much more toxic could it be?

"We don't do things the same way your society does, Rosie," put in Danny in his mild, feeble way.

Her society? He'd inherited this land thanks to society and its laws. And thanks to her own generosity he lived here rent free. The commune used electricity from the grid and drove on the roads the council maintained. Self sufficient? Who were they trying to kid? They didn't even have solar hot water. Tom was more self sufficient next door and he wasn't even trying. Or at least he wasn't boasting about it the way these people did. And they had nothing to boast about.

She grabbed her water glass and downed most of it in an attempt to quell the internal fire. Her hand was very steady, very controlled, when she placed the glass on the table. "Nirupam and I are going to the doctor tomorrow whether you have a communal vote on it or not."

Kurt glowered but kept his mouth closed for once. No-one offered to help paint. So much for communal assistance.

****

Primrose sat with Nirupam in the crowded doctor's waiting room feeling slim and agile. Pregnant lady day. She'd never seen so many in one place, had no idea how envious she would feel surrounded by this display of fecundity. Now here she was with a sister-in-law giving birth in a month and babies everywhere she looked. The mummy hormones were a palpable force in the room. Supporting Nirupam was essential but at the same time a trial on a deeply emotional and primal level, one that wrenched at her core and drove home how far from achieving this desirable state she really was.

"Nirupam?" White coated, rotund Doctor Singh in gold rimmed spectacles stood in the doorway, scanning the assembled mothers.

"Come with me," whispered Nirupam.

The doctor extended an arm and guided them to his room. He weighed Nirupam, took her blood pressure, then sent her behind a curtained area to settle herself on the examining table.

Primrose waited, listening to the murmured remarks from the doctor and Nirupam's barely audible responses. His head appeared through a gap in the curtain. "Would you like to hear the heartbeat?"

Would she? She jumped to her feet. Nirupam reached for her hand and clung on. Doctor Singh pressed a gadget to Nirupam's stomach and a rapid, light but steady thump, thump burst into the room.

"Very strong." He beamed at them both but Primrose could barely see through the tears which had flooded her eyes.

Doctor Singh indicated Primrose should leave them to it so she returned to her chair, her mind reeling from the reality of the life thriving in her sister-in-law's belly. It was staggeringly amazing. Astonishing. Wonderful and exhilarating. And she wanted a baby too, more than ever.

When they reappeared Nirupam was smiling properly for the first time since Primrose had arrived at the commune.

"Nirupam is anaemic and a little underweight but her blood pressure is good. When she eats better she will feel more energetic although the last stages of pregnancy are always tiring. Ellie Fletcher is a midwife in your area who can call in to see you." Dr Singh scribbled on his notepad and tore off the page, then handed it to Primrose along with a booklet and two leaflets.

"I want to have my baby at home." Nirupam's

words came in a breathless little rush. She stopped with an anxious expression. It would be nothing to the fear on Primrose's face.

Nothing threw Doctor Singh. "You will need to talk to the midwife but I would prefer you to be in the hospital."

"So would I," Primrose interjected.

"But you may not be able to get here in time so being prepared for a home birth is a good option." Another beaming smile split his face as Primrose's jaw dropped in horror.

"But isn't a home birth dangerous?"

"Not as long as there are no complications developing. Women have been giving birth for a very long time, you know?"

Maybe, but some other women, herself included, haven't been delivering them. Ever!

"Fern will be there. She knows what to do," said Nirupam happily.

Good old Fern with the crystals and the tarot readings. Still, there was a month to go yet. Plenty of time to bring Nirupam around to a more sensible decision.

****

Primrose stood back to admire her painting work. Clean, clear, crisp. Bit smelly but the pong would fade and was infinitely preferable to the stale, cloying odour of incense. Some of her edgings were rough around the window frame but the nudes had disappeared into oblivion. Today, to finish the second coat, she'd started at dawn. It would dry by mid morning.

A car engine roared outside. She negotiated her way round the furniture piled in the middle of the floor, to look out the window. Tom, getting out of his dusty white ute, confident, tanned and capable. Again the disabling surge of attraction. Her heart hopped and skipped a few beats. Or maybe that was paint fumes messing with her, or the fact she only had her brother and Kurt as comparison. What about the land deal? Had he cheated Danny? Hard to believe. He looked so upright and honest and he'd been genuinely angered by her tomato queries. He slammed the door and strode toward the house, stared toward her curtainless, open window.

Primrose gasped and jumped back. She was a total mess. Paint on her hands, probably in her hair, definitely on her clothes. No time to clean up. He'd laugh at her. He always did. She was a constant source of amusement for him. Good thing he hadn't dropped by yesterday when she'd trodden backward onto the paint tray. Good thing she'd been barefooted and very good thing the paint was water soluble.

"Come in," she called to his knock on the screen. No use pretending she was competent at this, no use pretending anything with Tom. He saw straight through her every time. His footsteps sounded in the hall, then the door was pushed wider and his face appeared round the frame.

"G'day." He stepped through and studied her handiwork. "How's it going?"

"Hello." Primrose waited ridiculously, childishly, apprehensive about his verdict. He filled the room. He made her breathing shallow. What did it matter what he thought? She was proud of herself.

Was he an opportunist or a man determined to expand his empire?

"Good job," he said with a grin. The lopsided, extremely attractive grin. He touched her cheek and scraped a wayward strand of hair aside with a surprisingly gentle finger. Her skin burned. "Did a good job on yourself too. Should wear a hat."

"I never thought of that." Barely breathing, her body suddenly pulsing with heat, Primrose stared into two deep grey eyes. Crinkly lines etched into the tanned skin by the glare of the outdoors gave a comforting solidity to his face. A kind man. A cheat? He tugged softly on her hair and moved across to examine the area previously occupied by Danny.

"Two coats?"

Primrose's brain lurched into action, spewing words. "Yes. It took ages. I started too late yesterday because I took Nirupam to the doctor and like you said, nearly passed out. Today I got up before dawn." She put the lid on the remains of the paint and gave it a thump. "I'm going to paint the baby's room, too. Apparently the boy, Mojo, sleeps in it." She lowered her voice. "The others came back last night but I'd gone to bed so I haven't met them yet. A new person came with them."

Brendan, in his fifties with a scrawny body and vacant blue eyes. He and Danny had gone off to look at the leaky windmill this morning.

"I'll give you a hand clearing up if you like."

She caught his eye briefly, just enough to send hot blood to her cheeks. "Thanks. Then we can have a cup of tea."

"Deal."

With Tom's expert and muscular help the wardrobe was pushed into place, the bed shoved against the wall and the paint equipment cleaned in no time. Primrose scrubbed at her hands in the laundry, recovering her equilibrium after confined exposure to him devoid of scoffing or annoyance, while he filled the kettle in the kitchen. This Tom was a very desirable man. If she was in the market. She wasn't, but she really did need to know about the land sales and now was about as good a time as any to ask.

An unfamiliar woman's voice was just audible over the splashing. Must be Fern. Getting up late—nearly ten. She paused in the doorway so as to assess this psychic healer who knew better than the caring doctor they'd seen yesterday. Fern wore an Indian cotton skirt and a cheesecloth embroidered blouse with an abundance of jewellery around her neck and on her fingers. Short, dumpy, brown-haired. She turned to give Primrose an equally assessing stare.

"Hello, Rosie." The eyes narrowed with psychic awareness. "You're a Fire sign, aren't you?"

"Hello, Fern. I've no idea."

"What star sign are you?"

"Libra."

"Oh, no. Libra's Air." The brow creased in psychic confusion. "Strange."

"Is it?"

"It's a Cardinal sign, however." She smiled. All was now well in the cosmos. "Never mind. How lovely to meet you."

"Thank you. Tea?"

"I'm about to do my breathing exercises. Need an empty stomach for those or it upsets the internal energy flow." Fern went out toward the sculptures. Primrose watched her walk across the grass to a spot under a beautiful spreading gum and begin raising and lowering her arms rhythmically. Maybe she should ask Fern about Tom's character as dictated by the stars.

"I should learn meditation," she murmured.

"Do you need to?"

The kettle clicked off. Primrose poured boiling water into the big brown teapot.

"I need something. My brain's a pigsty." She tried to raise a smile. Failed. She took two mugs from the draining rack. "I suppose you think I'm as mad as the rest of them."

Tom took the mugs to the table. "No." He sat down. "If you've been in the wars you need to recover and that way is as good if not better than many others. Booze, pills, or dope, for example."

"Really? I thought you'd turn your nose up at alternative type therapies."

"Why? Because I'm a farmer?" His grey eyes studied her over the rim of his mug. He was no hayseed that was for sure. Primrose's neck prickled uncomfortably.

"No because of your attitude the whole time I've been here."

Tom straightened his shoulders. "I think I've been very neighbourly."

And she was being very bitchy. Again. "You have. Absolutely you have, but you've made your opinion of the commune very clear."

"Aah, yes, Nirvana. But what goes on here doesn't necessarily resemble the best in alternative methods in farming or in health care. A place like this tends to attract the lunatic fringe element. Fern's all right. She's very kind. And Danny won't have anything to do with

56

drugs." He sipped his tea and changed the subject before she could steer him toward the land deal. "What did the doc say about Nirupam?"

"She's lacking in iron and calcium and something else plus she's a bit underweight. If she won't eat meat she has to make sure she gets enough protein and iron in her diet. He gave her some diet plans and multivitamin supplements."

"Good."

"Nirupam told him she wants to have the baby at home. There's a midwife who covers this area. Ellie Fletcher. She'll come and see Nirupam and tell us what we need to have ready. I don't think it's a good idea at all. What if something goes wrong?"

"Did he say anything might go wrong?"

"No."

"Ellie's delivered lots of locals. She'll look after Nirupam."

"We heard the baby's heartbeat. It was so exciting! I wish Danny had come." Both in tears, clutching hands and beaming at each other like idiots. A wondrous moment. "I'm so envious."

"Do you want children?"

"Oh, yes, lots of babies. Maybe one day." She flicked him a tiny smile but his expression was unexpectedly solemn, almost sad. He didn't speak for a long moment, then said, "I'm glad Nirupam's doing well. I like her."

Primrose studied the dregs of her tea. Did he like her, too? She hadn't made a good impression so far. In the ensuing silence she looked up and discovered Tom studying her. Flustered, she said, "Tell me about you, Tom."

"Not much to tell." He plonked his mug on the table. "I farm the place next door. Been there seven years."

"What crops do you grow?" A reasonable question to ask a farmer. She couldn't ask him anything personal, like did he have a girlfriend? What did he do for entertainment? The things she really wanted to know all of a sudden.

He leaned forward eagerly and began telling her what she'd asked. After several minutes of mind boggling facts he finished with, "I'm developing a sustainable method of living, minimising carbon-based energy sources by using solar panels and wind turbines, and agriculture that doesn't rely on chemical fertilisers and pest control. I'm focussing on truffles at the moment. They're a niche market, could be very profitable if they're successful but I have a variety of crops which do well in this area and I'm part of a larger nationwide study run by the CSIRO. Climate change is forcing these changes upon us. All of us. Adapt or die. Water management is crucial."

Here was her opportunity. Ask the question nagging away at the back of her mind. "Is that why you *insisted* Danny sell you his river land? So *you'd* have plenty of water?" As soon as the words left her mouth she knew the emphasis was excessive, the accusation of wrongdoing implicit in the phrasing.

He swallowed tea and put his mug down with precise care. "I don't know what you're implying but it was a mutually beneficial arrangement."

"Not more beneficial to some than others?"

"In what way?" His voice was deadly calm. The grey eyes never left hers. Steely now. Primrose's mind groped for facts. They were scanty. Mostly based on Kurt's ravings and Danny's vaguely defensive comments.

"Doesn't the commune need water frontage too?"

"They have the creek. They don't irrigate much and they have two dams. Haven't you noticed?"

She hadn't. But seeing as she'd begun she may as well finish. "What about the price?"

"What *about* the price?"

"Was it fair?"

"We thought so. And Danny and I are the only ones involved." Blank faced, daring her to keep blundering on. "And I've made him an offer for his thirty acre block, too."

"You're buying more land?" Surprise shot up Primrose's spine like an electric current. Why hadn't Danny mentioned it?

Tom replied quietly, "He's *selling* more of his land."

"Why?"

"Ask him."

"Do the others know?"

He shrugged. "I haven't told anyone. Except you." He raised one eyebrow slightly and murmured, "Maybe I shouldn't have."

That startled her even more than the initial remark. "Why not?"

"Danny asked me not to broadcast the news but he didn't exactly ask me to keep it secret. Will *you*?" He leaned forward slightly, emphasising the question.

Primrose hesitated. Wasn't everyone supposed to take part in decision making on the commune? Why hadn't Danny discussed this with the others? No-one had mentioned it, not even Nirupam. Did she know?

Tom's eyes bored into hers. "I'll ask Danny about it," she said. "How many acres will he have left?"

He relaxed against the back of his chair. "Seventy. Plenty for what they do here."

She frowned at the scorn. "Mess around, you mean?"

He smiled the lopsided smile but it didn't linger. "I didn't say it, you did."

Primrose sat uncomprehending. Her brain thrashed the information about like a tumble dryer. Danny must be really short of money and despite all his protestations about not being part of the capitalist system he was selling land. Or was that why he was selling? Was he offloading possessions? And if he was, was Tom taking advantage of some predicament her brother was in? Did he know more than he was letting on?

"How much are you paying?"

"None of your business." The tone was polite but the smile had gone, replaced by a narrowing of the eyes.

"It is my business. I'm a joint owner."

"Really!" That shook some of the smugness from him.

"Yes, really."

"Doesn't he need your approval to sell?"

"No. When we inherited it we agreed he would live here and run it as a commune. I never imagined he'd start selling bits off without telling me."

"Well he has. You'll have to take it up with him. It's not my problem."

Primrose gritted her teeth. Another "not my

problem" from Mr. Fairbrother. "Have you signed on it yet?"

"No." Crisp, succinct and clearly not willing to discuss it. "Why?"

"I'm going to make sure Danny knows exactly what he's doing before he does any deal, this time. And I'm going to make quite sure we aren't being ripped off."

"By me, you mean?" The eyes pinioned her again. Primrose stared right back. She wasn't the pushover Danny was, and the sooner Tom Fairbrother realised it the better.

"Yes."

"Know all about land prices, do you?"

"I can find out."

Tom stood up. His voice came taut with fury but unlike Kurt he didn't yell, which made his sudden anger more chilling. "You do that. Thanks for the tea. I'll be going now before I'm accused of anything else, but as you've been here all of four days I suggest you talk to your brother and get your facts straight before you start interfering."

Primrose swallowed the lump in her throat. She groped helplessly for words to apologise to this man she barely knew and who had done nothing but treat her with friendly helpfulness. More so than the people she was living with. More than the brother she was protecting with such vehemence. A brother she hadn't ever been close to and hadn't seen for six years. A brother with secrets.

"Who are you?" The piping, belligerent voice came from the doorway. Hot- faced and humiliated under the weight of Tom's disgust Primrose twisted round to see a plump little ginger-haired boy staring at them. Mojo. By the look on his freckled face she'd just gained another disapproving acquaintance.

"I'm Primrose, Danny's sister, and this is Tom from next door." She couldn't bring herself to face Tom, couldn't bear to see his disdain.

"I know. Hello, Tom."

From the corner of her vision Tom lifted a hand in greeting. "G'day, Mojo."

Mojo ventured into the kitchen, eyeing her with suspicion. "Is there any breakfast?"

Primrose's brain grappled with the change of gear, grabbing for an intelligent answer. "Does your Mum make it for you?"

"Anyone does. Mum or Nirupam. You can boil my egg. You're here."

Primrose glanced at Tom. He'd started moving toward the door but stopped to listen to the exchange with the hint of a familiar smirk on his otherwise stern face.

"There aren't any eggs," she said. "They haven't been collected yet."

"If I'm not here Nirupam does it." Mojo frowned. "Mum said she needs rest now so you should have."

"But you *are* here and I've been painting. Why don't you collect the eggs? Isn't it your job?" She accompanied the suggestion with what she hoped was a friendly smile although the muscles barely worked.

"I slept in. I'll have toast."

"Can you work the toaster yourself?"

He glared at her but deigned to admit he could by nodding. "Have you lived on a commune before?"

"No. Have you?"

"Lots. I was born on one in Mullumbimby. Mum says all the adults are my parents and my teachers." He raided the bread bin and emerged with two slices of bread. Fern couldn't have studied Kurt very closely.

"Don't you go to school?"

"No. I can learn much more from my parents and their friends. What can you teach me?"

Manners sprang to mind.

"Primrose plays the flute," interjected Tom. She flicked him a furious glance, but he was smiling at Mojo.

"You could teach me music." The plump face regarded her with satisfaction.

"Sorry. I'm not a teacher." Primrose stood up abruptly and headed for the doorway where Tom stood. If she ever had the great good fortune to have a child it wouldn't behave like this.

Mojo stuffed two slices into the toaster. "You won't like it here."

"Exactly what I think." Tom spoke up again. "She's not cut out to live in the country." Delivered with a large dollop of scorn. "See you later."

Mojo smiled at him, revealing missing front teeth and becoming quite sweetly childish for an instant instead of the little monster he'd resembled until that moment. "Bye, Tom."

Seething, Primrose led the way through the house to the front door. "Thanks a lot."

"What's your problem?" Tom said behind her.

His question seemed to encompass everything, her whole attitude, not just the exchange with Mojo. She pushed the screen door open and stepped onto the verandah. Heat radiated up from the bare, dry earth outside the thin line of shade provided by the overhang.

"I didn't come here to teach music." She brushed away a fly with a furious swipe. "There's no excuse for doing to your kid what they're doing. Farming him off on everyone else to educate. Is it legal?" It came out sounding too vicious. "Alienating him from society as well as preventing his education. Can he read and add up?"

"Don't know."

"I'd never do that to a child of my own. He wouldn't have any friends."

Tom placed his hand on her arm. "Calm down. I'm sure they love him."

Primrose dragged in a breath of rapidly heating air. She flashed him a sort of smile, conscious of the pressure on her skin, his touch warm, firm. Loving Mojo wasn't enough. Parents owed their children more.

"I guess so. I don't know them." A tiny squeeze and his fingers slid away to brush a fly from her hair. "Kurt thinks he's a genius."

A weak laugh covered the unexpected flutter of nerves caused by the casually intimate gestures, the unsmiling intensity of his scrutiny.

"Compared to Kurt he probably is." Tom walked down the steps leading to the yard. His ute waited by the gate with heat waves rippling from the white surface. "You can't expect everything to be laid on for you. It's not a holiday resort. It's a give and take system they work under."

"I give and they take, so far."

"Nothing keeping you here." The patronising mildness of his tone infuriated her.

"You'd be pleased if I left soon, wouldn't you?

You and Mojo." The sun beat down on their heads, cooking her brain.

"What do you care what I think? And Mojo is seven. He's a child. But seeing as you've asked. No, I don't think you'll last long. You're not the least bit interested in fitting in. I don't know what miracles you expected from them here, but from my experience personal problems follow you around no matter where you are. And until you admit to yourself *your attitude* may be the cause, you're stuck with them."

"But I came here to sort myself out!" Primrose cried. "I know I need to change."

"Fine! Good luck. But leave me out of it."

Tom turned on his heel and reached the ute in a couple of long strides. Primrose watched with a curious, hollow ache in her chest as he swung around and accelerated away, leaving a cloud of white dust hanging in the air. Disappointment? Uncertainty? Definite regret for the violently accusing way she'd spoken to him despite a lingering feeling something was being hidden. He had every right to be angry. She'd gone about it all wrong and made another impulsive attack.

Sammy the sheep peeped around the corner but she glared at him so fiercely he didn't dare venture further.

Why had Tom come over?

Chapter Four

Primrose trailed miserably back inside when Tom roared away. He was the only person she'd made any sort of connection with apart from Nirupam and Nirupam was in the slow, peaceful, self-centred world of late pregnancy. Danny disappeared early every day to work outdoors. They'd never talked easily and he showed no inclination to start now.

Mojo had been replaced in the kitchen by Nirupam when Primrose went to clear the tea mugs.

"Was that Tom?" She held a piece of cloth and had a selection of half moon shaped silver earrings spread before her for polishing.

"Yes."

"What did he want?"

"I don't know." Primrose sat down and examined the jewellery. Beautiful.

She'd first met Nirupam at Mum's bedside in the Emergency Department. She'd brought Mum in with a blinding headache which indicated the aneurysm the doctors realised too late. It was all over in ten hours. Danny only just made it in time, not that Mum knew.

First impressions of Danny's girlfriend weren't strong. A slim, calm girl in a loose white cotton dress, her pale, almost translucent skin dotted with light freckles. The light brown hair was still long and still hung straight from a centre parting. She and Danny had come into the ward holding hands and looking with anxious faces at the occupant of each bed they passed. Danny obviously adored Nirupam and vice versa. She remembered envying him. Envied the support his oddly named girlfriend gave without actually saying or doing much beyond being there.

Afterward, the following week, came the funeral and the accompanying legalities. There wasn't much to fight over even if they had been so inclined. Then, a couple of years later, they'd invited her to their wedding. Nirupam's doing, she suspected. Danny wouldn't have bothered. Again she was struck by the love. It hovered in the air between them as a tangible force. Inseparable then and inseparable now. Lucky people. Lucky child.

She'd felt out of place and uncomfortable despite the friendliness of the celebrating guests and the welcoming hugs from the bride and groom. She'd hung back and watched her brother marry the girl he would always love. Watched and remembered this happy, besotted man as a meek, quiet child cowering in fear of their father as he raised his fist. Watched with tears in her eyes and was glad he'd survived, glad he'd found this girl, the love of his life.

Nirupam broke into the reverie. "Tom hardly ever comes over but he's been here twice since you arrived." She kept her eyes focussed on the earring in her hands. Her expression gave no hint of any extra meaning behind her comment. She winced and placed her palm against her belly. "Kicking." A tiny smile lurked.

"I'm so envious." Primrose quickly put her own hand on the bulge. A firm lump moved vigorously under her fingers and disappeared. "I'd love to have a baby."

"You will, one day." The pale blue eyes regarded her for a moment. "You should ask Fern to do your cards."

"Maybe." Did it make any difference knowing what was going to happen? Or thinking you knew. If the cards told her she would meet her soul mate within the year would she be more likely to recognise him as such when he appeared? Doubtful. Unless the cards gave her a name, time, and date she'd wouldn't trust her judgement of men any more than she could at the moment. Primrose sat back. "I think Tom was checking on my painting."

"He's nice." The casual remark was like a slap in the face, snapping her out of the maudlin haze of self pity. He'd done nothing wrong. All the mess was in her own head. She was an overflowing toxic waste dump and he'd copped the spillage.

"Yes, he is nice." And nice looking. But she mustn't let a slow-burning lopsided smile and a sexy work-hardened body distract her. "Why is Danny selling land to him?"

The worried look flitted across her face. "We need the money. I'm sorry he didn't ask you but, well..."

Primrose smiled and shook her head. "It's fine. Danny's right. I never had anything to do with this place. But aren't you self sufficient here? I thought the idea was to grow your own food."

Nirupam put one earring down and picked up another. "Yes, it was. But it's very difficult. The drought hasn't helped. Birds eat the fruit and we can't afford netting. Plus we need money for rates and electricity, and we don't always earn enough. For a while it was all right because we still had some of the inheritance money to draw on but it's all gone now."

"Do the people who stay here contribute?"

"Not all of them. It's harder to get the dole nowadays. Danny lets everyone come regardless."

"You mean you're always supporting a whole lot of useless people?"

Nirupam nodded. "I agreed with him at first. The idea was everyone would work on the land and contribute in kind. Give what they could. But now there's the baby. And everything's getting more expensive. I'd like to have a home for just us."

"Of course you would! Is Danny getting the best possible price for the land?"

"I suppose so. It's Danny's business."

"Have you discussed asking everyone to leave?"

Nirupam shook her head. "It goes against everything Danny wanted to do." She looked Primrose in the eye. "I think he's always been trying to build a substitute family for the one you never had."

"Ours wasn't very good." There was no denying that as families went theirs was pretty woeful. A drunken abusive father, a weak-willed mother keeping the horrors at bay with prayer and Valium. Primrose bit her lip. "I think maybe that's why I've come here, too."

Nirupam smiled tentatively, waiting for her to continue but there was no solution to be had there. Nirupam had her own problems.

Primrose said, "But bad as he was, Dad wasn't as insane as Kurt. He thinks you should just squat down in a paddock for the birth. Can you imagine what crazy ideas he'll have about how to care for the baby? And he won't keep them to himself."

Nirupam's eyes opened wide and she nodded. Her hand went unconsciously, protectively, to her belly.

"He really has to go," said Primrose.

"We can discuss it tonight at the meeting."

Discuss it? We? Cripes! Didn't she get it? "No. We have to talk to Danny. Alone. He's the boss. He can kick someone out, no discussion needed."

Nirupam bent her head over her jewellery. "Did you meet the others?" she asked after a few moments of intense polishing.

"Only Fern and Mojo."

"They brought someone else in with them. Brendan." She glanced up and then down again before Primrose caught her eye.

"I met him. Do you know him?" Skinny with a face like a melting candle.

Nirupam shook her head. She straightened her back and edged her bottom forward, wincing.

Primrose exhaled. Maybe this unknown quantity Brendan, despite the unlikely packaging, would offer something useful and offset the ravings of Kurt.

****

The communal meeting began after dinner.

"First we should welcome our newest members, Rosie and Brendan." Kurt had appointed himself chairman.

"Thanks," Primrose said amidst the chorus of greetings. She was perched on one end of the saggy couch thigh to skinny thigh with Jason who squeezed in next to Fern. Mojo sat on the floor amidst the fading threadbare pink roses.

The scrawny, grey-haired hippy nodded and smiled. He wore a vacant expression most of the time, alleviated occasionally by either a slightly bewildered frown or a vague smile. At lunch he hadn't said much but afterward, with surprising alacrity, he offered to wash the dishes. Harmless, willing, and not altogether useless, but the extent of his abilities remained to be seen. He'd been helping Danny earlier but when they came in for lunch Danny hadn't looked happy.

Kurt, with a style of delivery reminiscent of the best in Hollywood Nazi oratory, addressed Primrose directly. "Our ideal here is equality for all. No-one has less say than the others. Everyone has equal voting on decisions which affect us all. Those who don't like this system can leave whenever they want." The last sentence was accompanied by a glower from under the wild, hedge-like eyebrows.

"Everyone contributes what they can. Everyone brings different skills," explained Fern with a smile at Brendan who now resembled a terrified basset hound even though Kurt ignored him completely, focussing on Primrose.

The crazy German appeared to assume she couldn't grasp the basics of a democratic society. She did. The question was, did anyone else? "Can I ask how the bills like rates and electricity are paid? Are they equally divided?"

"We figure things out." Danny, peeved and showing it. "Don't worry about it."

"I'd like to know."

"It all works out," said Kurt. "Some people contribute in kind. Money isn't everything. Society has brainwashed you into thinking that way. Here we do away with those capitalist notions."

"Right," muttered Primrose. And who was the most

upset about Danny's land price? Not Danny or herself. "Remind me of that when the next bill comes."

"Can we have reports for the week, please?" said Kurt. "I will go first. The dry weather has affected the crops very badly and without the windmill it's hard to water. The birds are eating everything. I collected five tomatoes today." Five small misshapen tomatoes with splits and marks.

"I fixed the windmill today," said Danny in a flat voice. "The dam is about half full."

Hah! No more excuses for the miserable quality and quantity of vegetables.

"Well done, Danny," said Fern.

"Anyway" he added with what could almost pass as a glare at Kurt. "It's only been out of action for a week. I haven't had the time to go into Braidwood for the parts."

Kurt's oblivious gaze swung around the room. "Who's next?"

"I collected six eggs," piped up Mojo. "And before we went away I collected twenty three."

"Ten came since," said Nirupam. "So the chooks laid thirty nine eggs this week."

Primrose had fossicked around in the undergrowth for some of those. The free thinking commune hens didn't believe in laying in their boxes in the fenced in part of the shed where they were locked up each night. Goodness knew how many she'd missed, or how old the eggs were she'd found. Now that Mojo was home he could resume his poultry duties and be welcome to them.

"Very good," said Kurt. "Well done, Mojo." Everyone clapped.

"Do the goats do anything?" asked Primrose. "No-one milks them, do they?" No milk, no yoghurt, no cheese. No nothing from that pair of malingerers. Tom's attitude to the communalists made more and more sense. No wonder he'd laughed at her that first day.

"They've never given milk," said Nirupam.

"Perhaps they should be sold."

"No." Kurt's dictatoresque stare swung away from Primrose. "We've already decided. Danny? Have you anything else to say?"

"The water tanks are three quarters full but the second dam is getting low. I took Nirupam's jewellery to Braidwood and collected nearly twelve hundred dollars from sales for the last batch. That's how I managed to repair the windmill."

Danny's little show of bravado had worn off and now the big bully had her brother sounding like an employee. Why should he be reporting in to anyone?

"I had no idea you were selling so well, Nirupam."

"A craft gallery has a standing order and a new shop took some this time."

"Maybe you could take your work further afield. Along the coast there are heaps of craft shops."

"I'm not sure we want to rely on my jewellery income. It's really my way of contributing."

Primrose gasped. Her work was supporting everyone. "Your way of contrib...."

"We can buy more vegetable plants with that money," interrupted Kurt. "And fix the tractor."

"It may only need new spark plugs," said Danny.

"Good. That will be cheap."

"I'd like to buy baby things," Nirupam offered in a

soft voice. "And some other nursery things." She looked at Primrose as though her request was a ridiculous self indulgence.

"Of course you should," she cried. The lack of preparation had seriously alarmed her. "We can go shopping."

"Babies don't need much," said Kurt. "No point wasting good money on new. Secondhand clothing is best, they grow so fast."

"She can have new if she wants." Primrose fixed him with a hard-eyed stare. "She earned the money."

"I agree," said Fern. "A first baby is special."

Kurt glared at them like a cornered bull, but Jason said in a bored voice, "Vote. Who agrees Nirupam spends the money on baby gear?"

All hands went up except Kurt's. Mojo put up both of his. Nirupam produced a shy little smile. "Thanks."

"Anything else to report?" Kurt snapped.

"We earned one hundred and thirty dollars at the workshops." Jason yawned, folded his arms and stretched his legs out.

"Is that all?" The shaggy brows drew together in disgust.

"After expenses." Fern stared right back at him. "There are three of us." Primrose's estimation of her character rose dramatically. But what exactly were they contributing? Jason hadn't lifted a finger today except to strum the guitar strings and raise his beer to his mouth. No wonder he was yawning.

"Right." Kurt made a sound like a draught horse with chaff up its nose. "Now we have complaints. Who goes first?"

"I think the men should do more of the household

chores," said Primrose. "Brendan helped wash up but he's the only one who's done anything."

"I don't mind cleaning," he said with an eager smile. "I worked as a cleaner once."

"I don't think you have the right attitude," Kurt said to Primrose with a vast sigh. Patient and all knowing.

"Because I don't agree with everything you say? You know what I think, Kurt? I think you run this commune like a dictatorship and from what I've seen you don't contribute much at all. Nirvana? It's more like Animal Farm and you're Napoleon."

Kurt gave her a pitying smirk and shook his head.

"I think Rosie is doing her best to fit in," said Danny. "It's hard for her, remember. She has to adapt."

Kurt growled, "She's brainwashed by society. They get inside your head like worms. The money men. Everything money. Money, money, money." He shook his shaggy head again. "Stupid bastards."

"Any other complaints?" asked Danny.

"Kurt, why are you so upset about the price Danny and Tom agreed on for his land?" Primrose demanded. "You weren't even here at the time."

"I can't stand a man who cheats his friend."

"It's in the past, Rosie," said Danny with unexpected strength. "Leave it. You too, Kurt."

Two maniacal eyes bored into her head. She bored right back with what she hoped was a laser beam of dislike. How could she have doubted Tom's honesty, taken this lunatic's word over his?

"If that's everything, we'll do a mantra to finish," said Fern brightly into the pulsating, overheated air. "We need to cleanse our thoughts and minds of negative energies."

The thoughts whirling about would need a good dose of industrial strength bleach to cleanse them.

Jason took incense burners and candles from the cupboard and lit them. Everyone stood up, pushed the furniture back, and sat crosslegged in a circle on the worn carpet. Fern turned the light off. She took her place and began to intone something.

Primrose glanced around. Everyone had their eyes shut, even little Mojo. Brendan, next to her, wore an expression of complete tranquillity and acceptance and he'd only just arrived. Either he was unaffected by the negative vibes or he'd drifted blissfully into his own hazy world. They all had their hands clasped in their laps so she did the same. Fern's voice became quite hypnotic. Peaceful. Tom's angry face flashed into her mind as her knees began to ache.

****

Despite the energy cleansing meditation session, tension hovered in the air the next morning. Primrose cleaned the house in a purely physical way and left the spiritual and metaphysical side to Fern. Nirupam was incapable and no-body else cared about the layers of grit lining the bookshelves, or the dust bunnies having group meetings in the corners behind the chairs.

Kurt ignored her. Fern and Jason were polite but seemed to take it as a personal insult that she refused to give Mojo music lessons. Mojo gave her baleful looks when their paths crossed which wasn't often because he spent most of the time either swinging listlessly on the tyre swing or sprawled on the old couch in the living room reading a tattered Harry Potter book. Brendan cleaned the bathroom and toilet in a flurry of activity then trailed around after Danny, but late on Friday afternoon, announced he was leaving. Jason drove him to the main road where he intended hitching a lift north.

At least one of them had moved on voluntarily. The wrong one but better than none.

Primrose went to her room straight after dinner, exhausted from cleaning in the heat and the strain of pretending the tense atmosphere wasn't bothering her. Far from a haven of peace and tranquillity, this place was worse than the orchestra pit in the last show she'd done. The show which had put the finishing touches on her disillusionment with an orchestral career. Unbearable as Kurt was he didn't have the caustic tongue and acid wit of the conductor. The man who had taken an active dislike to the flute section and to her in particular. A misogynistic bastard who made every rehearsal a nightmare and every performance a terrifying ordeal of nerves.

In the middle of the night, awakened from a fretful, uneasy sleep, Primrose sat up in bed, heart pounding. Squawks and screeches erupted into the quiet. Feet pounded down the corridor outside her door. The screen door slammed. Kurt's roar of rage echoed around the yard.

Primrose leapt out of bed and flung on a robe and scuffs. Light shone under her door and when she opened it Danny pushed past, shoving her against the wall in his haste.

"What's wrong?" she called.

"Fox." The door slammed as he raced through.

A fox? Eating the chooks? She rushed out to the verandah. The outside light only reached partway to the sheds. Kurt and Danny had torches but the beams flashed in random arcs and she couldn't see anything. More squawks and yells. She ran across the yard toward the lights. Danny and Kurt were pulling wire netting back into place, cursing in a fluent duet of German and Australian.

"Fox killed four hens," said Kurt with a ferocious scowl her way. "You have to make sure the door is shut properly. Every night. Otherwise this happens."

"Me? I thought it was Mojo's job." Assumed he'd taken over again now he was home. He was the egg collector.

"He's only a little child."

"I know but...I thought seeing he was home again he'd do it."

"It's a job for an adult," said Danny abruptly.

"I'm sorry," she murmured, stricken by the enormity of her assumption. She hadn't properly discussed it with Mojo. Quite honestly she hadn't given the chooks a second thought. Last night they must have been lucky because she hadn't locked them up then, either.

Primrose returned to the house to lie in bed, sleepless for the remainder of the night with nightmare visions of shredded hen's bodies whirling in her mind like bloodstained feathers, interspersed with her harsh words to Tom and his furious face hovering over the mayhem like an ancient god ready to pronounce judgement.

****

Mojo burst into tears at breakfast when he learned of the night raid, and rushed outside to discover which of his brood had survived. Kurt followed him after more smouldering, rage-laden glances at Primrose.

Primrose sat with Fern and Jason, toying with a piece of toast and honey. "Will he be all right?"

"He has to learn about death." Jason poured himself more tea. "It's a natural part of life."

"Yes, but I was supposed to lock up the henhouse."

"Mojo was supposed to," said Fern. "He has to learn responsibility."

"But he probably thought I'd do it. I feel terrible."

"Don't. It's always been his job. He'll be fine. We'll have a burial ceremony." Fern shoved in a mouthful of homemade muesli. "Maybe you could play your flute."

A funeral for some chooks. Why not? This place was forcing her mind wide open.

"Nirupam said you wanted to learn some relaxation techniques," said Fern.

"Oh! Yes, I would, but I don't like to ask her at the moment."

"I can show you some Chinese exercises. Chi Kung."

"Is that what you do each morning?" When she'd got up early to paint she'd spied Jason and Fern doing their exercises under the trees near the sculptures. They looked peaceful and calm, quite in contrast to the daily emotional mayhem of Nirvana.

"Yes. We do it early when the Chi is freshest."

Did Chi go stale? "What's Chi?"

"The life force," said Jason. "These exercises cultivate our natural energy, our life force."

Fern added, "They also incorporate meditation for calming the monkey mind. That's what the Chinese call the mind. Always leaping from thought to thought. Never still."

Primrose smiled. "That's the inside of my head exactly."

"Join us tomorrow morning."

"Thanks, I will. Where did you learn?"

"We went to a weekend workshop given by a Tai Chi instructor from Canberra. He learns from a Grandmaster in China."

"Goodness." Maybe they really did know about it. They certainly looked as though they did and they practised diligently which was something she understood, having devoted many hours every day to practising the flute. Odd how her flute held no appeal right at the moment yet she'd loved it since she was a teenager.

"You'll enjoy it and it'll help you a lot." Fern gave her a knowing smile.

****

The chook funeral was held behind the goat shed with the two goats peering inquisitively through the railings. Sammy the sheep wandered about and finally stopped to pick at the grass along the back of the shed. Kurt had dug a hole in the dry, hard-baked earth with a great deal of sweating and the occasional curse. He leaned on the shovel while the mourners assembled.

Danny didn't stop whatever he was doing on the tractor to take part. Nirupam stood in the patchy shade of a gum tree, while Jason and Fern held the deceased's bodies, wrapped in sacking.

Primrose, flute in hand, waited by the hole. She had no idea what to play. Mojo sniffed.

"I'm sorry," she said to him. Watery eyes looked up at her but he didn't say anything.

"We commend these bodies to the deep," said

Jason.

"Isn't that for burials at sea?" asked Primrose.

"Ssh," Kurt hissed. "Mojo, would you like to say something? They were your friends, these chooks."

Poor kid if his only friends were chooks. Primrose put a hand lightly on his shoulder.

"Goodbye Treasure, Ruby, Mrs. Cluck and Princess Leia. I'm sorry the fox got you. I'm sorry I left the gate open." A tear dripped down his cheek.

Primrose's heart lurched. She slipped her arm around his tubby little body and hugged him. "*I* didn't lock them up, Mojo. It was my fault."

He sniffed again and wiped a hand across his face but he stayed in the circle of her arm as Fern and Jason lowered their bundles into the hole. Primrose's throat tightened and a tear pushed against her lids.

"Rest in peace, chookies," she said.

Fern straightened. She stepped back a pace and nodded to Primrose. "Play." Kurt began filling the hole.

Primrose raised her flute and began the slow movement from a Handel Flute Sonata. One of her favourite pieces. The sound wound up through the trees, borne on the warm air, mingling with the wind chimes and the cicadas. She closed her eyes, blocking out the steady thud of the shovel, focussing on the melody and the fact her fingers were stiff and unwieldy, her tone a little rough.

She reached the end, opened her eyes, lowered her flute, grimaced in apology for the lacklustre performance. The others were standing watching her, blank-faced. Even Kurt was bereft of comment. A neat mound of earth covered the final resting place.

"That was absolutely beautiful," said Fern after a

long silence.

"Thanks for playing, Rosie." Mojo gave her a little smile.

"Very good," was Kurt's grudging praise.

"I'm a bit rusty."

"We had no idea you were so good," said Nirupam. "You didn't sound rusty to me."

"Or me. It was perfect." Fern held out her hand to Mojo. "Let's get cleaned up for lunch."

The men headed for the sheds. Primrose and Nirupam walked slowly to the house.

"Was I really all right? I haven't played for a few weeks."

"It was absolutely beautiful. You're really, really good."

"Thanks, I'm so pleased. For Mojo's sake." And also because she'd been able to render Kurt speechless.

****

After lunch Primrose managed to corner Danny putting on his boots in the laundry.

"We want to talk to you."

"What about?" His eyes flicked from her to his wife standing behind her. He licked his lips. Nirupam smiled uncertainly but didn't object.

"In private," said Primrose. "In my room."

Under the surprised gazes of the others they trooped along the corridor and into the fresh whiteness of her bedroom. A faint tang of paint still lingered.

"It's lovely." Nirupam stared around in surprise.

"I'll do the baby's room as soon as the others leave," said Primrose. "Sit down."

Nirupam lowered herself carefully onto the bed. Danny stood against the closed door with his arms folded. "What's up?"

"We have some things to discuss," said Primrose.

"Everyone should be involved."

"No!" Nirupam's tone startled them both. "I'm sick of discussing everything we do with them. They're not our friends. We haven't known any of them longer than a year. Kurt makes all the decisions and you never object to anything he says or does."

"Maybe I agree with him," he said.

"Rubbish," Primrose interrupted. "He's mad! He can't grow vegetables and Tom says he won't listen to any advice. He's a loudmouth know it all and Nirupam and I think he should go. You have to tell him to leave, Danny."

Danny's mouth fell open and he sucked in two great breaths before he said, "I won't tell him to leave. This place is for everyone." His arms flailed wide as he took two strides toward her. "You just don't understand, Rosie. You come here bossing us around and telling us what we're doing wrong, and upsetting Nirupam. We were doing well until you came barging in. You've always been the same. Telling everyone what to do. Why don't you leave us alone? Why don't *you* leave?"

Nirupam heaved herself off the bed. Two pink spots burned in her cheeks contrasting starkly with the alabaster of the surrounding skin. "Rosie hasn't upset me. She's said what I should have said ages ago. I don't like Kurt and I want him to leave. I don't want him anywhere near my baby. If Rosie goes, I'll go with her."

Primrose's head whipped round in alarm. Where could she take eight months pregnant Nirupam? She didn't have anywhere to live herself except here.

Nirupam had an unusually determined expression. Danny must have recognised it as one demanding conciliation because he said, "Sweets, calm down. I'll...I'll...think about it."

"Good. I need to lie down." Her anger deflated as quickly as it rose. She shuffled toward the door. "Thanks, Rosie," she whispered as she passed. Primrose squeezed her hand.

When the door closed behind her, Danny, lips white with fury hissed, "This is all your fault. Why can't you mind your own business?"

"This *is* my business, Danny. You're my brother and Nirupam's the closest to a sister I'll ever have."

"We haven't seen each other for years," he spat in disgust. "Now, when you need help, you come swanning in here and expect us to change everything to suit you."

"I don't! Can't you see what's happening? Nirupam's not happy."

"She was until you arrived and started telling her she wasn't."

"Give her some credit. She's not stupid. She's worried about her baby. She wants to have a normal family life, not strangers dropping in and out. Surely you can understand that?"

He dropped his head, sighed in exasperation. "I don't think I can do that sort of family. A normal one. Whatever that is." He glared at her again.

"You're more along the way to it than I am," Primrose said in a frustrated burst of candour. "You have a wife who loves you and a child on the way. I can't even get a man to marry me." The last words hung in the air. Where had they come from? Envy? Bitterness? She didn't begrudge Danny and Nirupam their happiness. They deserved every bit of it. Danny certainly did.

He studied her for a long, uncomfortable moment and the dislike in his green eyes chilled her to the bone. "Maybe you should try being less of a controlling bitch."

****

Primrose stayed in her room the rest of the afternoon, alternating lying on the bed and pacing about, sometimes peering out the window, sometimes sitting on the floor, her back against the cool of the wall, hot tears trickling down her cheeks. Leave? Every fibre in her body screamed clear out as fast as she could. No-one would miss her, no-one would care. Except one.

She couldn't walk out on Nirupam, not now, however much she may want to. If she did, Kurt would continue to rave and impose his idiocies and poor Nirupam would lose any control she had. Plus if she left, Tom would have a smug chuckle and congratulate himself for being right once more. She'd be damned if she'd give him the satisfaction. And on one level she had every right to stay. This land was half hers.

But if she didn't bust out of the house she'd go madder than she already was. Stir crazy. Time to hit the town for some night life. It was Saturday. The boldly advertised Trivia Night at the Kullanurra pub she'd seen on the way through town should offer some form of entertainment. No way was she spending another evening in the company of Kurt. Whatever the locals were like they had to be more fun than the nightmare crew she was living with. Pubs served good food. Steak or a roast, most likely. Her mouth watered at the thought.

At six thirty she showered, donned the lacy black panties Tom had spilled in the yard and applied make-up with the greatest of care. An image of his fingers running over the fabric, touching her skin, caressing, sent goosebumps up her spine. His grey eyes held more than a hint of interest when he looked at her body despite the words on his tongue. Perhaps he could be persuaded to have some fun, too. Sexy, lean, strong man. She chose a snug-fitting black dress with spaghetti straps and a plunging neckline, slipped her feet into high-heeled sandals, grabbed her purse and headed for the car.

Chapter Five

Tom looked up as the mutter of conversation in the bar faded to silence. Seated at a table in the corner of the L-shaped room he had a good view of Primrose as she made her entrance.

Kullanurra hadn't seen anything as well-proportioned and sexy since...ever. She knew exactly the effect she was having and lapped it up. Green eyes sparkled beneath the artfully tousled mop of multicoloured hair and she flashed those dimples about like invitations as she sashayed between gawping admirers toward Ted behind the bar. He grinned and adopted what he probably thought was a sophisticated barman's pose. Pity about the shirt buttons straining over the expanse of belly.

"G'day, love. What can I get you?"

"I'm buying," interjected Mike, a self-styled Casanova from the peach orchard just out of town, swiftly edging alongside Primrose.

"White wine, please," Primrose said. "Thank you." She smiled up into Mike's weatherbeaten face with an intimate little glance which socked Tom in the solar plexus. Desire surged. He half rose from his seat then subsided as he remembered what she was really like. Mike wouldn't know what hit him when she got revved up.

She scanned the room curiously as Mike ordered

the drinks. Found Tom. He offered a half smile but didn't stir, tamped down an outrageous attack of intense physical attraction. If she wanted to say anything— apologise, for example—she could come to him. Mike turned so his large shoulders blocked Tom's view of her face. All he could see was half her trim body and one sleek leg ending in another of those silly high heeled sandals she liked. The ones that showed off her ankles and calves. He could almost encircle one of those ankles with the fingers of one hand. Then he'd move on up over the rounded calf to the tender skin at the back of her knee...

Mike shifted. She raised her glass of wine and clicked it gently against his beer. They turned and headed toward Tom's corner table. Mike had a grin like Delilah's when Tom gave her a bone.

"G'day Mike. How's it going?" Tom rose slowly and stretched out his hand to first one then the other. "Primrose." Mike's hand was firm and tough, callused and hard like his own. Primrose's handshake was firm but the skin was soft and the hand small, cool—hard to let go. She released his fingers, removing her hand from his grasp with a little tug. He said abruptly, "Care to join me?"

She said, "Thanks," and they pulled out chairs, Mike large and cumbersome, she as gorgeous and exotic as a tropical bird settling amongst a motley pair of drab workaday pigeons.

"I was hoping to have dinner here. Do they serve food?" A sweetly innocent smile at Mike.

"Yeah," he replied. "Not bad, either."

"Fed up with vegetables?" asked Tom. She'd done something to her eyelids and lashes so the green of her eyes was emphasised. The nail polish had gone. Painting was rough on the hands. And kitchen work.

She didn't rise to his remark. Cool jade regarded him for a moment. "I thought a night out would be fun."

"Trivia night's always a riot. The whole town comes," said Mike, oblivious to nuance as usual. "You might win the Meat Tray." He roared with laughter. "Be a real hit at the commune." Tom snorted into his beer and Primrose grinned.

"When does it start?"

"Eight," said Tom. "You can have dinner first."

"Are you eating here?" Primrose spoke to Mike, then slowly switched her gaze to Tom. Heat rippled in his groin again. Was there an invitation in her eyes? She seemed different tonight. Although she sat apparently relaxed across from him, an air of tension hung about her like an invisible electrical field.

Mike said, "Yeah. You, Tom?"

"I'd planned on it." Funny how that worked out. He'd planned on inviting Primrose to dinner when he went over day before yesterday, changed his mind when she accused him of nefarious dealings, and now here she was, asking to have dinner with him. And Mike.

"I'll grab a menu." Mike stood up and headed for the bar.

"How are you?" Primrose asked, not meeting his eye. She twirled the stem of her glass. Abba blared on the jukebox.

And here he was, lusting after her like a fifteen year old. "Fine." He sipped his beer thoughtfully. Yep, tense as piano wire. She looked about to break. "How are things in Nirvana?"

She looked up then and for the first time the internal tension was blatantly revealed. A tightness around the eyes, a tremor in the mouth. "Terrible." Her lips wobbled. "I'm sorry I was rude to you, Tom. Really sorry."

Keep it light. If that was her problem, easily fixed. "Apology accepted." Terrible? Her week would be up in a day or two. She'd almost proved him wrong.

"I had a fight with Danny this afternoon."

"Not Kurt?" His attempt at lightening the mood fell flat.

"No." She didn't even raise an attempt at a smile. "I had a stoush with him on Thursday."

"First me then Kurt. Quite a day for you—Thursday," he said. "So what did you fight with Danny about?"

"He said I was...I should...he said..." He waited while she thrashed words about incoherently. Must have been a humdinger of a fight to render her speechless. Perhaps she'd stirred Danny up enough to tell her what she should have been told years ago, "Mind your own business," and the shock had incapacitated her vocal chords. He pursed his lips to stop himself chuckling. She was very upset. But it *was* her business. Very surprising, the joint ownership news.

Mike slapped a sheet of paper on the table. "You can have chicken curry, roast lamb, or a steak."

"Roast lamb," Primrose said instantly.

Tom grinned and met her eye. "Me, too."

"Right, I'll put our orders in. This is on me, love," Mike said as Primrose opened her purse. Tom firmed his mouth and found his wallet. Mike was a bloody fast worker. He'd known her five minutes.

"Thanks, Mike, but no, I prefer to pay my own way." She accompanied the refusal with another sweetly dimpled smile. "You can buy me a glass of wine, though."

She handed him some money and he almost drooled all over her. Tom gave him two twenties. "Here, mate."

"Thanks. Same again?" He charged away.

Tom studied Primrose. "So? Are you going to tell me?"

"What?"

"What Danny said you were, should, whatever it was."

She frowned. "Do you really want to know?"

"If you want to tell me, I'll listen." She bit her lower lip and pulled it inside her mouth, considering, probably trying to decide if he was having a go at her. "If you need to get it off your chest, tell me. Who else is there?" he prompted. Not that he was avidly interested but it was obviously something which had shaken her previously uncrackable composure, and she'd chosen him to confide in.

She met his gaze with such a naked, open expression of misery he gulped and had to swallow a mouthful of beer while he regained his equilibrium.

"No-one else," she said hoarsely. "I have no-one."

He thought for one horrible moment she was going to cry, here in the public bar of the Kullanurra pub surrounded by his friends and neighbours, all of whom would immediately assume he was responsible. He opened and closed his mouth, impotently groping for words to soothe and stave off the inevitable flood but she forged on. He'd underestimated her once more. The words poured out in a torrent of indignation.

"I thought I had Danny on my side—he is my brother, after all—but he's furious with me. He accused me of coming here to the commune and trying to change everything to suit myself. Can you believe it?" She stared at him. He shook his head. Unbelievable, all right. As if she'd expect that. Miss Do It My Way. "Nirupam and I are worried about Kurt—like you say he's a raving lunatic. Nirupam doesn't want him around after the baby is born and I told Danny he should kick Kurt off the place."

"And he got upset?" No wonder. And no doubt she did it in her usual tactless, blunt style.

"Yes. Very. He thought it was just me but Nirupam backed me up." She smiled, a little off-kilter but still a smile. "Danny said if I didn't like it I should leave, but Nirupam said if I left she'd go too."

"You've certainly shaken them up over there." He leaned back, casual and unconcerned but the suddenly crucial question burned in his mind. "*Are* you leaving?"

Her eyes narrowed and she leaned forward slightly. A wicked gleam shone in her eyes now. "No. But you'd like it if I did, wouldn't you?"

Tom leaned forward too and stared right into the deep greeny brown pools. "I wouldn't like it at all." The truth, he realised. Amazingly so. He wanted her to stay. He wanted to know more about her, discover the depths of her. Explore her delicious body with his.

She held his gaze. "Won't last a week?" One delicate eyebrow arched upward. "Week's up on Monday."

"Are you flirting with my date?" Mike dumped a

92

handful of paper napkin-wrapped cutlery on the table. Primrose sat back with a little grin, her eyes still fixed on Tom's.

"I'm not your date, Mike, but he is flirting," she said demurely.

Tom drained his beer with a nonchalant flick of the wrist. The intensity of the look belying the casualness of her words twisted his brain in knots. *Who* was flirting?

Mike flung himself into the chair next to hers. "Bloody typical. Turn my back for an instant and he's in like Flynn."

"Does Tom have a reputation with the girls?" Primrose grinned at Mike and the dimples danced.

He leaned toward her with what could only be classed as a leer. "He has his share of admirers. Can't imagine why. Go and get the drinks, Tom. It's my turn to chat with Primrose."

Tom stood up. He hadn't met this Primrose. Now that she'd offloaded her hurt concerning Danny a flirty girl in party mode emerged, complete with sexy black dress. Wearing the lacy underwear he'd found in his bathroom? Hadn't been close enough to smell if she was wearing the same perfume. Her dress revealed acres of smooth, tempting skin and one honey brown knee and half her thigh was exposed as she crossed her legs. He turned for the bar and heard her say, "Everyone calls me Rosie, Mike." Not everyone. She hadn't asked *him* to call her Rosie! He pushed through the gathering crowd.

Tom gathered the drinks carefully between his hands and edged toward the corner table. Mike and Primrose were laughing. God, she was gorgeous! Black lace knickers—barely a scrap of fabric. She wouldn't need much to cover that neat behind of hers. No bra? Or the lacy thing he'd found in his bathroom?

She reached out to remove the precariously balanced glass of wine. A special little smile from shiny red lips. A flash from those sparkling eyes. "Thanks." Was she doing this deliberately? Did she know the effect she was having and did he look as stupidly obvious in his desire as Mike?

"Rosie's been telling me about the paintings in her bedroom," said Mike. "Always wondered what went on in that place."

"Rosie?" asked Tom.

"Danny called me that when we were little. Now all my friends do." She shrugged. "It's stuck."

"You don't strike me as being a Rosie." Tom started in on his new beer. He obviously didn't rate as a friend. He studied her solemnly. "We had a big chestnut draught horse called Rosie when I was a kid."

"This Rosie is no draught horse, she's a thoroughbred, through and through," cried Mike.

"What name do you think suits me?" She ignored Mike's blatant attempt to wrest her attention away. This girl was all his. He wanted her with a gut-wrenching intensity which shook him to the core.

"I prefer Rose." He put his glass down precisely on the coaster.

"Why?" She was all attention now, leaning forward slightly, lightly tanned skin of her throat and chest on display, soft swell of her breasts tantalisingly visible before the black dress obscured further delights. No straps, definitely not that bra. Not prim like the first part of her name.

He tore his eyes and his mind away from temptation. "It's elegant and refined." Unlike his thoughts.

A slow smile spread across her face. "Thank you." Unless he imagined it her eyes blurred momentarily. She blinked and turned to Mike.

"So how smart are you? Is it worth being on your team for trivia?"

"Sport's my specialty," he declared. "And peach growing."

"Excellent! I know all about music. What about you, Tom?"

"Tom's the local science boffin," said Mike.

"Really?" She turned a very surprised face toward him. "Did you study science at Uni?"

"I have a PhD."

"So you're doing all that stuff on your place with a scientific basis?"

Her amazement could be taken as insulting. If he chose. "What did you think I was doing? Messing about?" He raised an eyebrow.

Primrose's mouth dropped open and a warm pink tinged her cheeks. He caught her eyes and held. Mike interrupted. "Tom's the local expert on new agricultural methods. He's improved my crop yield over the last couple of seasons." He frowned. "And if that German bastard would see some sense we'd all be better off."

"Kurt?" Still holding Tom's gaze.

Tom nodded. He shifted in his chair, broke the contact because this subject was close to his heart and he wanted her to understand. "He farts about with his organic style methods, refusing to intervene on disease control saying it's unnatural, and all he does is attract every pest known to man. His version of organic is do bugger all. Then he complains when the professional fruit growers in the area dob him in to the authorities. Blames me because I'm closest."

"Doesn't he bother you?"

"Nah. He gives me a laugh sometimes. Apart from the farming menace aspect. But we've got it under control, now." He looked at her pointedly. "I don't have anything to do with him. And I don't have to live with him."

"If you can get him to leave, Rosie, you'll be the local hero," Mike exclaimed.

"Evening, folks. Who's having what?" Maureen appeared with their meals.

"Thanks." Primrose inspected her roast lamb, peas, carrots, and baked potatoes.

Tom smiled. "Nothing like a good old-fashioned roast. My Mum's are the best, though."

"Where are your parents, Tom?" No tension, no flirting. Just plain interest.

"Cowra. I grew up on a farm. Not big enough to support more than one family, though. Dad still works it." He shook pepper over his spuds.

"Do you have brothers and sisters?"

"One brother still at home helping Dad. Two sisters. Both married."

Primrose nodded and continued to eat in silence. Tom came from a happy family, she could tell just by the way his face changed and softened when he thought of them. They'd given him a solid base to build his life on. She and Danny had grown up with sand slipping and sliding under their childish feet, never sure where home would be from one week to the next, never sure whether their father would be there and if he was what state he'd be in or who would be the target of his rage.

"So quiet," murmured Tom under cover of Mike requesting chutney from Maureen.

Startled, Primrose swallowed the mouthful she was chewing. "I'm concentrating on my food. It's delicious."

Tom nodded but the expression on his face implied he didn't accept her glib excuse. His grey eyes watched and assessed. She shifted uncomfortably. She didn't want to be serious tonight. He'd accepted her apology, surprised her by listening to her gripe, and even more by flirting earlier, and it was fun. So was Mike's attention although his big bear-like build wasn't nearly as sexy as Tom's lithe muscular frame.

"How's your curry, Mike?"

"Tasty but not as hot as the ones I had in Thailand. Reckon you could strip paint with them." With that he proceeded to tell them all about his two week Thai holiday, which effectively prevented Tom probing any further into her mental state. Tonight she wanted to forget the crappy childhood, the crappy fiancé, her crappy life and the mess she'd made at the commune. She wanted to drink wine, flirt with Mike and Tom and have a good time. Tomorrow could take care of itself. Same for yesterday and all the yesterdays before it.

****

Their table picked up two extra contestants in the form of Mike's brother and sister-in-law but even with the boosted brain power the Meat Tray prize went to another loudly cheering team.

"Miserable effort," cried Mike as everyone pushed chairs back and prepared to leave. "Remind me to get a better team next time. I'm off home." He yawned. "Early start in the morning. Make sure you come to visit, Rosie."

"Will do." Primrose gave him a salute followed by a kiss on the cheek.

He grinned and went off with his relatives.

"Home time?" asked Tom.

Primrose wrinkled her nose. The lumpy mattress wasn't calling yet. It was only just after eleven but the crowd had thinned. "Is there anything else to do?"

"Not unless you want another drink."

"No, thanks." Primrose picked up her bag. "Guess that's it then."

"Are you all right to drive?" Tom followed as she walked across the near empty room, his voice anxious. He held the door for her and she stepped out into the oppressive warmth of the still night. Headlights splashed across her body as cars turned for home, doors slammed, and voices called final goodnights. Tom's white ute was across the street. Her Golf was around the corner opposite the little town park.

"Sure. But I feel like some fresh air."

"Like some company?"

"Yours?" Primrose smiled, standing close, looking up into cool grey eyes, head tilted. Had she wanted him to be the one? Had she come into town tonight hoping he'd be here? Somewhere deep inside the answer was yes. She'd known as soon as she turned and saw him watching her from his corner table. Known he wanted her. And vice versa.

"I can catch Mike if you'd prefer."

She shook her head slowly, holding his eyes with hers, then turned and headed for the corner with a deliberate sway in the hips. If she wasn't very much mistaken Tom had lust in his eye and what better way to lose herself tonight?

He caught up in a couple of swift strides and took her hand when they turned into the side street where the light didn't reach. She stumbled slightly in her heels in the sudden darkness and his arm slipped around her waist to support her. Strong. Comforting. She leaned into his body and slid her arm around him as they walked on. He smelled nice. Soap and freshly laundered shirt mixed with his own scent and a slight tang of beer. Trees rustled softly overhead. They passed the last of the three houses in the street, cocooned in the warm night air. A dog barked somewhere. A million stars spangled the black velvet sky. Their steps sounded loud on the tarmac and then the road turned to gravel. Tom stopped.

"Bit rough here for you. You wear such silly shoes."

Her eyes had adjusted to the soft summer night so when she glanced up she could see his face illuminated by the half moon, looking down at her. All sharp planes and angles, deep shadows and silvery skin. Inches away.

"Do I?"

He turned her in his arms and his fingers stroked her cheek and gently traced her mouth, cupped her chin. Without a word he bent his head and kissed her softly.

Primrose held her breath. Not what she expected. A kiss so light and sweet from a man like Tom. A man who observed her with reserve and a measure of cynical humour despite his obvious desire for her as a female. Not what she'd expected at all, especially tonight when she'd deliberately dressed to attract, to party. When she wanted to forget.

"Tom," she murmured into his lips. He drew away. "Sorry."

"Don't be sorry." She grasped his face between her hands and stood on tiptoe to press her mouth on his. He responded instantly, pulling her hard against his body, all soft sweetness lost in a torrent of passion and hot skin.

Primrose closed her eyes and flew with him. This was what she craved—oblivion, sensory delight to the point of overload, a blotting out of the mess of her life. His hands roamed her body and one found its way to her breasts. She moaned into his mouth at the caress. Then he was speaking, murmuring words she didn't understand, couldn't decipher through the haze of lust. He dragged his mouth away from hers.

"Not here." His voice was hoarse with craving.

"Home?"

He kissed her again, fiercely, and groaned with frustration. "Do you want to?" he muttered in between more demanding, devouring kisses.

"Yes."

One word was all he needed to hear. He took her hand and they ran, giggling, for the main street. Primrose paused as they passed her car. Some sense filtered through the rush of hormones and supercharged blood.

"I'll take mine." No telling what gossip would arise if she left her car and went home with Tom in his. Not that she cared right at this moment. But he might.

Tom pulled her into his arms. "My place. Promise? My Rose." His eyes locked with hers then he dived in for another soul searing kiss. Primrose clung to him. She could barely stand up for desire. Tom released her abruptly. "Get in."

Primrose unlocked the car with shaking fingers and collapsed into the driver's seat. He waited while she started the engine then strode toward his ute. The car was stifling and she lowered the window for cool night air to fan her face. The imprint of Tom was on her body, on her lips, the taste of him in her mouth. She stared at his receding figure—tall, slim hipped. Breathed hard. Wanted him with every fibre.

"Ten minutes," he threw over his shoulder. "Follow me."

Primrose drove carefully in the dark. The way was still unfamiliar but the twin red taillights of Tom's ute reassured her through the twists of the mountain road. He slowed for the turn into their road. A few minutes later he swung left through his gate. Primrose braked, hesitated. Was this wise? Here was the point of no return. She could easily continue to the commune.

And do what? Lie in her lumpy, hot, single bed, remembering how it felt to be in Tom's arms? Reliving his kisses. Impotently reliving the passion. Frustrated. Filled with regret.

She swung onto the driveway.

A light shone from the front window of the house, throwing a shaft of yellow across the verandah, dimly illuminating the yard. Tom walked straight toward her as she parked. She got out with a pounding heart and weak legs. Had *he* had second thoughts? His expression was impossible to read in the darkness.

"I thought you might change your mind."

"So did I." A mere whisper.

"But you didn't." He slipped his arms around her and pulled her close. Her pulse leapt. "You can still leave." But his mouth found hers and she couldn't have left if she'd tried.

He took her hand and led her unprotesting inside the house. His bedroom. Tom released his hold to flick on a bedside lamp and suddenly she was blinking in the soft light. He gazed at her with eyes dark with desire.

"You're so beautiful, so sexy. Beautiful Rose." He held her face between his palms and touched her lips with light nibbling kisses until she whimpered in frustration. She wanted more, wanted his kiss deep with passion, wanted his body slamming hard against hers.

Her hands found his shirt and tugged it loose from his pants. She yanked the buttons undone and dragged the garment off still tasting his lips, pressing harder to hold him to her. The kisses slowed to one long, slow exploration of her mouth which weakened her legs so much his arms moved to hold her upright. His attention switched to her throat and neck but his skin was hers to enjoy. So firm and hard, strong from physical labour, exciting. She nuzzled with her mouth, tasted his neck, his throat, his chest with the covering of fine dark hair while her fingers found the buttons to his pants, and then the evidence of his desire.

Tom kicked free of the jeans. His hands dragged her face to his again, his mouth sought hers, devoured and plunged then traced a molten path to her breasts. He eased the thin straps of her dress aside, his fingertips leaving a trail of sparks on her bare shoulders. The fabric slipped away to the floor, revealing her body naked in the dim light. "Mmm," he growled deep in his throat as his fingers slid to the black panties and pulled them down her legs.

He lifted her against his body, hard and unyielding the way she'd craved, and tumbled her onto the bed where her limbs entwined with his, his lips on hers, hands setting her on fire. Only sensation mattered. No thinking, only now, her yearning body joining with his, forging together toward the same destination, toward oblivion. Time lost meaning, place ceased to exist. He paused briefly, frustratingly, as he fumbled for a condom then he was with her again, sailing and soaring, surfing the crashing waves of passion. Together.

****

Primrose came awake curled against a solid wall of hot flesh. Tom. She remembered in short, sharp flashes. How she'd wanted to attract, intended to seduce. Succeeded. And all without a moment's hesitation. Apart from one fleeting, negligible pause at his gate. He'd been as eager as she. No need to feel guilty. No need for regret.

But she had to leave before he woke.

Soft rumbling indicated the depths of his sleep. She eased herself to a cooler patch of sheet. Heat radiated from his bare skin. Her own body was hot and sticky with perspiration. A sheet lay half off the bed, covering her legs.

Her throat rasped with thirst. She sat up carefully, so as not to disturb him. A glimmer of pale light came through the curtains. Her eyes gradually accustomed themselves and she slipped her legs from under the sheet and slid out of the bed. Something tangled in her foot. Familiar fabric beneath her groping fingers. Her dress. She snatched it up and felt about with her hand. A shoe and further on its pair. Panties? No idea where they were. Hadn't worn a bra, a fact which had fascinated and enticed him all evening, he said, in the midst of the passion.

She crept from the room guided by the paler rectangle indicating the door. What time? No idea. No sound from the bedroom. No time for a drink of water. Go home. She dragged her dress over her head and carrying her shoes, scurried for the front door.

On the verandah Primrose dragged in a deep breath of cool, dewy morning air. A faint line of light showed on the horizon. Must be about four. She'd left her bag and keys in the car. Perfectly safe out here. Plus the fact no thoughts beyond Tom entered her head as soon as he walked toward her.

He'd be upset when he woke and found her gone. But she couldn't stay. There'd be nothing to say. He already thought she was a misfit here so this wouldn't disillusion him in that respect. Even as she thought it she knew it wasn't fair but she really couldn't face him this morning. She'd had an itch, he'd scratched it and vice versa. Magnificently well. But that was it. Done. If he thought there was more—tough. There was no more. She knew what men and relationships were like.

She held her breath as the engine burst into life and held it until she was over the rise and out of sight of the house. Then she exhaled noisily. Her body smelled—heat, sex, and Tom. Reminding her of last night's craziness, the irresistible urge to drown herself in a man's arms. She needed a hot shower and sleep. Her foot pressed harder on the accelerator and the car leapt forward. He'd be very upset. Under the cynical exterior lay a sensitive, caring man. But he was a man and men liked sex without strings. Tom wasn't ready for another partner. He should be pleased.

The commune lay in darkness. Primrose crept inside, thankful her room was at the front of the house. She grabbed a nightie and headed for the bathroom.

Ten minutes later, clean and exhausted, she collapsed into bed.

****

Someone was knocking. Primrose's eyes flickered open. Insistent tapping more than knocking. It stopped. Her eyes drifted closed. Tap, tap, tap. Persistent, annoying. Her brain clanked into action. Memories crashed through her head like an avalanche. Boulders of memory. Tom. Sweet, loving. His Rose. Tap, tap, tap. At the window. She sat up.

"Primrose," hissed a voice. An angry voice.

She sprang out of bed and pulled the curtain aside with dread an indigestible lump in her stomach. How angry was he? And how did his anger manifest itself?

"Tom?" She kept her voice low. The last thing she, and undoubtedly Tom, wanted was a communal discussion on the subject.

A tall, dark shape blocked the early morning light. The window was open enough for conversation. Not enough for him to get physical if such was his inclination. Although she seriously doubted he would. Not Tom.

He leaned into the gap between the window and the frame and said with quiet vehemence, "Why did you leave without waking me?"

"I wanted to go home." Now she sounded like a petulant child.

"Fine. But why not wake me?" The words came at her from the dark shadow of his face. Could he see hers? Yellowy grey morning light crept furtively over the far hills, silhouetting him.

"I didn't think there was any need."

"Are you ashamed of what we did?"

"No, of course not."

"What then?"

"I wanted to avoid the sort of conversation we're having now," she said harshly.

"Keep your voice down unless you want bloody Kurt to join in," he hissed. "And we wouldn't be having this sort of conversation if you'd stayed."

"I'm sorry." She folded her arms across the flimsy nightie, conscious of how exposed she was the stronger the light became. "I don't need any extra complications in my life. I thought you'd be pleased I didn't hang around." Why didn't he go home? Why didn't he just accept the situation?

He stared at her and it was as if her unspoken thoughts somehow transferred themselves to his mind. "So this was just sex to you."

"What was it to you? Don't tell me you love me," she whispered with as much derision as she could muster. "We've known each other a week. What else could it be but just sex?"

He said, after a long moment, "I never thought of you as callous."

"You don't know me at all," retorted Primrose. "We were attracted to each other, we acted on it and it was fun. I don't want any more. You didn't object, I might add."

"So any man would have done last night, is this what you're saying?"

She hesitated, faltered at the hurt in his tone. The

male pride she'd trampled. "Not any man, no."

He looked away down the verandah, then his head snapped back and his eyes pierced her like knives. "Thank you very much. I suppose that's a compliment."

"You're welcome."

He stepped closer to the window, yanking it wider, leaning in even further. "Can I just tell you, Primrose, next time you want a man to screw you, find someone else."

A core of anger rose from deep inside. "Tell *me* something, Tom. Why is it when a man does what I've done it's okay but when I do it, it's not?"

His words hit like ball bearings. "I can't answer for other men but I've never used a woman the way you've used me. I don't think it's ever okay."

"Like I said before," she said, struggling, drowning. Losing. "You didn't object. Where were your scruples last night?"

He licked his lips and firmed them briefly. "I find you," a pause emphasised the next word, "physically, very attractive. You seemed to feel the same about me. Last night I thought maybe we'd discovered something a bit special. Obviously you didn't."

Primrose stared up at him. All her carefully constructed justifications shattered around her, leaving her speechless, bereft of cohesive thought. The dawn light had strengthened and cast rosy fingers of light across the verandah. She could see his expression now, deadly serious. She had to look away from the disappointed disgust on his face or the sudden and furious welling of tears would undermine her completely.

"I'm sorry," she whispered. "I didn't set out to hurt

you. I'm in a mess at the moment."

His expression softened. "I know you're in a mess, Rose, but sex without love never solved anything. Even if you are on the rebound."

He turned and before she could summon any form of response he'd gone. His ute started up and bounded away, quickly disappearing between the trees. She extended her arm to push the window even wider, seeking the fresh morning air, hoping the shame would dissipate in the vastness of the outdoors. The frame screeched and the upper hinges parted from the dry, rotten wood, leaving the window hanging precariously.

"Oh, bugger!" And that summed up the whole hideous situation. "Bugger, bugger, bugger." And if Kurt heard her, too bloody bad!

Tom's words seared themselves into her brain. Love. He'd said "sex without love". Did that mean he'd made love to her? Really made love? Something special, he'd said. He *was* special but he couldn't have fallen in love so quickly, could he? Was she on the rebound from Martin? He'd barely entered her head since she'd arrived. She swallowed and blinked hard. Salty tears scalded her throat. Tom called her his Rose.

Something black slipped from the windowsill to the floor at her feet. Her black panties. He'd returned them—again.

Chapter Six

Primrose surfaced from fragmented and unsettling dreams late in the morning. She lay sprawled across the bed like a discarded rag doll, heavy-limbed, cotton wool brained, mouth dry as the yard outside. Thoughts scrolled across her mind in an endless, unbearable, unstoppable torrent. She dragged her hands to her ears in a vain attempt to stop the voices in her head. Voices telling her she was a selfish idiot—thoughtless, cruel, crass, callous, promiscuous, wanton and all the other horrible things Tom had obviously wanted, but had been too gentlemanly, to say out loud. Gentleman. That was Tom—a gentle man. A special man. A proud man.

She groaned into her hot pillow. How could she face him ever again? How could she face anyone? News travelled fast in this town. Everyone would know—probably already did—how she'd broken the heart of the town hero. Too strong, broken-hearted? How she'd messed him around.

She dragged herself upright. It was stiflingly hot again. Slept too long. Blast Kurt and his rules of one miniscule shower per day, she'd have another. He'd never know and if he did—tough. She could say it was a trade-off for the ones he never took.

Twenty minutes later she staggered into the kitchen seeking water and caffeine. They only ran to instant coffee but it was better than Nirupam's herbal tea which tasted like something scratched up in the goat's yard.

Nirupam. Danny! The whole of yesterday's toxic dispute erupted in her brain. Everyone. She'd upset everyone. Even innocent little Mojo who simply wanted to learn about music. Plus she'd caused death and destruction in the chook community.

Fern was standing at the sink washing vegetables. She threw a smiling glance over her shoulder. Lunch time already.

"Morning."

"G'morn'n'," Primrose mumbled as she made a beeline for the kettle.

"Big night, last night?"

With the kettle safely doing its thing, Primrose slumped onto a chair. "Trivia night at the pub. I think I drank too much wine."

Fern nodded and returned her attention to a lettuce.

Primrose breathed deeply. May as well make a start on atonement. Little things first. "Fern, I'm sorry what I said—about not wanting to teach Mojo music."

"Don't worry about it. We all walk our own path in life. Sometimes we're destined to share the route, other times we aren't." A benign smile accompanied her words. Could anyone really be so unflappable? Maybe if you can read the future it gives you an edge—or if you believe you can read the future. Such certainty in the angels, whoever and whatever they were, and the cards, eluded Primrose.

"I think my route must be a very narrow single track at the moment. I've had a...a difficult time lately—musically. I've been wondering whether I should give it away altogether." Apart from the funeral when she'd been asked, she hadn't even thought about playing her flute since she'd arrived. That must mean something.

"Maybe you need a break. Rosehip tea for me, please."

"Maybe." The kettle clicked off. Primrose took two cups from the shelf and opened the tin of assorted tea bags. "Trouble is I can't do anything else." She picked up the kettle and poured.

"If you relax and allow yourself to open up to new experiences something will present itself."

Primrose's hand jerked so she half missed the cup and boiling water spread across the bench. If Fern knew how she'd opened up to a new experience last night...She finished pouring and wiped up the spillage.

"What I'd really love is a baby. I'm so envious of Nirupam."

"It's a truly wonderful thing." Fern lowered her voice. "And I'm glad you're here to stick up for her. We'll be leaving in a few days and I was worried how she'd cope."

"I thought you'd be here for the birth!" Primrose stared at Fern in shock. It was her idea for Nirupam to have no medical intervention and now she calmly says they're leaving? What if Ellie couldn't get here for the birth?

"So did we but something's come up." She began ripping the leaves from the lettuce and placing them in a bowl. "You're here and that lovely midwife will manage. Nirupam and the baby will be fine. I've seen it in the cards."

Right. So there'd be a cosy little group of four left in Nirvana. Danny and Kurt who detested her, and

Nirupam who mistakenly regarded her as a saviour, a Joan of Arc. And not forgetting the man next door who despised her as well.

"Have you seen Nirupam this morning? Or Danny?"

"Danny's gone over to see Tom, and Nirupam's working on her jewellery."

Luckily Fern's back was turned so she didn't witness the guilty start and the hot flush burning across Primrose's face. What would those two be discussing? How friendly were they? Would Tom blurt out his disgust for Danny's sister and confirm everything Danny always thought?

Fern went on, "It's come over very cloudy. Maybe we'll get a storm." It *was* dark now Fern had mentioned it. "It's incredibly hot. Building up to something. By the way I brought the washing in yesterday. Your things are in the laundry."

"Thanks."

Primrose wandered across to the back door. In the far yard Mojo was patting one of the useless goats with Sammy hovering at his side. A couple of hens scratched about by the wall of the shed. The survivors. She squinted up at the sky. Clear blue to the north but overhead dark grey and white bundles were piling up at an alarming rate. She walked further out and looked south and east. A thick wall of purple black. Strangely, the air was perfectly still, crushingly hot with a malevolent air of brooding.

The Golf was parked under a tree where she'd left it in her mad rush early this morning. Better off in a shed in case of falling branches or hail. Primrose hurried inside for her keys. "Massive storm's brewing," she said to Fern in passing.

"Did you see Mojo?"

"He's with the goats. I'll tell him to come in."

She drove the Golf under shelter beside Danny's ute and Jason's battered station wagon. Mojo came round the corner as she closed the door.

"You'd better come inside," she said. "Don't want to be out in the storm that's coming."

A low rumble in the distance underlined her words. "Ooh." Wide-eyed. "I don't like storms."

"Me neither."

To her surprise he grasped her hand in his small grimy one as they started for the house. A flash of sheet lightning illuminated the bruised clouds building up over the roof line. Another, closer, burst of thunder grumbled threateningly, rolling around the hills. Mojo gave a squeak of alarm and broke into a jog, tugging Primrose along with him. Together they dashed up the steps and in through the front door.

"Are the others inside?"

"They'll come in soon. Don't worry."

"They might get struck by lightning." His anxious face peered up at her in the gloomy hallway.

"It's very unlikely. You should wash your hands. Lunch is ready."

"Kurt already did get struck by lightning." Mojo turned and headed for the bathroom. More thunder cracked overhead.

"Really?"

"He got struck by a great big bolt of lightning and it made him deaf in one ear. That's why he shouts all the time."

And perhaps explained some of Kurt's other

peculiarities. "When?"

"Ages ago in Germany when he was young." Mojo's smile displayed great satisfaction at having so totally stunned her. He disappeared into the bathroom.

Primrose stood in the doorway watching him splash water about.

"Mojo, would you like to look at my flute after lunch?"

His eyes opened wide. "Yes, please. I'd love to play like you do."

"There's no reason why you shouldn't be even better at it than I am."

The hail started just as they sat down to eat. Big stones dropped one by one, loud on the corrugated iron roof.

"Damn hail will ruin the crops." Kurt sat glowering at his sandwich as the crashes on the roof increased to a steady deafening roar.

"Danny must have decided to stay at Tom's," said Nirupam. "I hope he did."

"He's not silly. He won't ride in this." Primrose stood up and peered out the kitchen window. Hail fell in a white sheet completely obscuring the sheds and the yard fence. Mojo ran to the back door.

"It's like snow," he yelled.

"He said he'd be back before lunch." A worried frown creased Nirupam's pale brow. "What if he's had an accident?"

Primrose resumed her place at the table.

"He's fine." Fern took a large bite of salad.

Nirupam didn't look convinced. "He was only going over for a quick visit, he said. Half an hour at most. Will you go in the car, Rosie? Please?"

114

Primrose studied her plate. If she refused she'd seem unnecessarily stubborn. A pregnant woman, especially Nirupam, didn't need extra worry and stress. She needn't speak to Tom beyond civilities. He wouldn't want to talk to her that was for sure. "All right. Do you want to come?"

"You stay here in the dry." Fern patted Nirupam's arm. "Rosie will bring him home safe and sound."

"The roof's leaking," Mojo shouted. A steady stream of water ran down the wall by the back door and even as they all leapt to their feet big drops began plummeting into the salad bowl on the table.

Fifteen minutes later, after mopping and helping place bowls and buckets strategically through the house, Primrose sprinted to her car sheltering from the downpour under a wonky black umbrella someone unearthed in the laundry. Everything from the thighs down was drenched within five paces of the verandah. Her yellow cotton pants stuck uncomfortably to her legs and her oldest sandals were mud soaked and ruined almost instantly.

Muttering dire things about Danny, the weather, the rotten, leaky house and anything else which sprang to mind she scrambled into the shed and lowered the umbrella. The wheels slipped and slid in soft mud as she backed out. Rain pelted onto the windscreen and even with the wipers on double speed visibility was minimal. The track up the hill presented a challenge beyond anything she'd encountered on the way in. The rear end fishtailed alarmingly as the wheels spun and gripped and spun some more. With one side on the rough grass verge she discovered traction was marginally improved and reached the top of the rise safely. Here the trees sheltered her from the worst of the rain but the hail had shredded leaves and downed smaller twigs and branches to create a different hazard. If Danny had been caught half way home he could be in trouble on the motorbike.

She drove peering intently through the sheeting grey rain not only to keep the car on the track but also, she admitted to herself with a sick sensation, for any sign of a wrecked motorbike or a huddled motionless figure. Her brother.

The little white bridge appeared dimly through the grey wall after fifteen minutes of tense, finger cramping travel. The halfway point, the river—down a slight dip and up on the other side. She could barely see the bridge let alone the flood level beneath the flimsy structure. The roar on the roof pounded relentlessly into her brain, making her ears ring. She crawled across the wooden bridge holding her breath until the wheels once again sank into the soft muddy surface on the far side.

Puddles stretched across the road at each curve and undulation. Some were shallow and she bravely ploughed straight through. Around others she edged as wide as possible to skirt the unknown depths, always conscious of the soft verge and the possibility of becoming bogged.

Tom's gate finally, thankfully, emerged on the right. She turned in with a sigh of relief. A few more minutes and the house appeared squat and solid through the grey curtain. Primrose drove as close as she could to the honeysuckle-covered gate and turned off the engine. She sagged against the seat and released her death-grip on the steering wheel. Her hands were aching. She flexed the fingers and shook her wrists. Rain thundered onto the car, deafening.

Primrose manoeuvred the umbrella out unfurling it against the drenching onslaught. Along the path, up the three big steps, and suddenly the rain pounded onto the verandah roof instead of her. She kicked off her filthy shoes which were already leaving unsightly muddy footprints on Tom's decking, and eased the cotton pants away from her legs. Spotted with mud they clung sodden and chilly and dripped pools of water onto the verandah. At least her top half was dry.

She knocked on the door. And waited. Knocked again. Hard. Still no answer. She pulled wide the screen and opened the front door.

"Hello? Tom?" Her feet were clammy and cold. Drips fell to the floor from her pants.

No answer. The silence invited her to walk boldly through to the kitchen, passing Tom's bedroom and its roiling memories with averted eyes. No-body. She opened the back door and peered out. Rain lashed down. The closest building was about fifty metres across a soggy stretch of ground.

She walked around the covered verandah to her umbrella and shoes. May as well make a run for it, she'd come this far and couldn't go home to report nothing to Nirupam without checking.

Half way across to the shed her right shoe slipped then stuck, throwing her off balance. Rain belted into her face as the umbrella flailed wildly and next thing she was falling. "Aah," she screeched as her left knee crashed into the boggy ground. "Urgh," as her hip landed on a hidden stone. "Bugger," as she rolled sideways into a puddle.

Primrose righted herself slowly. Her backside was

soaked through. Cold, clammy cloth clung to her skin. Her previously dry T-shirt was now artfully decorated with slimy tan mud and her hair straggled down over her face. She used the umbrella as a prop and hauled herself to her feet. One knee hurt but it was functioning and her hip would have a bruise. No point running now.

She hobbled the remaining distance to the open doorway through which she could now see a glimmer of yellowy light. The first thing she saw was Tom's white ute, the second, Danny's motorbike and the third, two familiar male faces staring at her in astonishment which turned very swiftly to amusement, complete with huge guffaws of laughter.

"What the hell are you doing here?" Danny gasped when he'd recovered enough to speak. Tom rose from the chair where he'd been sitting casually with legs stretched out before him, and came toward her grinning. There was some sort of engine on a bench beside them. Boy stuff.

"Here." He tossed her a small blue striped hand towel he'd plucked from a cardboard box on the floor.

"I came to find you, and I fell over," Primrose snarled at Danny. She wiped her face and neck, eyes averted from the two heartless idiots who were enjoying the spectacle so immensely. "And it was a horrible drive. I didn't think I'd make it. The bridge is nearly flooded." Only a slight exaggeration.

"Why did you come?" Laughter gone in an instant, replaced by an angry curl of the lip.

"It wasn't my idea! Nirupam was worried and she mustn't be worried. You shouldn't stay away so long when you tell her you'll be half an hour, Danny." Chilly droplets ran down her neck from her saturated hair. She blotted at them with the now uselessly damp towel. It had grease marks on it, she noticed for the first time. Maybe she'd applied grease to her person to go with the mud. "She thought you'd had an accident on the bike in the rain."

Her brother had the grace to look slightly ashamed. "I forgot the time. We were talking." He glanced at Tom for assistance but Primrose was in no mood for explanations. They'd been sitting cosily drinking coffee and chatting while everyone else was either worrying about being flooded or worrying he'd had an accident.

"Don't tell me, tell Nirupam," she exclaimed as the fury rose like molten lava. "And by the way the roof's leaking. I don't know how you expect a baby to survive in a dump like that."

"Hey!" Danny leapt to his feet. "How dare you come here telling me what to do. You don't have to stay—just leave us alone. Clear off back to the city."

Tom stepped forward with raised hands. "Calm down, you're like a couple of little kids, for Christ's sake!" He frowned at Primrose then Danny. "Danny maybe you should go home and see Nirupam. Rosie's right, she doesn't need any extra stress at the moment."

Danny glowered but retreated under Tom's stern gaze. "I can't ride home in this." He gestured at the sheeting rain.

"I'll drive you," said Primrose with clenched jaw, but the thought of the return journey filled her with dread. And all Danny would do was criticise her driving. Or throttle her and throw her in the river.

Tom said, "Let Danny take your car and you come in and get cleaned up." He looked her up and down, skating past the wet T-shirt plastered to her breasts and focussing on the mud on her hips. "You're a mess. Your car seats'll be ruined."

Primrose hesitated. Car seats? What did he care? She glanced at Danny standing with a face like murder. "You look just like Dad," she blurted and immediately regretted it. His expression changed to one she recognised from childhood—lost bewilderment, almost fearful. "I'm sorry," she whispered. "Danny, I'm sorry. You're not like him at all. I didn't mean it."

"Where are your keys?" Blank-faced now.

"In the car."

Danny pulled on his leather jacket. "See you later, Tom." Head down he ran for the car.

Primrose took two hurried steps after him and called, "Drive safely," but he either didn't hear or chose not to acknowledge her.

Tom flicked a switch and the shed was plunged into gloom. He hoisted the umbrella overhead. "Let's go." He strode out into the deluge.

Primrose scurried after him. "Wait a minute. What about me?" she shouted through the onslaught.

"You're already wet," he called over his shoulder. "You can't get any wetter. I'm dry, so far."

She had no comeback to the indisputable fact other than contemplating a shove in the small of the back to send him into the mud as well. But that would be far too nasty, although very tempting, so she splashed after him meekly instead.

Primrose stood shivering in the laundry washing her feet in a bucket while Tom went for a towel and dry clothes. What he'd produce for her to wear was anyone's guess.

Even though they'd both left their boots and shoes

respectively outside on the verandah her feet and ankles were covered in mud. He told her to clean up before trekking through to the bathroom, as if she was in the habit of leaving a trail of filth wherever she went.

"You know where the bathroom is, don't you?" he asked as he disappeared through the kitchen door. Primrose poked her tongue out in his general direction.

She left the bucket of muddy water standing in case she got into trouble for pouring it wastefully down the drain, and headed for the bathroom, carefully negotiating the doorway so as not to leave muddy decorations. Tom met her in the hallway with an armful of clothing. "Sweatshirt and track pants with a drawstring waist. Best I can do." He shoved the lot into her hands. "Use the green towel. I'll make a cup of tea."

"Thanks."

He turned away. Primrose, for the second time, luxuriated in Tom's shower.

Tom busied himself with the tea, his mind awhirl. He wasn't prepared for her. Not so soon. He hadn't recovered from last night, hadn't got his thoughts in order and his armour in place. Having Danny turn up this morning threw him as well. For a moment he thought he'd come to defend his sister and tell Tom not to come bothering her any more. The next moment he'd realised that was ridiculous. Danny went out of his way to avoid confrontation, which was his main problem.

Perhaps he shouldn't have chased after her as soon as he realised she'd left. But it infuriated him she should sneak away without even so much as a goodbye kiss or word of farewell. After a night like theirs. So bloody insulting! Her scathing words had stalled him, though, "Don't tell me you love me." Did he? If he didn't, what was he doing there at four fifteen in the morning? If he didn't love her she was right, he should be pleased she wasn't clinging and wanting more.

Of course he didn't love her! Tom thumped two mugs on to the bench. She was just the first woman he'd been intimate with for a while. He'd forgotten how it felt to be so close...

Whatever had happened last night he wasn't going to be the one clinging and wanting more. She'd made her position very, very clear. Anyway, a woman less suitable for the hard life on a rural property he had yet to meet. And underpinning any runaway fantasies he may have was the inescapable fact he couldn't give her children. And she made no secret of the fact she wanted babies. No doubt she'd go after that goal with the same determination she pursued everything else she wanted. Thank God he hadn't told her that.

The shower stopped. A few minutes later Primrose appeared, rosy cheeked from the hot water, towel dried hair already wisping about her cheeks and neck, his sweatshirt draped over her slender frame and the track pants bundled around her waist with the legs rolled up around her ankles. A delicious, fragrant armful.

"Better?" He grasped the teapot to avoid grabbing her and kissing both of them senseless.

"Thanks. I left my wet clothes in the laundry tub."

"Fine. How do you like your tea?"

"Same as you."

Of course, she'd made tea when he called in the other day. The day she'd offended him with her accusations. Should have held that thought and they'd both be better off. Trouble was she'd set out to seduce someone last night and he was easy game, already halfway there. He put her mug on the table and she sat down.

"What's with you and Danny?"

Primrose lifted the tea and drank. She'd better give him an answer. He deserved one, especially after witnessing that incredible explosion of bitterness and anger. "We weren't ever very close. He's four years older."

"He never mentioned you."

Primrose raised her eyes to meet his, defiant, as though he'd accused her, implied that the omission was her fault. "He hates me."

"I don't think he does. Perhaps he feels you're judging him all the time." He said it mildly but his message was clear. "Nobody likes to be judged." Tom returned her gaze calmly.

She looked away out the window to where rain still fell. Less heavily now but solid, like drops of lead nailing her to this place, imprisoning her in his house. Her expression screamed, *What did he know*?

"I came here for his help."

"Why, if he hates you?"

"There isn't anyone else. We're all we have left of our family." She blinked. "After Martin dumped me I realised I wasn't going to have a family of my own in the foreseeable future. I really wanted, I still really want, babies." She shrugged as though helpless to explain something she didn't fully comprehend herself. "I don't know. I wanted to see if anything could be saved."

"You might have your own family one day. You're not old." He must sound at a loss as to how to react, withdrawn and distant, uninterested but this topic was too uncomfortable Way too intimate despite having spent half a night together.

"I'll need a permanent man for that. I don't want to be a single mother. It's a Catch 22." Primrose stared at him. "I'm not about to sign up for commitment again in a hurry."

Right. She'd made her situation clear. He changed the subject abruptly. "Tell me about your father."

"Dad was a drunk. A violent one." She waited for his reaction but his mind went blank. Too surprised to speak. "I haven't told anyone before. Not so plainly. I don't know why I'm telling you. I didn't even tell Martin."

She spoke as if it was a curious situation, one she didn't understand, or hadn't thought about before. Why was that? Shame?

"What happened to him?"

"When I was twelve he dropped dead of a heart attack and we were all secretly pleased. Relieved, at least."

"Did he hit you?"

"Not me. Danny and Mum. I don't know why Dad picked on him but he did." She paused then added, "Maybe he figured bashing a little girl was out of bounds."

He absorbed the information. It went in and disappeared into his mind for processing later. He couldn't react. Not with shock, horror, or anything else. He'd had no idea of the horrendous life she and Danny had endured as children. A life both of them wanted to forget but couldn't escape. It explained a lot.

"What about your Mum?"

"She followed him around, getting him out of

trouble, getting beaten up for it and trying to keep the family in one piece. She wasn't exactly stable, either— bi-polar, I think, looking back. She died when I was nineteen. Aneurism." She spoke harshly. "Those people mean nothing to me now. They're just dim memories of a miserable time. They failed both of us, especially Danny. We owe them nothing."

"Hard childhood." To put it mildly.

Primrose shrugged. "It was the only one we had. We survived. Other kids have it worse. At least he didn't molest us. Danny left home as soon as he could. So did I."

Tom tilted his head, grimaced. No wonder Primrose was tough and independent. No wonder Danny had a haunted, insecure look. "I can't imagine what it must have been like."

"Like I said, we survived. It's gone now. They've gone." She smiled but not her wide dimpled grin. This one was forced. "What deep dark secrets do you have, Tom?"

He took her cue, sat back with an offended expression. "I'm pure as the driven snow."

"I'll bet. What engrossed you and Danny so much he didn't notice the storm brewing?" Her eyes narrowed.

Tom pursed his lips and met her gaze. A ripple of anger stirred deep inside. "Are you still on about the land price? Do you still think I'm trying to cheat you?"

"You tell *me*."

"No, I'm not trying to cheat anyone and I'm even more offended now that you still think I would."

"Now?" A bewildered shadow passed across her face.

"Since we slept together. Or had you forgotten? I think sharing someone's bed implies a measure of trust in that person, don't you?" Colour rose to her cheeks. Her eyes slipped away, but he held his gaze on her face until the intensity forced her to look back. "Well? Do you trust me or not?"

She nodded briefly, reluctantly.

The reticence infuriated him, rising in his body, forcing him to his feet to gather the tea mugs, saying, "I should damn well think so. I've given you paint, saved you from an attack sheep, made love to you, given you the use of my bathroom and you're wearing my clothes! What more do you want from me?"

Her response startled him. "Nothing!" She jumped up, the chair legs scraping violently on the tiled floor. "I don't want anything from you. I told you this morning. I don't want to put my faith in any man ever again. Spending a few hours in someone's bed doesn't give you any rights over them."

He glared at her then turned and dumped the mugs in the sink, breathing hard. He gripped the edge of the bench tightly, eyes closed, back toward her so she couldn't see the confusion and havoc she'd created in his head in such a short space of time. Driving him crazy. And so easily. He released pent up air slowly.

"You'll need a ride home."

She didn't answer for a moment and he turned to see her watching him with a measure of alarm on her face, arms tensed, body ready for flight. He laughed shortly. "Don't worry. I won't hit you. I've never hit anyone in my life."

Her expression switched to wide-eyed concern. "Oh no! I'd never think...of course, I don't think you'd

126

ever..." Tripping over herself to reassure him. She stopped suddenly, spoke softly. "I'm sorry, Tom."

"Sorry for what?"

"Being so stupid." She lifted one hand in a vague gesture. "Messing you around last night. I probably am on the rebound from Martin. You're a nice man. I should never have come in. I should have kept going at the gate."

"Maybe you should have but you didn't," he said briskly. "And that's that. Nothing more." That "nice" was like a slap in the face. A cup of tea was nice, a hot shower was nice. A lover should be more than nice.

She smiled, properly this time. Relieved. A cheeky dimple appeared in her cheek. "Right."

He strode to the window facing the yard and peered out, anxious to get rid of her, remove her from his home where she fitted so well. Anxious to remove the temptation of her. She wanted children. Bottom line. Remember that. "The rain's eased a bit. I'll drive you home."

She didn't fit into his home any more than she fitted into his life. His Rose was a daydream, a fantasy, no more than wishful thinking. In reality Primrose wasn't meant to be here anymore than she was meant to be on the commune.

"Thanks. I'll get my clothes. Can I have a plastic bag, please?"

"Sure. I've got a coat you can wear and there might be some gumboots that'll fit."

Primrose collected her wet clothes and followed him to the laundry where he rummaged in a store cupboard, emerging with dusty rubber boots and a red anorak.

"Alison left these," he said.

She pulled the boots on. A bit big but the anorak was perfect.

"Keep them."

"Thanks."

Tom put on his own coat and opened the door. The rain had settled to a steady fall but patches of brighter sky showed across the hills to the east. He stood on the steps and squinted up at the heavens. "Seems to be clearing. Pity. We could do with a week of it."

"Not hail, though."

"Didn't get any hail here. Did you?" He set off for the garage.

"Yes, heaps." Primrose lumbered after him in the awkward boots.

"It must have been a really isolated, specific storm. That's why the house leaked. Hail clogs up the gutters and the water seeps in under the eaves."

"Plus it's a dump."

He tossed her a grin across the top of the ute before opening the door. The lopsided, sexy grin that went straight to her belly like a punch despite the ever-widening chasm between them. "There is that."

The powerful ute bounced and slid over the muddy, puddled driveway, wipers sloshing cascades of water from side to side. Primrose clung to her seatbelt grimly. Tom seemed keen to be rid of her but home, such as it was, wasn't an appealing prospect. Danny would still be furious with her for many reasons, Kurt would still be Kurt, the house would still be uncomfortable. But she'd promised to show Mojo her flute.

"Fern and Jason are leaving on Wednesday," she said over the roar of the engine and the sudden firmer staccato rattle of rain on the roof. Her glance strayed to his hands on the steering wheel. Strong and capable, just like he was. A shiver of memory—of caring, gentle hands, touching, exciting. Don't. Tom was not for her. She looked out the window at the sodden paddocks, suddenly too conscious of him beside her. Too aware that he'd never touch her that way again and it was her fault.

"Anyone moving in?"

Primrose whipped her face toward him in shock. "I don't know. Did Danny say something?" Not more freeloaders, please! Surely not after the discussion they'd had about Nirupam and the baby.

"No. But they usually have a steady stream coming and going. That's why they never get anywhere. There's no focus. Everyone who lives there has their own ideas about what to do, and Danny lets them all have an equal say. Then they pack up and move on and leave him with the shambles of their half-baked ideas."

"Did you know he supports most of them financially, too?"

"You're kidding! That's bloody ridiculous." He stared out the smeary windscreen which had begun to fog up, concentrating on the route. They reached the road and turned left. The rain plummeted down suddenly harder than ever as though it had waited for them to arrive on this particular spot before letting loose. Tom switched the aircon on and the windscreen slowly cleared.

"That's why he's selling land. He needs the money to pay the bills! Didn't you realise? Didn't you ever ask him?"

Tom didn't answer. He leaned forward slightly as

they neared the river and the little white bridge. "Wonder if the road's cut." Not listening to her.

"Tom!" demanded Primrose. "Didn't you ever ask Danny why he needed money?"

"Primrose! It's none of your business," he snapped. "Just leave it, will you? We've other things to think about at the moment. Namely...this. Damn!" He stomped on the brake and indicated the road in front. Except there wasn't a road any more, there was a lake spreading brown and muddy before them, filling the dip and covering the bridge so only the yellow tops of the flood indicator poles were visible.

"Oh!" Primrose gasped. "Can we drive through?"

"No way. It's over a metre deep and the current's too strong. Water comes down fast from the mountains, but it runs away pretty quickly too." He threw the ute into reverse. The wheels churned mud and stones before gripping. Tom twisted to peer through the rear window, manoeuvring back to a wide enough place to turn.

"So Danny would have made it home all right?" He wouldn't have tried to drive through, not Danny. He wasn't stupid. But he'd been angry and maybe his judgement was off. No. He wouldn't. He'd lived here for years. He'd know the dangers.

Tom muttered, "Must have or he would've come back." He concentrated on the tight turn, face tense, mouth a grim line.

"Looks like you're stuck with me." She grimaced and bit at her lower lip.

"Yes," he replied tersely. "For a few hours at least."

"You don't need to entertain me." Stung by his

obvious annoyance. "I can read a book or something. You do have books, I take it?"

He threw her a pained glance then ignored her for the rest of the slow return trip.

Tom disappeared outside almost immediately after he'd shown Primrose indoors again. She, left to her own devices, prowled about the living room investigating his book shelves and music collection. To her surprise he liked classical and jazz with an assortment of rock and country bands. She picked out a Bob Dylan album, a legend she wasn't very familiar with but felt she should be, set it in action and settled into an armchair with a Clive Cussler yarn.

****

Tom woke her by slamming the back door and clumping into the house via the laundry. Primrose's eyes flicked open. She yawned. The book had slipped to the floor, Dylan had sung himself to silence, the light had gone from the day. Still raining with a gentle but solid patter of drops on the roof.

She stretched and stood up. Her feet were cold.

"Hello." He stood in the doorway, a dark figure in the gloomy evening light.

"I went to sleep." She yawned again. A sudden explosion of light made her blink as he turned on a lamp then moved across and switched off the CD player. He glanced at the open CD cover but didn't comment.

"Still raining," he said. "You'll have to stay overnight."

"I'm sorry." And she was. Now she was a burden, not a dalliance. Staying overnight, invited and willing in his bed was one thing. Staying because she had no

131

choice was another. By his expression he evidently thought the same thing.

"I've only got sausages for dinner," he said. "And mash."

"Fine. I'll cook."

"No need, I can manage."

"It's the least I can do."

He shrugged. "If you want."

"Could I borrow some socks as well, please?" Eating his sausages and potatoes, wearing his track pants and sweatshirt, staying the night. Was asking for socks stretching the relationship just that little bit too far?

"Sure." He turned and left the room. It looked very much like an escape. Primrose went to the kitchen and searched for a saucepan and potatoes. Tom was being unnervingly polite, had been all afternoon. The easy banter of the preceding week had gone, the relaxed amusement had disappeared, replaced by a tense, watchful reticence.

Her fault. The truth crashed in on her with the force of the hailstorm. She'd caused this distance between them. Everything she'd done and said virtually since she'd arrived in Kullanurra had been wrong. Harmfully wrong. Pain causingly wrong. Danny was right, she was a bitch and Tom had had enough after only a few days in her company. And one wonderful night which she'd thrown back at him like dirty dishwater.

He was distancing himself and who could blame him? Shouldn't that please her? It would mean they could sleep peacefully in separate beds with no obligation on either part to recreate last night's ill-judged activity. Strangely it didn't please her at all. On the contrary, it sent a shaft of hot, burning shame searing through her. Shame tinged with regret. She'd never had a night like that with Martin. His lovemaking was pedestrian by comparison, and he wasn't as in tune with her body after a whole year together as Tom was in minutes. It was instinctive and it worked both ways. He knew precisely what turned her on and she took great delight in. . .

"Here." A pair of grey wool socks was thrust at her. He studied her flushed face curiously but didn't probe. Her eyes went straight to his mouth, with those lips that did such exciting things. She swallowed. Her breathing was way too fast. He had to notice.

"Thanks." She grabbed the socks and bent quickly to pull them on, straightened. "Where are the potatoes?"

"In that cupboard. Do lots. I'm hungry."

He pointed and she looked. That sounded more like the old Tom but when she turned with a smile and her hands full of potatoes he had his back to her and the fridge door open. "Like a beer?"

"No, thanks. I had enough to drink last night."

"Yes," he said. "You were pretty pissed."

That was a low blow! And *he* hadn't been drinking water all night.

"I wasn't drunk. I wouldn't have driven if I had been. I knew exactly what I was doing, Tom," she countered swiftly.

He spun about and impaled her with a steely-eyed gaze. "I wish *I'd* known exactly what you were doing." He twisted the cap off the stubbie with a vicious snap of the wrist and tossed it into the sink.

"Would it have made any difference?" she asked softly, anger dissipating under the reminder of her harsh words of early this morning.

He stared at her, considering his reply. "Of course it would." He gave a tiny shake of his head, lips twisted into a wry grimace, and left the kitchen.

Primrose filled a saucepan with water, head bowed, trying in vain to prevent the fat tears which rolled slowly down her cheeks like boulders. She heaved the pan across to the stove top and wiped her face on the sleeve of Tom's sweatshirt. The fabric smelled of him. Each time she moved he moved with her, reminding her all afternoon of the warmth and strength of his body and the comfort of his arms. Taken for granted until now.

He was the only person in the place who'd treated her well and befriended her apart from Nirupam and more recently Mike, and she'd done what in return? Used and abused him. She'd have to be on best behaviour from now on. Prove to him she wasn't a bitch, prove she was the sort of woman he originally thought she was, the one he wanted to take to bed. The one he wanted to make love to.

For starters she'd cook him the best sausages and mash he'd ever eaten.

Chapter Seven

Tom went to the living room and switched on the TV for the news. An earnest-faced woman was describing the disastrous effects of storms in Canberra where huge amounts of hail had ripped through the city centre, causing millions of dollars worth of damage.

Nature in all its glory. Powerful and unstoppable. If it wasn't drought or fires it was hail and flooding. Who'd be a farmer in this country?

He sucked on his beer. Who'd be a farmer's wife in this country? Certainly not the girl bashing pots and pans around in his kitchen. How was he supposed to spend a night with her in the house but not in his bed? She'd have to lock her door. He grunted in silent, cynical amusement. If he so much as ventured near her he'd be sent packing. She'd made that very clear. A *nice* man. Great.

Yep, a girl who didn't know what she was doing was as dangerous and mad as a cut snake. Trouble was he had the sneaking suspicion he'd begun to fall for her in a big way. A very big way. Something about her made him want to protect her. The aggression and defiance were a front she put up to compensate for the lost, bewildered little girl struggling to survive by herself in a world which hadn't done her any favours so far.

Despite the run-ins with Dad, being estranged from

his family was unthinkable, as was being separated the way she and Danny were from each other and had been from their parents. To have become a professional anything from her background showed how tough she was. Danny said she had completed a performing degree on flute at the Sydney Conservatorium of Music. What had gone wrong? There must be more to this change than the dud fiancé.

The news moved on to the cricket results. Tom concentrated until the bulletin was over and the weather girl announced a day of patchy showers then a return to the heat. The river would go down in no time once the rain stopped. Primrose could go home tomorrow. Just as well. He couldn't afford to get used to having her in his house.

"Dinner's ready." She stood in the doorway, face pink from cooking, the too large clothes making her look like a child playing dress-ups. "I set the table in the kitchen. Is that where you eat?"

Tom rose to his feet. "Yep. Thanks."

"It's my pleasure," she said, her expression solemn. "It's the least I can do for landing on you this way." He followed her to the kitchen where she'd laid two places opposite each other, neatly arranged knife and fork, salt and pepper. He found the tomato sauce in the fridge, and sat down.

"You didn't have much choice."

"Neither did you, although you could have driven me in to the pub," she said. "How many sausages?"

"Three for starters." He hadn't even considered taking her into town. "Would have been a rough trip over the ridge in this weather."

"Heavens, yes." Primrose shuddered in agreement

as she placed a heaped plate of grilled sausages, creamy white mashed potato and a dollop of something reddish with tomato and capsicums in it. Smelled delicious. Tasted even better. "What's this?"

"Ratatouille. Plus some herbs."

"Very good."

"It tastes so much better with home grown vegetables and herbs. They're fantastic. Do you grow everything yourself?"

"Pretty much," he said with his mouth full of sausage.

"Do you have help?"

He shook his head. "Not any more. I did when I was getting started. I hire people when I need. Fruit pickers, truffle sniffing dogs, for example."

She smiled. "I've seen stuff on TV about truffle growers in France. They use pigs."

"Yes but dogs don't eat the truffles. It's hard to argue with a hungry pig." He grinned and she laughed.

"So you're truly self sufficient." He nodded. He'd told her that already. "Can you handle more land?" Her smile faded. "Do you need it?"

He didn't rise to her bait, didn't want to travel that well worn path again. "I want to try truffles on a broad scale. They can make a lot of money. To be viable I need a larger plantation so I can test different host trees. Plus there are other crops I'd like to test. Strawberries using a variety of mulching methods. Olives." He shoved in another chunk of sausage and potato.

Primrose finished her single sausage in silence. Tom was amazing. He was doing what Danny had dreamed of, tried and so far, failed to achieve. He'd created a self sustaining, flourishing property, a home.

Danny came to Kullanurra with little knowledge of the land, she knew for a fact. His dream bore scant relationship to reality.

"Who died and left you that place?" His question startled her.

"Mum's stepfather."

"Les Cochrane?"

"Yes. Did you know him?"

"No-body knew him very well. He died about a year after I bought this place. Took a week before anyone found him."

"How sad!" She gazed at him in dismay. "We never knew him, either. Gran died years before and he never kept in touch with any of us. Danny and I were amazed when they told us he'd left us his land. I suppose we were the only relatives he had and we weren't even properly related." Her mouth quivered slightly and she bit her lip. "It's so sad."

He nodded. "I'd have a chat occasionally but he didn't socialise."

"I don't want to end up like Les. All alone, no-body knowing or caring whether I'm dead or alive." A shudder rippled through her body.

He laughed. "Why on earth would you end up like him?"

"Danny's my only relative. And Nirupam. But they don't really want me around. At least, Danny doesn't. And I won't be able to stay after the baby's born. Not after telling him to kick everyone out."

Tom frowned. "You're his sister. It's a bit different."

"Not to Danny. In your family it might be different but we...we don't agree on much. You saw today."

"I doubt whether he'll chuck you out. Nirupam will need help with the baby."

"For a while, but later. . ."

"Why would he turf you out when he welcomes everybody and his flea bitten dog?" Tom got up and helped himself to more ratatouille and another sausage. Primrose shook her head when he offered her a second helping.

She said with an intense quiet determination, "I won't let him sell any more of our land, Tom."

He almost laughed aloud at the craziness of her sudden intense attachment to a block of land she'd never even seen before last week. "Why not? You just said yourself he won't want you here. Why on earth should you care what he does with it? He'll give you half the money, I'm sure."

Her voice rose indignantly, "It's not the money. Neither of you get it! It's the land. It's a place that's ours. A place we actually own. We never had security as kids. We moved all the time. That's why Danny came here."

"Fair enough." His own family felt exactly the same way about the land in Cowra, handed down from father to son. The line had to start somewhere. Why not with Danny and his child?

Then she said, "I want to stay here too. Maybe build my own house."

Tom stared at her in astonishment, mid chew. "And do what? You know even less about farming than Danny."

"I can learn."

Learn? Who from? Danny the idealist, Kurt the lunatic? "You're a flute player for heaven's sake!"

139

"Not anymore."

"Why not anymore?"

She pushed mashed potato around on her plate, scraping and scooping little piles and flattening them with her fork. "It's very stressful. I couldn't cope. I don't want to live my life that way—I started having migraines, not sleeping. It was stress."

"Can't you teach or something?"

She shrugged. "I suppose I could." Mojo's pleased little face flashed through her mind. He'd be disappointed she hadn't returned to show him her flute and surprisingly, she was disappointed at having let him down. "I taught a bit when I was a student—for the money. I never had time when I freelanced."

Tom went on, "I imagine you'd find a lot of students in this area. We don't have much in the way of proper musicians. Can you play anything else?"

"Piano—a bit."

"See." He gestured with his fork. "Use the talent you've got. You might surprise yourself."

"But I want a complete change."

"You'll find being a farmer pretty stressful. Specially if you don't know anything about it. Look at Danny."

He was right. Primrose sagged in her chair. She didn't have the knowledge to become a farmer, she wouldn't know where to start. But even so. "I won't let him sell you any more land."

Tom met her gaze with equal firmness. "I understand what you're saying but I think you'll find you don't have much choice. Unless you can help Danny enough to make a go of the place, or you've enough money to support him and his family."

Primrose collected the dirty plates and stood up. "How we manage isn't any of your business."

"No. Thanks for cooking dinner. It was very nice." He used the word deliberately but she didn't get the reference. She wouldn't. He meant nothing to her and the night they'd spent together had slipped from her mind completely. He wished he could dismiss the memory as easily, but the silky smoothness of her skin was imprinted into his fingers, and the perfume of her body taunted him every time she moved close.

"You're welcome." She turned away to the sink. Tom grabbed a tea towel and dried while she washed, making occasional comments about the weather and how his dams and tanks would fill up if the rain held on a little longer. Safe, mundane topics to keep his mind away from the dangerous, impossible one.

"I've never thought about the weather much," Primrose said as she scrubbed the mashed potato pan.

"It's crucial for us," said Tom. "Means success or failure. A comfortable living or ruin."

"Why do you do it?" She paused mid scrub. "If it's such a lottery?"

"Because I think I can make a difference to the way farmers operate. An improvement. My father worked like a slave on his land and it nearly killed him. Years of drought meant he had to sell off his livestock or watch them die of starvation because he couldn't afford to buy feed. He switched to crops but the same thing happened. Too much rain or too little too late."

"Why did he keep at it?"

"Because he didn't know how to do anything else and he loved the land. It was where he grew up."

"His home," said Primrose softly.

"Our home. He couldn't turn his back on the place his parents had worked so hard for."

"But why aren't you working there with him?"

Tom said, after a pause, "My brother Sean is. He'll take over when Dad retires. If he ever does, the tough old devil. They're doing all right now apart from the drought. I've made a few suggestions and they've taken them on board. Seems to be working."

"He must be proud of you, your Dad."

Tom sucked in air and let it out through pursed lips. "Dad's pretty set in his ways. He's an old school farmer. He's not convinced radically new methods and science will make a difference. "You smart buggers still can't make it rain when we need it," he says."

"So you have something to prove here, on your place." Primrose faced him, eyebrows raised. "You need to show your father you know what you're doing." She turned back to the sink full of dirty water while he grappled with the sudden insane desire he'd had to kiss her. The way she looked at him with the fervour of her opinion making her eyes glow, lips parted, brow wrinkled with the intensity—her oblique support of his worth—was almost irresistible. Almost. If he hadn't already given in once and suffered the consequences.

He frowned, considering her remark. "Maybe. I don't think of it that way."

"Maybe you don't but it doesn't negate the fact that's what you're doing. You want to show him you can do better than he can. And that you haven't been wasting your time."

Her words prickled like a handful of thistles. "Rubbish! I'm sharing my knowledge with Sean. He's receptive. I want to help them make a go of the place."

"And of your own."

"Of course!" Tom turned away and slung the tea towel over the oven door handle. Primrose's remarks struck a sore spot all right but he wasn't going to let her see just how close to the truth she was. His father's angry face flashed before his eyes, the tanned skin lined and marked by years of heat, dust, and heartbreak. The reproach in his grey eyes saying one more pain had been added to his burden—the fact his eldest son didn't want to stay and work the family property. Wanted instead to go to the city and do some fancy university degree that was all academic books, and no practical use to man nor beast. Giving up, turning his back on the Fairbrother heritage.

Sean had stepped in eager to placate their father and eager to have a purpose when he left school. Eight years younger than Tom, he loved the land with as much of a passion as his father. Fortunately he also admired his big brother and understood the value of his knowledge.

"Don't you get lonely out here on your own?" Primrose asked, interrupting his meandering thoughts with an abrupt change of subject. Her tone suggested she'd be bored rigid stuck in such a backwater. Probably already was. After a week.

Tom leaned against the table, arms folded. When she tossed in remarks such as that it was much easier to ignore the urge he had to hold her face between his hands and kiss the words from her lips. Those comments reminded him very smartly how superficial the country girl layer was and how deeply different they really were. "Too busy to get lonely. Anyway, I've got plenty of friends about the place."

"Do you miss your girlfriend?" Another change of tack catching him unawares.

"Sometimes," he admitted before he thought about denial. It was true, though. But surprisingly, now he *had* thought, it wasn't so much Alison he missed as the little feminine touches. He liked the softening effect in his life.

Primrose nodded. "I miss Martin though I'd strangle him if he came near me." And he didn't doubt that for a minute. She wiped down the bench briskly and dried her hands. "Coffee?"

"I'll make it. You sit down."

She yawned and quickly covered her mouth. "Thanks. I'm tired all of a sudden."

"Not much sleep last night," Tom commented and couldn't prevent a sly smile. An image of her sexy body beneath his fingers made him catch his breath. The memory would probably keep him awake on many nights to come.

"Mmm." She met his eye fearlessly. "But I'll be getting plenty of sleep tonight so don't get any ideas."

"Me? I have no intention of going anywhere near you tonight or any other night." Sleepless nights or not, the emotional price tag attached to Primrose Pretty was way out of his reach. "I was thinking the same about you as a matter of fact. Don't be getting any ideas."

"Likewise," she confirmed.

"Agreed." Tom turned his back on her while he finished making the coffee. She really meant what she said. A one night stand. Cool as ice. He firmed his mouth into a hard line. Toughen up, country boy. She doesn't know what love is. Don't show her any weakness.

"Which is my bedroom?"

He jerked his head in the direction of the spare room. Primrose strolled across and looked in. "Nice. Where are the extra sheets and things?"

"Hall cupboard second shelf. There's a doona already on the bed."

He heard her open the cupboard. The door always squeaked. He never remembered to oil it. Do it now. He left the coffee brewing in the plunger pot and went to the laundry for the little oilcan. Primrose was busy flapping a sheet about in the spare room. He squatted down and applied a few drops of oil to the top hinge then the lower, swung the door experimentally. Silent.

Tom straightened to find her standing behind him, watching. He looked down into her face and smiled. "Been meaning to do that."

She returned his smile, genuine and warm. He wanted to kiss her. An incredibly strong pull, irresistible. She was very close, her eyes shining in the softer hall light, hair tousled around her face, body enveloped in his clothes, fragrant and desirable, the more so because he knew exactly the taste and feel of her. He swallowed.

"I need a pillowslip. Excuse me." She extended her hand to the shelf behind him.

"Right, sorry. I'll get out of your way," he babbled like a fool, and barged past her for the laundry. Total idiot!

While he poured their coffee. Primrose said, "Would it be all right if I washed my clothes? They might dry overnight."

"Go ahead. I've some work to do on the computer." Nothing that couldn't wait but the

145

alternative was sitting here making small talk with her when all he wanted to do was throw her into his bed again. Agony. He took his coffee to the study.

The washing machine sloshed and gurgled Primrose's mud spattered clothes about enthusiastically. She had a feeling the clayey brown earth would stain her lemon coloured pants but Tom didn't have any stain removal powder so there was no choice. At least they'd be wearable. Pity. His clothes were snug and warm. She wrapped her arms around herself. Almost like being hugged by Tom. His sweatshirt enveloped her with his smell and she closed her eyes momentarily, remembering.

He needn't have sounded so convincing when he said he had no intention of hopping into her bed tonight. And so determined to keep her out of his. As if she'd be doing any midnight visiting...The look in his eyes when she went to the linen cupboard for a pillowslip. So sure he wanted to kiss her. But he didn't, even though she'd waited, giving him time. Wrong. Not interested. He'd ensconced himself in his study with the door half closed. Clearly not wanting to be disturbed by his enforced visitor.

She wandered into the living room and found the book she'd been reading. Rain pattered softly on the roof. Cosy inside Tom's house. This roof wouldn't leak. She liked his taste in furnishings and his taste in music. Gentle, soothing Mozart this time. Violins quivered into the room. She sat on the comfortable old sofa, tucked her legs underneath her and began to read.

At about ten thirty Tom finally gave up on pretending to do his accounts and trying to concentrate on articles in the latest issue of *Good Fruit*. The Mozart

CD had long since finished and Primrose hadn't put on another one. Maybe she'd gone to bed.

He stood up and stretched, yawned widely. He hadn't slept much either last night and a farmer couldn't sleep in. The cow had to be milked, eggs collected, and the hens fed every morning. Plus Danny had arrived with his usual swag of questions and problems. Somehow Tom had unwittingly become Danny's confidante and sounding board. Sworn to secrecy. Not that Tom was given to gossip—but the things he'd confided over the years were things Tom would have preferred not to know. Still, Danny was a good bloke all round, and Tom understood his reluctance to divulge certain information to his wife. Secrets, though, had a habit of coming back to bite you on the bum.

The money aspect was already causing trouble with Primrose. She wasn't one to be fobbed off, not like innocently vague Nirupam. And given her current mental state Primrose was highly unlikely to understand or be amenable to any of Danny's muddled reasoning.

Tom sighed. Life was simple until she arrived. Simple but duller. He switched off the light and headed for the living room.

She hadn't gone to bed, she'd gone to sleep on the couch again, curled up with her head on a couple of cushions. Tom walked across and turned off the CD player. He picked up the book from the floor and placed it on the coffee table. Primrose didn't stir.

He studied her for a moment. His Rose. She was lovely in sleep. Sweet faced, soft skinned, hands clasped lightly by her cheek. Silent. He smiled ruefully. If she could keep as quiet as this when she was awake they'd have no problems—he or Danny. But then she wouldn't be the woman he found so exciting. A secret definitely worth keeping to himself.

"Rose," he said gently. "Rose, wake up."

No reaction. He shook her shoulder lightly. She stirred but didn't wake. "Rosie, bedtime."

"Mmmph."

"Come on." Louder.

Her eyes flickered open, focussed. She smiled slowly. "Tom." In a whisper of sound. The lids closed again and she sighed, a contented, happy sound.

In one swift movement Tom bent and scooped her into his arms. She nuzzled her face into his neck as he strode to the spare bedroom. Her hair tickled his nose, smelling of herbal shampoo. Her body, warm and fragrantly desirable, tempted him to change course for his own bedroom but he resisted. He wouldn't succumb a second time. Especially not when she was so sleepy she didn't know where she was. The consequences of bedroom action taken in those circumstances would be catastrophic.

He dumped her gently onto the bed and rolled her so he could pull the doona aside then roll her back under the covers. She sighed and snuggled in. Tom bent and dropped a gentle kiss on her exposed cheek right where the cheeky dimple lived. Such a beautiful, complicated, dangerous woman.

He went to bed and lay listening to the rain pattering on the roof until sleep came.

The smell of frying bacon curled into Tom's nostrils when he awoke the next morning. Hot sunlight streamed in through the window. A furious bellow from the paddock meant Daisy was waiting to be milked and angry about the delay. He glanced at the clock. Quarter to seven. Late. Primrose must have woken early. He threw on shorts and went to the bathroom.

"Hi," she said when he emerged dressed and ready for breakfast. "Sleep well?"

"Yes, overslept. Haven't done that for years."

"It's a lovely morning. Rain's all gone. Eggs and bacon?"

"Yes, please." He eyed her curiously as she fussed with the spatula and the eggs. Very domesticated. How long would it last? Primrose placed a heaped plate in front of him.

"Do you have a cow?" she asked after another loud moo from outside.

"Daisy. She wants to be milked. I'm late."

"Really?" Her eyes opened wide in astonishment. "You're kidding. How does she know what time it is?"

"No, I'm not kidding. Cows like routine. Their udders get uncomfortably full of milk."

"Does all the cream in the fridge come from Daisy?"

Tom nodded with his mouth full of bacon. To go with her other delectable attributes she could cook like a champion, and this chatty friendliness could very easily undermine his security system which had been lulled by the night's sleep. Beware. A smiling Primrose in the morning was a treat he couldn't afford to get used to.

"How come Danny doesn't have a cow? All they have are those goats who don't do anything except eat."

Tom shrugged. "They prefer goat's milk. Lot of people do. Plus goats are cheaper to buy and feed. They eat anything."

"They're not cheap if they don't produce anything." Primrose poured him tea and sat opposite with her own toast and one egg.

"True."

"Can I watch you milk the cow?"

"If you like. You can collect the eggs for me."

"Okay. I was on egg collecting duty while Mojo was away." She smiled a big happy smile which made his breath catch, but faded abruptly.

"What went wrong?" He hid a smile at the spontaneous indignation on her face, but she grimaced almost immediately.

"I didn't lock up the chooks and a fox killed four."

Air hissed between his teeth.

"I thought Mojo would take over when he got home and he thought I...anyway."

"They're a real problem, foxes. I shot a couple last year. They won't do that next door though, of course." Much safer to discuss predators than dwell on her smiling mouth, and the perfect body he'd wanted to take to his bed last night.

"No!" Kurt might. No telling what he would do but the thought of him wielding a gun was terrifying. "There aren't any guns at Nirvana. Thank goodness. Why do you need a gun?"

"Farmers are allowed to have them for just that reason. Culling feral animals and sometimes destroying injured stock. What would you do about it? Foxes and rabbits aren't native animals and they kill off the natural wildlife and plants. They don't have any predators. Except humans. Feral cats are just as bad," he added.

Primrose bit her lip. "I don't know," she muttered.

"Trap them?"

"And then what? Take them somewhere else to bug some other poor bloke? Farming life is harsh."

Primrose ate the last of her egg in silence. She was wearing her own clothes. Crumpled but clean. How did she manage to look so sexy? When he'd first seen her she was attractive but city slick, now, relatively dishevelled, relaxed and natural she looked even better. He took a gulp of hot tea in an effort to curb thoughts which should have been on the day's work but circled constantly around the minefield of a woman across the table.

She finished her toast and looked up.

"Did you put me to bed?"

"Yes."

"Thank you." She studied him for a moment but didn't comment further. No probing into his mental state or accusations of anything untoward. "Have you got lots to do today?"

"Fair bit. I'll have to check the fences along the river in case of flood damage, and I'll need to have a look at the crops in the far paddocks for the same reason."

"Will the bridge be clear?"

"Not sure."

Tom scraped the last of his toast around the plate collecting up smears of egg yolk, and shoved the lot in his mouth. He stood up, anxious to remove himself from the temptation which had roared back powerful as ever. "Thanks for breakfast. I'd better get a move on."

"I'll clean up here and come down in a little while."

"The cowshed is behind the garage and round the

151

back past the chook run."

"I'll find it." Another brilliant smile. So co-operative. What was she up to?

Primrose hummed to herself as she washed and dried the dishes. Tom's spare bed was very comfortable. She hadn't slept so well since she'd arrived in the valley. Tom's whole house was comfortable—much nicer than the commune. Tom's house felt like a home. The commune felt like a hostel for the homeless. Animal Farm.

But it needn't! Primrose hung the tea towel neatly on the oven door. If Danny kicked out all the hangers on and made the big old place his own instead of sharing it with all and sundry it would take on a completely different aura. She could help. Painting her bedroom had made a terrific difference. Poor Nirupam had been amazed. She needed better treatment. The nursery would have to be the priority now. Shopping for baby things. Primrose smiled in anticipation. Fun. Maybe there'd be more babies and the Pretty family would totter on into the future.

She went to the back door and pulled on the rubber boots for the trek to the cowshed. The yard was muddy and slippery despite the heat of today's sun. Primrose breathed deeply of the fresh air as she walked. Country air had a marvellous quality, invigorating and refreshing. Deeply cleansing for the lungs. She'd only had two sessions but Fern's Chinese exercises had awakened her to the subtleties of such things. Cleared her head of city fumes and city stress.

Nature was absolutely amazing. Drops of water sparkled from the deep green of the fruit trees, diamonds quivered on the grass, puddles reflected blue mirrors. She spread her arms wide as if to embrace the earth and the sky and the sun and the whole wonderful world. Lovely. She really could live the rest of her life out here. Plus she'd got off to a very good start with Tom this morning. Nothing like a good feed to cheer a man up.

She followed a well worn path beside the garage and workshop and around the corner. On the right was a shed with a wire mesh front. Brown and black speckled white hens scratched about inside muttering to themselves and each other. Primrose peered in and the hens peered back expectantly with cocked heads, clucking softly. Along the rear wall was a raised bench with a row of separate little boxes. She couldn't see any eggs. At the commune the hens laid eggs where they felt like it because they wandered about freely. This was a much better arrangement. No fox would break into this pen.

She continued on past the henhouse to a barn and what must be the cowshed next to it. A field lay beyond with a black horse grazing peacefully. It lifted its head and stared, munching, ears pricked. She didn't know Tom had a horse. She didn't know lots of thing about him. Delilah the dog stood up from the shadow of the shed and came forward wagging her tail. Primrose went to the gate leading into a small yard and the open-sided cow shed. Tom sat on a stool milking a brown cow whose head was deep in a bundle of hay. A leather halter with a length of rope attached the cow to a metal ring on the wall.

"Hello," she said.

He raised his head and smiled. "Meet Daisy." That smile did it to her every time, turned her brain to dough.

She had to drag her eyes away to focus on the cow.

Daisy shifted her back leg and twisted her head around to have a look at the visitor.

"Hello, Daisy."

Daisy snorted, flapped her big hairy ears then turned back to her hay and recommenced chewing.

"Is that your horse?"

"Yes. Cindy."

"Do you ride much?"

"Not a lot. I use her to get around the property. I'll take her out later when I look at the fences."

Primrose considered the idea of a horse. She'd wanted to have a pony when she was a child but knew very early on it wasn't going to happen. Maybe she could have one now. Tom could teach her to ride. A vision of the two of them on the horse, his arms around her, his body warm against her back, breath in her ear...

"Like to try milking?" Not what she'd anticipated but by the look on his face he was expecting her to decline the offer. Still thought she wouldn't cope with farm stuff. Think again, Tom.

"Can I? Would she mind?"

"Not if you're gentle."

"Okay."

Primrose took Tom's place on the stool, squeezing past him in the confined space, holding her breath at the sudden proximity of that broad chest. She steadied the milk bucket between her rubber booted feet the way he'd done. Daisy took another look and snorted softly. A big grey tongue emerged and licked a nostril. She went back to her food. Warm cow smell flooded Primrose's nose. Not unpleasant at all. "What do I do?"

"Grasp the front left teat between your thumb and

forefinger and pull down firmly. Not too tight or you'll hurt her and she'll kick. Like this." His fingers closed over hers. She tried to concentrate on his words but her whole being centred on the sudden, unexpected contact. So close, and totally oblivious to the effect on her. "You try."

She did as instructed. To her surprise a feeble jet of milk squirted into the bucket. "Gosh. I did it."

"Keep going."

Primrose kept on. After a few tries she settled to a steady rhythm producing a strong stream of milk.

"Try both teats with two hands. Alternate," Tom said.

She managed to co-ordinate left and right hands. He watched for a minute. "You can finish her off. I've done the rear teats. Just go until you can't get much out." He patted Daisy on her bony rump. "I'll be in the workshop."

"Hang on," she cried as he opened the gate. Surely he was being overly confident in her ability. Recklessly so. "What do I do with Daisy?"

"Take off her halter and make sure you shut the gate when you leave. Take the milk up to the laundry."

"But..." began Primrose but he'd gone. Was this his way of showing her how useless she'd be as a farmer? Throwing her in the deep end? "Stinker," she said aloud. Daisy snuffled and tossed her head. "Not you." This milking business was pretty easy once you had the knack.

But knack or not, soon her hands began to ache and she had to keep stopping to flex her stiff fingers. Daisy finished the hay by which time she apparently decided the milking should be finished too. She began to fidget and shake her head, pulling at the rope. The round belly loomed over Primrose. Daisy was very big from her low angle.

"I'm trying, Daisy. Calm down."

The left teat was almost empty but the right still flowed copiously. Primrose tried switching hands. Daisy wasn't happy. She shuffled her feet. Her tail which had been hooked out of the way on a nail on the wall, came loose and flicked across Primrose's face with a stinging swipe.

"Owww." Primrose lurched sideways, her hand to her cheek. The little three legged stool tilted but she managed to right it before crashing over. Daisy rumba-ed sideways and one hoof caught the bucket, spilling a frothy wave of creamy white milk over the dirty concrete floor.

Chapter Eight

"Daisy! Oh, my goodness!" Primrose scrambled to safety as the cow swung her bony backside round, kicking out wildly and sending the bucket flying. "Jeepers!"

No way was she going any closer to that lunatic animal. Where was Tom? How could he leave her alone with a cow? How irresponsible was that? All the milk was gone, spread in a vast lake over the floor, stomped on and churned up by the mad cow and it served him right!

Primrose flung the gate open and stormed along the path to the workshop. Tom was busy with some unrecognisable farming implement. He looked up when she appeared in the doorway. "Finished?"

"Sure am! Your mad cow just booted the bucket out of the shed and your milk is all over the ground."

Tom straightened. For a second she could have sworn he was about to laugh in which case she would have clocked him with something. But his expression darkened. "Where's Daisy?"

"Trying to get herself out of the halter."

"You just left her there?" He didn't wait for her reply, hurried to the door, pushed past Primrose and jogged for the cowshed. Delilah jogged after him. Primrose trailed behind both of them.

"I wasn't going near her. Not the way she was

acting."

"You must have upset her," he tossed over his shoulder. "And you didn't close the gate like I told you. I hope she's still tied up."

"I must have upset *her*?" yelled Primrose. "She nearly knocked me over and kicked me."

But Tom wasn't listening to her excuses. He was muttering soothing things to his precious cow. He slapped her on the rump and edged in beside her. "Shove over," he said, giving her a push. Daisy moved sideways snorting and blowing in her indignation. Tom undid the halter buckle and slipped it off her head. Daisy backed out quietly and wandered innocently off into the paddock, pausing to snatch mouthfuls of grass as she went. Tom hung the halter over the metal ring.

"She's very placid, usually." He eyed the mess on the floor. Daisy had made her own sloppy, smelly contribution to the milk while she waited. "You can hose that out."

He pointed to a hose attached to a tap beside the water trough against the shed wall. Primrose glowered at him with her hands on her hips. He stared back, blank faced.

"She wouldn't have hurt you. She doesn't even have any horns. I wouldn't leave you with her if I thought either of you would be in danger." Nice. She and the cow, equal in his eyes. He picked up the empty bucket. "This'll need a good wash." He put it down again.

Her job, no doubt.

He turned to go but paused. "The egg collecting bucket is in the barn by the side door. Should be safe enough. Make sure you shut the chook run gate when you go in and out. Don't want to be chasing chooks all day. Or letting foxes in."

Primrose was left staring at his retreating back. She gritted her teeth and walked over to the hose. Right. Hose the crap out of the cowshed. That she could manage. She turned on the tap and aimed the nozzle at the floor. A feeble trickle emerged. She turned the tap on full. The pressure increased slightly. A finger half over the end helped. Milky water sloshed out onto the already muddy ground. Daisy strolled over to watch, chewing, ears flapped forward inquisitively.

"This is your fault," Primrose told her. "You should be doing this."

A coarse bristled broom stood in the corner. She grabbed it to clear the hay and the cow poo away. More hosing and the floor was done. She picked up the dirty milking bucket, carefully latching the gate behind her and giving it a few good tugs to make sure. Next chore.

She left the bucket outside the barn. Masses of little yellow, white, and purple flowers grew haphazardly between the path and the wall of the old wooden building. Drops of moisture sparkled on the petals. Primrose bent to sniff the faint perfume rising on the warming air then went inside. The interior was all cool shadows. Quiet, peaceful with dust motes floating in the shaft of sunlight streaming in through the door.

Inside the barn door, he'd said. There to the right on a waist high workbench. Egg cartons and a white metal pail with a layer of straw in the base. Primrose set off for the henhouse swinging the bucket. Chooks would be no trouble. For a start they were smaller than she was and judging by the ones at the commune they were timid creatures, ran away when people came near.

Tom owned about twelve. They clucked and darted about when she opened the door. Some of them made a dash for freedom but she pulled the door closed smartly behind her.

"Not so fast, ladies." One of them pecked at her boot but the tough rubber stopped the beak from achieving more than a firm poke at her foot. "You can cut that out."

She discovered that by walking slowly the cluster of chooks around her feet fluttered aside. One egg was on the floor in the corner. The other hens had used the nesting boxes the way they were supposed to and laid their eggs neatly in the straw. She scooped up four more eggs. The third box was occupied but the hen hopped out as Primrose neared. Two brown eggs lay nestled together, warm to the touch. New laid. She always had doubts about the commune eggs.

No eggs in the next. "Someone's been slacking off," she said sternly to the little flock. They clucked and scratched and ignored her. Box number five had a white occupant hunched solidly in place. Primrose extended her hand tentatively and flapped it about so the sitter would get the message. The hen eyed her with a beady gaze. It settled itself more firmly into the box.

"Are you sitting on something?" She pushed her hand gently under the warm feathery body, feeling about for an egg. The hen pounced, pecking viciously at her wrist.

"Ouch." Three red marks appeared on her skin. No blood fortunately. She put the egg bucket carefully on the ground. Good thing she hadn't dropped it in shock. Primrose studied the hen. It glared at her through a suspicious yellow eye.

"I'm not giving in to you." She tried to lift it with two hands but the hen swung its head about and connected with the base of her thumb this time. "You horrible thing! I'm having your egg, so there."

Time for an all out assault regardless of consequences. Primrose drew a deep breath and plunged her hand underneath the chook's body, feeling desperately about as the beak attacked her wrist. One egg. She pulled her prize out swiftly. One little white egg.

"Pathetic effort." She put the egg in the bucket and rubbed her wounds. "I've one thing to say to you," she said fiercely to the hen which was now standing, fluffing its feathers indignantly. "Christmas dinner."

"I don't think chooks understand very much." Tom—standing outside the hen run with a smirk on his face and a bucket in his hand. "Their brains are about the size of a pea."

"This one has an overdeveloped defence system." Had he seen the attack? She checked the remaining boxes. Five more eggs.

"Didn't you see the gloves on the bench?" Tom opened the door and stepped in as she stepped out. He tossed handfuls of grass all over the floor and the hens raced about frantically pecking at the new pickings.

"Do you need gloves? *I* didn't."

He grinned and upended the bucket for the last of the greenstuff to drop.

"I didn't know they ate grass?"

"It makes their egg yolks rich and yellow." He took the egg bucket from her and headed for the barn. Delilah trotted behind him, faithful as a shadow. "We'll take a walk down to the river and have a look at the water level."

"Can I see the truffle crop?"

"Not much to see. Just trees." Tom left the eggs on a shelf in the barn. "But we walk through the plantation to the river."

He led her toward the house then swung left following the drive for a few metres before cutting across to a gate in the wire fence. The land sloped down gently to the willows lining the path of the river. Orderly rows of young trees filled the paddock. Primrose walked by Tom's side through the damp grass. His arm brushed hers lightly every few paces, leaving a trail of tingling sparks. Did he notice? His eyes were fixed on the ground ahead. The dog snuffled about running backward and forward around them, checking out interesting smells.

"The rain was handy," he said. "Truffles need a decent rainfall."

"Where exactly are they growing?" She stared at the rough grass underfoot. "Are we walking on them?"

"Truffles are a fungus. They grow under the ground as a result of a symbiotic relationship with the roots of particular trees infected with the appropriate mycorrhiza—literally, fungus root," he added as he saw the expression on her face. "These are oak trees. They seem to work best in Australia but the industry is only young so no-one's really sure yet."

"When will they be ready?"

"About March."

"Is Delilah your truffle hunter?" The grey ears pricked up at the mention of her name.

Tom laughed. "No, she's a bit past it. I've hired in an expert for the last crops but I think I'll buy another dog and train it myself. Doesn't take long apparently."

Primrose gazed around the field. The trees stretched along the river bank and back up the slope toward the buildings. Must have taken ages to plant them all. By comparison Danny had done nothing. His land was all natural bush or cleared pasture land—empty of stock apart from the small orchard and the garden patch. Now Tom owned the land on the far side of the river as well and he'd put it to good use. Profitable use from what he'd told her. Even she knew truffles were an expensive and highly sought after delicacy.

Didn't seem to need much cultivation. They grew themselves. Why couldn't she and Danny plant their land the same way?

"Could Danny grow truffles?"

Tom tilted his head in thought. "He could. It's like any other crop, takes hard work, knowledge and luck with the weather." He scanned the newly washed blue sky, empty save for a few billowy white puffs of cloud over the hilltops.

"But you could advise him, couldn't you?"

His gaze swung from the heavens down to her, assessing. Very sceptical. "If he wants to go into it, sure. The trees aren't cheap to buy and there's a fair bit of work to get things started. It's pretty hit and miss crop wise. May not get anything for years. I've been lucky, but it's been five years."

"But he'll have the money you're paying him for the land."

He raised an eyebrow. "He might have other ideas about where to spend it. Anyway, I thought he wasn't going to be selling any more land. And if he does where are his trees going to go?"

Why couldn't he be a little bit positive? "We wouldn't need as many acres as you."

"True." Tom nodded. "In theory there's no problem."

"In practice?" His calm stonewalling made her want to grab the front of his shirt and give him a good shake. Where was that passionate man who could barely wait to make love to her? He spoke to her as though she was an interested stranger rather than a woman he'd chased after in the middle of the night. How could he switch it off so completely?

"Danny may not want to grow truffles. It's very risky. It's really an untried crop and market in Australia. All speculation. And he may want the money for something else."

He'd said that before. Did he know something she didn't? They'd looked very comfortable together in the shed yesterday. Tom and Danny had some man thing going. Secrets. "What something else?"

"The baby? Fixing the roof?" He shrugged and strode away down the slope to the river. Primrose clumped after him in her large boots which were fine in the henhouse but too sloppy for comfortable walking on the uneven ground. "Water level's dropped," he called. He turned and came back. "I'll drive you home."

Home? She'd forgotten about leaving, forgotten she was a visitor here. Nirvana didn't feel like home. Fairview did. Maybe the bridge would still be impassable. With any luck. Except Tom didn't want her here. What was she thinking? Of course he didn't want her here, and she didn't want to be any more beholden to him than she already was.

"Or you could go cross country," he suggested with a little snort of laughter. "Much shorter."

"Is the river passable?" Was he serious? Did he expect her to swim?

"There's a ford—the water comes to Cindy's knees normally but the current's up today and there's a fair bit of storm debris so no, it's probably too rough." His glance caught hers with an unmistakably amused glint. "Unless you feel like a swim." He continued tramping solidly up the slope.

Primrose jerked her legs into action. Uphill was harder work. Her feet slipped about inside the boots so she floundered along behind his competent figure like a beginner ice skater. "Not really. Do you swim in there?"

"Yep. There's a good deep pool just near the bend." He stopped and pointed to the right. A small shed stood on the bank and irrigation pipes meandered out across the paddock.

"Kurt swims in the creek. It's his bath."

"No leeches?"

Primrose stopped, adjusting her posture to relaxed casual before he turned around. "Yes but they don't bother him." Smiled. "So he says."

"It'd be the other way around, I reckon." Tom grinned and she giggled.

But the whole Kurt issue loomed in her mind, a dirty, foul-smelling cloud of pollution. Returning to the commune meant returning to the tension and the mania and the total uncomfortable lunacy of the situation. "I wonder if Danny's done anything about him yet." Impossible to keep the unease and dread from her voice.

They reached the gate to the driveway. Tom swung it open and waited for Primrose to walk through. He slipped the chain back on the hook. "No idea." So calm, so uninterested. No, that wasn't the word—disinterested was more like it. The goings on next door didn't affect Tom one way or another, other than to provide the occasional entertainment. *She* didn't affect him one way or the other. Except in regard to his friendship with Danny.

Maybe he'd give her a straight answer if she took him by surprise.

"What did Danny come to see you about, Tom?"

He didn't, he took evasive action. "He often comes over for a chat."

Primrose gave up. "I'll get my shoes," she said as they walked around to the back door.

"Keep those boots if you like."

"Thanks, I will." She levered them off on the step before going into the house to retrieve her ruined sandals.

She nipped into the bathroom. What a mess. Her hair was all over the place and somehow the clean T-shirt had dirty marks on it. That would be from hosing cow poo. And her face! A streak of what she hoped was plain mud and not something worse stretched from eyebrow to chin. Courtesy of Daisy's tail. Tom hadn't even commented. Probably just laughed to himself. She scrubbed her face, hands, and wrists. That nasty chook hadn't broken the skin, thank heavens.

She dried herself with the green towel but hesitated before hanging it up. Should strip her bed and wash the sheets and towel before she left. Tom didn't need extra work. She went to the spare room.

"What are you doing?" Tom from outside. He sounded annoyed.

"I'm stripping the bed," she yelled.

The back door banged and his feet sounded in the hallway. "Don't bother." He lounged in the doorway watching.

"Too late." She faced him with her arms full of bedding. Why did he have to be so sexy, and so relaxed, and so nice, and so frustrating, and so...so...downright annoying. "I'll put it in the machine and you can hang it out later."

He straightened, frowning. "I can do it."

"So can I." Primrose marched toward him so he had to step aside quickly and allow her space with her bundle of linen. He followed her to the laundry.

"Why do you have to be so bossy?"

Primrose dumped the washing on the floor. "I thought I was being helpful by not leaving you with my dirty sheets." She opened the lid of the machine and crammed in the bedding and the towel. As an afterthought she yanked off the socks and dropped them on top.

"You are, thanks. It's not..." The hesitation made her pause with the washing powder ready to pour. He sucked in air and folded his arms. Grey eyes studied her from under the flop of brown hair. If she had scissors she'd give him a quick trim. "You won't let people do their own thing. It's as if you think you know best about everything."

More powder fell in than necessary. "I don't! It's obvious I don't know anything about cows, for example." She glared at him. "And only an idiot would leave me alone with one."

He unfolded his arms and stuck his hands on his hips. "So you think I'm an idiot."

Primrose slammed the lid closed and pressed the start button. "In that respect, yes." He was too close and too good-looking and the memory of their night together flared suddenly, far too fresh in her mind. Would he ever want to kiss her again? Her lips tingled.

"You always manage to turn things around so in your mind someone else is in the wrong."

Anyone looking less inclined to kiss her she had yet to see. She braced herself against the washing machine. "You're still angry because I went home without waking you, aren't you?"

"See?" he cried. "You've just done it again. *You* planned your way into my bed, *you* sneaked off and somehow it's all my fault for finding you sexy and desirable and wanting..."

"Wanting what?" she demanded harshly as the guilt crashed in. He was right. She'd behaved abominably. She didn't dare look into his eyes. Afraid if she did she'd cry because of how kind he was and how nasty she was. How petty and small his straightforward honesty made her seem. And how he wouldn't want her again and how deeply that hurt. Really hurt.

He didn't answer the question—he shook his head. "I don't mean just me, we've been all through that. I mean Danny, too." He wasn't a man to waste his time where he thought he wasn't appreciated. Once bitten stay right away. "You're somehow trying to blame Danny for the situation you've caused next door."

Safer topic. Unpleasant, uncomfortable too, but much safer. The best defence is attack. "What about

Danny, Tom? You're not telling me something. What is it?" Maybe you should try being less of a controlling bitch. Danny's words. Had he reported the fight to Tom or had Tom had the same thought?

"Why do you have to know everything? Why should I tell you what Danny and I discuss?"

"Because if it's about the land it's my business."

"And if it's not about the land?"

"What else would it be?" The words sprang out, stupid and ill-considered, and unreturnable.

"Oh, Christ." Tom emitted a laugh completely devoid of humour. "Get your shoes, I'll drive you home."

****

The hail had flattened Kurt's vegetable garden.

"All gone. Kaput," he said with a sweep of his arm. He glared at Tom's ute bounding back up the slippery driveway and over the ridge as if Tom had brought on the deluge and aimed it deliberately at this derelict patch of ground.

"Gosh, that's awful."

Two heads were silhouetted in the rear window. Danny had gone back with Tom to collect his motorbike. He'd emerged from the house, greeted Tom and ignored Primrose before climbing into the seat she'd just vacated. Kurt came charging up from the veggie patch too late to do his usual growl and bark at Tom. He looked so miserable when he stopped glaring she almost felt sorry for him, standing there in the muddy yard with a woebegone expression and a battered wheelbarrow load of shredded plants.

"Ja. Farming is a mug's game." The wheel squeaked as he gave the barrow a shove and trundled away toward the goat pen.

Primrose went straight to her room to change. She pulled on a blouse and skirt and, grabbing one of her two towels, went to the bathroom to clean her teeth and rewash her face with cleanser and toner. Tom's facilities were much better but he didn't run to moisturiser and deodorant.

And at Tom's place the bathroom wasn't shared with six other people. No way was she leaving her cosmetics and either of her precious, thick, expensive blue towels in there. Someone else was just as likely to grab her toothbrush by mistake.

She tucked her towel onto the rail next to the other one. The other one? Thick and blue. Hers! It should have been in the laundry basket with the clean clothes, brought in by Fern the day before the storm. The day she'd been fighting her brother and sulking all afternoon in her room. The day she'd set out to seduce Tom and ruined a promising friendship. Bringing in the washing was the last thing on her mind that day.

She stared at the blue towel then assessed the others hanging on hooks and railings. Fern's family used large striped towels, Nirupam and Danny had plain purple or blue, Kurt's were striped but smaller, cheap, threadbare and instantly recognisable. His was missing. He'd pinched her towel. The bastard! She eyed it with distaste. It would need soaking for days, maybe disinfecting. She snatched it off the railing and bundled it with her cow muddied clothes to take to the laundry for a lengthy session in stain remover.

Nirupam and Fern were in the kitchen.

"Hi."

"Hello. Have a good time at Tom's?" Fern and

Nirupam exchanged glances and smiled knowing smiles.

They didn't know anything whatever they thought. "Fine, thank you. Kurt used my towel!"

"Don't change the subject," said Nirupam.

"What subject?" Primrose strode into the laundry and dumped her dirty clothes in the sink.

"The subject of you and Tom alone in his house for twenty four hours," called Fern. Nirupam giggled.

Primrose attacked the stained yellow pants with Sard's soap. "He lent me dry clothes, I cooked sausages for dinner, I slept in his spare room, I cooked him bacon and eggs for breakfast, he showed me the truffle paddock, and he drove me home. End of story."

"Hah. If that's the end of the story I'll be very disappointed."

"Prepare yourself for a big disappointment."

Fern appeared in the doorway with her big psychic smile. "The cards say otherwise, Rosie."

Primrose stuck the plug in the sink, shook the stain removing powder in and turned on the tap full bore. She rammed the towel down into the cleansing suds with a shudder of distaste.

"I doubt it very much."

"I don't and neither does Nirupam."

"Well you both know more than I do. Or Tom." She turned off the tap. "Especially Tom."

"Sometimes others can see something far more clearly than those involved."

"Sometimes others are just stickybeaks." She pushed past Fern into the kitchen but stopped, turned, biting her lip. Fern was gazing at her with sympathetic eyes, all-knowing and all-seeing, the soothsaying expression. Except fortunately she wasn't any of those things. She was just a kind, well-meaning woman. A friend. "I'm sorry. I didn't mean to be rude."

A hand heavy with rings raised in protest, bangles jingled. "Don't worry, Rosie. When a soul is troubled words often come out the wrong way."

A troubled soul? Maybe that was true. She gave Fern a feeble smile. Nirupam sat smiling like a pregnant Buddha both hands resting on her belly.

"We'll do some Chi Kung when you're ready." Fern patted her shoulder in passing. "You need some inner cleansing."

"Thanks." Just like her clothes. Stain removal. Her soul would be a dirty grey colour.

Primrose dragged a chair out and sat down opposite Nirupam. "How's Danny?"

"He's calmed down."

"Good. He ignored me just now when he went with Tom to get his bike."

"We had a flood in here after you left. It's a good thing Danny had your car to get home."

"I was worried he mightn't have made it when Tom and I saw the bridge was underwater. Tom said he wouldn't have tried to drive across if it was dangerous."

"He said it was just coming up to the road level. The bathroom roof leaked and it got flooded. So did Kurt's bedroom."

"Just Kurt's?"

Nirupam nodded, eyes twinkling with suppressed delight.

"Oh, dear, and the vegetable garden got flattened by the hail."

"Must be a sign," said Nirupam.

"But will he recognise it?" Was that why he'd taken her towel? Because his were soaked in the flood? No. Because one of his was still clean and dry in the laundry basket. She'd have it out with him later and make quite sure he understood her things were hers, communal property, sharing or not. No way was she pussy footing around him the way Danny did.

****

Jason, Fern, and Mojo left on Wednesday morning amidst hugs and one or two tears from Nirupam and Fern.

"I'll write and give you our address so you can tell us about the baby. It's a girl." Fern touched Nirupam's belly lightly.

Primrose hid a smile. Tarot cards or palm reading? But she'd miss Fern's quiet strength, her passive resistance to Kurt's lunacies. There was only Nirupam for back-up now. And her loyalty was always to Danny, which was right. The balance of power would shift. But where?

Primrose went to the house for her shopping list and bag. Nirupam was staying home to rest. With Fern gone the idea of a home birth grew even less appealing. The more she thought about it the worse it got. They wouldn't be able to call Ellie without going to Tom's which would take time and if the midwife couldn't get here, what then? This would need gentle coaxing over the next week. Time was running out.

Primrose strode into the yard in search of Kurt, determined to wrest some grocery money from him. He wasn't in the vegetable ruins but clanking came from one of the sheds, a derelict one she'd never explored.

"Kurt?" The open door swung gently to and fro in

the breeze. She grabbed hold of it and peered into the dark interior. "Kurt?"

"Ja," came from somewhere behind a pile of old wooden fruit boxes.

Primrose took a step inside. A black snake lay coiled in a patch of sunlight right in the doorway.

"Snake!" She hurled herself backward and slammed the door then hurtled for the orchard screaming for Danny on her headlong flight through the tangle of weeds and grass on the path. A roar of rage emanated from the shed behind her.

Danny emerged running from between the trees. "Is it Nirupam? The baby? Is she all right? What is it?" he yelled.

"Snake." Primrose leaned over panting in big shuddery breaths. Her legs were shaking so much they barely held her up.

"Where?"

"In the shed with the boxes."

Another Germanic roar sounded from the shed.

"Where's Kurt?"

"In the shed."

"With the snake?"

Her eyes opened wide as she grimaced. "Cripes! I shut him in with it."

For a moment Danny froze then he started to laugh. "My God, you're hopeless, Rosie. It'll be pitch dark in there and there's no handle on the inside."

He started running again but this time he was laughing so much he could barely keep on the path. The closer they came to the shed the louder the cursing.

"He's still alive, then," Danny said between gasps.

Primrose stopped well back from the door. She

wasn't laughing and neither was Kurt. Best be prepared for a quick getaway from both him and the snake.

Danny was almost hysterical but he managed to control himself enough to ask, "Where was it?"

"Right in the doorway. I couldn't see Kurt. He was up the back somewhere. It's not funny!"

"Right. No. Could have been lethal." Danny heaved in a deep breath and then another. "Kurt, you okay?"

A stream of furious German issued forth in response.

"I'd take that as a yes," said Primrose softly.

Danny grabbed the door and pulled it open, jumping back as he did so. The snake had disappeared. "It's not in the doorway," he called. "I can't see it."

Something crashed over and a moment later Kurt came barrelling out of the shed, red-faced and roaring like a furious bull. Danny and Primrose sprang aside as he shot past and headed for the house, legs pounding faster even than the day she'd arrived and he'd charged across to attack Tom.

Danny all but collapsed with laughter again, bent double, gasping and wheezing, arms wrapped around his body, tears streaming down his face.

Primrose stared after the runaway train in amazement, then switched her attention to Danny. She'd never seen him laugh like this. Ever. It was infectious. Tears sprang to her own eyes as she began to laugh too.

"Not a good time to ask him for food money," she said. "I'd better wait a bit."

****

To Primrose's complete and utter astonishment

Kurt left in the beaten up old Kombi van two days later, immediately after breakfast.

She'd been too gobsmacked to ask why or how this miracle had occurred. After he'd calmed down about the snake incident and accepted her truly heartfelt apology he'd even forked over twenty dollars for the shopping with barely a grumble when she asked. At least she hadn't laughed like Danny. That appeared to upset Kurt more than the closed door.

"Did you tell him he had to go?" asked Primrose when she stood with Nirupam and Danny waving as Kurt roared away over the brow of the hill. Sammy the sheep uttered several plaintive bleats as he forlornly watched a kindred spirit depart.

"No."

"Was it the snake episode? It really was an accident. I didn't shut him in there with it deliberately."

"Could've been but he said he didn't feel comfortable here anymore. The vibe had changed and he had to free himself from the bad aura." Danny turned away, Sammy with him. "He said it was sucking the life essence from him, made it impossible to live here."

"I'm glad he's gone," Nirupam said with a little smile. Then, in a pleasant maternal world of her own, she waddled slowly toward to the house with one hand pressing against her lower back.

Primrose stared from one retreating back to the other. Danny's implication sank in. Kurt had raved on once about Tom creating bad vibes next door. But Tom hadn't changed...

"Me? Did he mean I was the bad vibe?" Sammy skittered away as Primrose darted after her brother.

He didn't slacken his pace as he tossed his reply at

her like a hand grenade. "What do you think, Rosie? Is it a coincidence everyone left within a fortnight of you turning up? Tells you something, doesn't it?"

"No, it doesn't! You've had people coming and going the whole time you've been here. I'm glad he's gone and so is Nirupam."

"Only problem now is we don't have enough people to work the place. I can't do everything."

"I'm here! I want to help." Primrose glared at him. "What's the problem anyway? Tom manages all by himself next door."

He ignored her crack. "Can you handle the vegetable garden?"

"I bet I can do as well as that idiot. After the hailstorm most of his plants have been flattened anyway, so I'll have to start again."

"We'll see."

Primrose restrained herself from remarking as far as she could judge no-body did anything much in the way of work, Danny included. Compared to Tom.

"We need a plan, Danny. We need to sit down and work out some proper farming strategy to make money on this place. I was talking to Tom," she began, eager to promote the truffle growing idea but Danny threw his hands in the air and continued walking toward the sheds.

"You still don't get it, do you?" he hissed furiously. "I didn't come here to make money. I came to get away from that scene. It's crippling."

"But why do you keep selling off land?" Primrose ran after him yelling at his back when he didn't stop. "You keep going on about not needing money and money being evil and all that crap yet you take what

Tom offers you. Where does it go, Danny?" He spun around, fury turning his face to granite. She waved her arm in a wide arc taking in the dilapidated sheds, the land, and the ramshackle house. "What do you spend it on? It's obviously not around here. I painted my room and I bought the paint for the front door and the windows." And what a lovely job she'd done on Tuesday with Mojo's enthusiastic assistance—glossy rich green to cover the ugly graffiti-like peace symbol.

Danny followed the sweep of her gesture but his gaze stopped on his wife painstakingly hanging up washing with her swollen baby belly making every movement awkward and clumsy. He couldn't have missed the relief and her pleased smile when Kurt made his dramatic declaration last night.

Nirupam took the empty washing basket inside and the back door banged behind her. Primrose lowered her voice. "Tell me, Danny. What's going on? I'm your sister. I love you. We're family."

He started walking again but slower, heading for the tractor shed. Primrose followed, sensing an imminent change of attitude, an acceptance of her presence. For better or worse.

She said, "I want to invite Tom to dinner. I owe him one." Then the topic of truffle viability and farm plans could casually be raised in conversation.

"Fine. Invite whoever you like. We have an open house."

"Tonight?"

"Fine."

Primrose grinned and received a small, somewhat guarded smile in response but the smile didn't reach his eyes and was switched off almost immediately. She hurried back to the house to tell Nirupam so they could discuss the menu. With the departure of Kurt an incredible weight had lifted from the communal house. Fancy blaming her for the bad vibe!

Having decided upon a variety of salads, rice, and a vegetable, nut, and tofu curry Nirupam went to lie on the couch reading a baby care book while Primrose prepared to walk across the paddocks to issue the invitation to Tom.

Another shopping trip to Moruya had resulted in a raid on the secondhand bookshop plus a secondhand bassinet from the Salvation Army store. Transforming Mojo's bedroom had begun with the remaining white paint and a change of curtains.

Nirupam positively glowed. With Kurt on the road the future was considerably brighter for the Pretty household.

Primrose changed into her bikini, dragged on shorts and a tank top, socks and joggers to guard against snakes, and jammed a wide-brimmed straw hat on her head. The river had dropped to its normal level during the week. Knee high he'd said the ford was, so if she wore shorts there'd be no problem. The temperature had soared once more after the brief relief of the storm. A swim in the deep pool sounded inviting. Perhaps on the way back.

"I'm off." She stood in the doorway.

"See you later." Nirupam smiled. "I can't wait to be slim again like you." She looked down at the bulge. "Come on baby. Get a move on."

"Do you think it's a girl?"

"Fern said so." Nirupam patted her tummy.

"You have to think of names, you know."

How could they not have discussed baby names? Wasn't it a natural thing for parents to do? Rupert was Primrose's preferred name for a boy but she doubted any man would go for it. Martin certainly hadn't. Would Tom? Dummy—why even think something like that? Nikki for a girl. Almost anything went with Fairbrother.

Nirupam gave her standard answer. "I'll know when I see her what her name is."

Chapter Nine

Primrose clambered carefully through the fence into Tom's land. A footworn track led through dry tussocky grass toward the line of willows which she assumed meant the ford was at the end of the path. Flies buzzed around her face. She swished them away. Heat radiated up from the barren ground baking her feet in the enclosing shoes and socks. The rain had been swallowed up by the parched earth in a few days. Only a tinge of green here and there indicated some plants had benefited from the soaking. They'd be brown and dry again within a week or two.

Tom said they needed steady rain for weeks at a time or at least regular rain over a long period leading into next summer. So much she needed to learn about the land. But she was willing to try. She'd promised Danny and she meant to honour her commitment. This was their land, their family, and their home.

The willows offered sudden release from the pounding of the sun. They had a distinctive smell, not unpleasant but mixed with a dank, muddy odour and they trailed long green fingers in the river which ran smooth and silent before her. Not as clear and pure as she'd envisaged. Branches and storm debris lay strewn along the shoreline or jammed into the bank, damming the brown water and creating eddies and whirlpools.

She stared across to the far bank. Hard to tell how

deep but she'd have to scale a metre high bank on the other side. Where was the ford? The river curved out of sight to the left. Tom had pointed in that direction to indicate the swimming hole.

Primrose went right. The bank rose higher above the waterline so she thought she'd gone the wrong way then through a thick cluster of trees it suddenly dropped to a stretch of coarse sandy gravel. The river spread its skirts lazily to become much shallower judging by the busy chattering of water running over rocks and stones.

She unlaced her shoes, stuffed her socks inside, knotted the laces together and slung the lot around her neck. Knee high on the horse? Thigh high on Primrose and getting deeper with a surprisingly strong undertow. Was this the ford? Maybe the bottom had shifted in the flood. Halfway across she stepped in a hole and went in to her waist. Lurched, slipped and slid for two tottery steps. Kept going with the water tugging at her body. Knee high suddenly and shallow to the edge.

Primrose dragged off her sodden shorts and screwed them up to wring out the water, draped them over a convenient branch and sat in the sun to rub her feet dry on tufts of grass. With the straw hat over her face she lay back to let the sun warm her body. The water had been downright cold. Her feet were freezing and her legs had goosebumps.

The sun soaked into her torso, soporific. Kurt had really and truly left. Now they could do something with the place. She and Danny and Nirupam plus the baby. Why would Danny kick her out when he ran an open house and put up with the likes of Kurt? Plus she part-owned the land. She smiled under the hat. The feeling of truly belonging was growing stronger by the day. A proper family. Their family. The family.

Wasn't that some sort of terrible cult? The Family? Evil. Not theirs.

"Sunbathing?"

Primrose jerked upright and her hat tipped to the grass. Tom's shadow fell across her belly. She squinted up at him looming above her in khaki work shorts, white shirt, and his battered hat. Two very sexy muscular legs were right at eye level, not to mention other parts she'd enjoyed exploring. His whole body was lean and firm, exciting beyond belief. She swallowed as the sudden searing burst of memory of that sexy hot night sent heat surging to her face.

"Hello. I'm just warming up. I waded across. The water's icy cold." She scrambled to her feet. "I was coming to see you."

"What about?" Not overjoyed by the prospect, judging by the look on his face. She'd had her chance with this man and well and truly blown it.

"We'd like your advice about crops and farming in general." She jammed the straw hat on her head. Would he notice the heavy breathing? Red face could be attributed to hot sun.

Tom studied her carefully before replying. Fancy finding a half naked girl in his bottom paddock. Especially this one. A dream come true. The last thing he expected when he came down to start the pump was Primrose sunning herself in a bikini. Presumably the red and white scrap of material was a bikini bottom. A pair of blue shorts was draped on a branch, drying. And he knew for a fact she preferred black lace knickers.

His fingers itched to reach out and touch that sunwarmed skin, draw her against his body, kiss her senseless. See if she could deny the attraction. Her breasts strained against the white tank top, perky little nipples inviting attention. He dragged his mind from the delights of sex in the bottom paddock to what she was saying. Her mind was on another track altogether. They wanted farming advice?

Here was a turnaround, especially from Danny. He'd never specifically asked for comprehensive advice on how to run the place. His questions had been more along the lines of what to do about the bird problem, or did Tom think peaches did better than nectarines.

Primrose must have followed through with her plan of taking over next door. She was serious about this farming business. Something deep inside glowed with secret pleasure. She'd be staying.

"What about Kurt?"

"He's gone. He left this morning."

Tom's eyebrows lifted in spontaneous unfeigned admiration. "Wow! You actually did it."

"I didn't do it. He left of his own accord." Primrose screwed up her face. "Although I..."

"You what?"

"I was going shopping so I went to screw some money out of him for a change. I wanted a capsicum too, but no-body else was allowed to pick stuff—although no-one would want to except for his cucumbers and capsicums and believe me there's definitely a limit to how many of those you can eat per week."

Tom nodded. He was having a hard time keeping his eyes off her legs. His mind kept straying to what lay beneath the clothes. Her beautiful naked body, in his bed, his for the taking. Maybe in time. He licked his lips.

"Is there a point coming soon?"

She ignored the interjection and forged on with the story. "He was in a shed with the door wide open. It's dark inside and he was in there finding something for that little tractor thing that breaks down all the time. Anyway, I was about to step inside—I called out his name—but right in the doorway there was a black snake. I got such a fright I yelled, "Snake!" and jumped out and slammed the door shut. It doesn't have a latch inside. But I didn't know that."

"So," said Tom with the beginnings of a wide grin. "You shut Kurt in the shed with a black snake. In the dark."

"Pretty much—yes." She laughed as Tom gave a loud guffaw. "I was terrified. I raced off to find Danny. He thought it was funny too."

In between bursts of laughter he said, "Possibly the reason Kurt decided to go, don't you think?"

"He was very angry but he forgave me when I apologised so it wasn't that. He told Danny the bad vibes round the place were sucking the life essence out of him. He meant me. *I'm* the bad vibe."

Tom stopped laughing enough to ask incredulously, "And you're upset?"

"Of course I am!" The delectable lips pouted in astonishment. He planted his hands on his hips to stop himself pouncing in for a kiss.

"Why? You didn't like him. He's a madman and he has more than enough bad vibes for the whole town. Remember what Mike said? If you can get Kurt to leave you'll be the Peach Princess."

"Right! I'd forgotten." Primrose relaxed, smiled.

Her green eyes lightened. "I should visit Mike."

"I went over on Tuesday. They were hit badly by hail too. Wiped out most of the fruit still on the trees." He hissed air in between his teeth as Mike's bitterly defeated face flashed into his mind. Another body blow to farmers already struggling to survive.

"That's terrible. We were hit but you weren't. It's so random."

Tom nodded. "I was lucky. We're in a drought and then we get a downpour and all it does is damage."

"It's not fair." She sat down and began hauling her socks on.

He exhaled noisily. Who said anything about Nature was supposed to be fair?

"What did you want to know? Specifically."

"We need a plan, don't you think?" The left foot was thrust into her shoe and the lace tied. On went the right shoe. Smooth brown thighs flashed before his eyes filling his vision with temptation.

"A plan?" Who was the "we"? She and Danny or was she thinking...

She jumped to her feet. His eyes moved to her face. "A five year plan. Like under Chairman Mao—the Chinese. It is a commune after all." She grinned. "We'd like you to come to dinner tonight so we can talk. Plus I owe you one."

Dinner? What were they eating over there? Capsicums?

"It's vegetable and tofu curry plus salad and rice. Very nice, I promise," she said, reading either his mind or the expression on his face. Fortunately she hadn't read his thoughts a moment or two before.

"All right. Thanks. I'll bring some fruit for dessert.

And cream." But a completely different sort of dessert would be far preferable.

"Daisy's cream? Lovely. Come about seven. Earlier if you like."

"I'd better get moving." He didn't want to get moving at all, much preferred to stand here chatting and surreptitiously ogling.

"I was going to have a swim. Why don't you join me?" She looked up at him from under the brim of her hat. The dimple flirted.

He shook his head. Oh, no, he wasn't falling for that. Hard enough keeping his hands off her as it was without them both stripping down to bare skin and frolicking about in the water. "Too much to do."

"Can I help?" His eyes travelled up her body from sneakers through bare legs to skimpy tank top, bare throat and shoulders already turning pink from the sun.

"I've got some fences to fix. Flood debris knocked them flat. Don't think you'd be much use."

"Where?"

He pointed vaguely along the river bank in the general direction of the long paddock. "I came down here to start the pump."

"Can I watch?"

"Yes." Tom began moving toward the pump shed. Primrose snatched her shorts from the branch and followed. He asked, to keep his mind from straying to thoughts of swimming—skinny dipping—bikini clad Primrose—naked Primrose, "How's Nirupam? Birth must be getting close."

"She's looking much better since we saw the doctor but she's had enough of being pregnant. Her back aches and the heat doesn't help. Ellie said it could come any time now. I so don't want her to have it at home and now that Fern's gone I think she's changing her mind. Do you know they haven't decided on names yet?"

"Must be hard to decide."

"I've already decided," she piped up.

"What? Are you having a baby?" Tom's legs, and almost his heart, stopped as ripples of shock cascaded through his body. Impossible.

Primrose walked several paces past him before she realised he'd frozen in place. She turned. "No, of course not." Then she saw his expression and burst out laughing. "Don't be ridiculous. It was only a week ago! And we used condoms. Several, actually," she added with a sly little lift of one eyebrow.

"Whew." He wiped his hand across his brow and his heart resumed its steady thumping. He grinned but Primrose had stopped laughing and was now frowning.

"Why would that be such a disaster?"

"You being pregnant with my baby?"

"Yes."

He stared while the gears in his mind whirled freely, totally unconnected with any worthwhile thoughts. Was she serious? Her expression would turn the milk. Where to start? Tell her? No way.

"We're not married or likely to be."

"Didn't stop you having sex with me."

"And vice versa. Afterward it was you who decided you don't want to have a relationship with me." He heard his voice rising with all the frustration and disappointment her callous dismissal of him had engendered. Sounding like every spurned lover that ever was. "You made that more than clear."

"But you don't want to have one with me, either."

"I didn't say that."

"You don't want a city girl for a wife. Or children."

"Wife? Where did wife come from? Who says I don't want children?" Treading water but sinking fast. Definitely in over his head.

"Generally speaking. You've made it very clear."

Tom started walking toward the pump shed. This was a crazy, painful conversation. How did she do it?

"Rupert," she said from behind him, "is the name I've chosen for a boy. And Nikki for a girl."

He shook his head and kept walking. Mad as a cut snake. And sexy and entertaining and surprising and totally desirable. And somehow she'd wound her way into his heart and his mind and he couldn't get her out again. Trouble was she enjoyed these games and he didn't know where he stood with her. Would he marry her? Yes. In a heartbeat. For better or, more than likely, for worse. But he'd never ask her. She'd play him like a puppet. And she'd drop him like a lead weight when she found out his problem.

"Rupert's a bloody awful name," he said.

****

Tom wasn't sure what to expect when he knocked on the commune door just after seven. He had time to examine the exterior while he waited to be let in. Primrose had painted over the peace symbol. Not with his leftover white but a smart, glossy forest green. She'd done the window frames too. Or someone had. Must have been her—no-one else had ever done any decorating round the place, except for Anne.

Danny opened the door with a grin. "G'day, mate.

Come in."

"G'day. Stick these in the fridge." He held out the six-pack he'd picked up that afternoon at the pub. The bag with fruit and a big jar of cream dangled from his other hand.

"Thanks. Primrose has wine for dinner. But we can crack one of these now."

Tom followed Danny into the house. Something tangy danced in his nostrils sending saliva flooding into his mouth. "Smells good."

"Rosie does most of the cooking. Has to now Fern's gone."

Tom grinned behind Danny's back. Always amused him how the women reverted to their stereotypical roles in this house. Men worked outside, women inside. Even Primrose hadn't objected. One of the few things she hadn't objected to.

Oddly, Danny didn't appear resentful of his presence. Overt hostility wasn't in Danny's nature but he might have been put out to have his lifestyle and methods threatened and, moreover, questioned and found wanting. Tom's father had been. But in this case, Primrose had asked or rather invited him on both their behalves. So she said.

Tom put a restraining hand on Danny's arm just before they stepped through into the kitchen. "Do you mind my coming over, Danny?"

"Why would I mind? You should have been over before. No need for an invitation."

"I guess I was brought up to wait to be asked." Wild horses wouldn't have dragged him here for a potluck meal surrounded by the likes of Kurt and Anne. "No, it's not the dinner part. I mean about the advice."

"What advice?" But before Tom could reply, comprehension fell like a curtain, wiping the smile from his face in an instant. "Rosie."

Tom nodded. "I thought you and she had talked about it. Geez, I'm sorry. I don't want to interfere in what you do over here."

"Not your fault, mate."

Blank-faced, Danny strode into the kitchen, unclipped two tinnies and jammed the remainder in the fridge. Primrose was nowhere to be seen. Nirupam sat fatly at the table. She looked up with a smile. More colour in her face, a brighter shine in her eyes, hair gleaming in the light. Happier than he'd ever seen her.

"Hello Nirupam. You're looking well."

"Thanks, Tom, but I'm fed up. It's too hot to be this size. Hear that, baby? Time's up." She directed the last remarks at her belly. Tom laughed. Had Primrose effected this change?

"They come when they're ready and not before," he said.

"Hi, Tom." Primrose walked in behind them. She came close and kissed his cheek, the brief touch jolting his senses like a lightning bolt.

"Hello." He caught a whiff of a familiar perfume which sent his mind reeling back to the previous weekend. The blue patterned dress displayed those shoulders and the neck he'd caressed and explored with such delight. Her walk and swim this morning had given the skin a sun kissed rosy tinge. She positively glowed and he wanted more than anything to drag her into her bedroom and taste the sweetness, bury himself in her, force her to feel what he felt. Admit it.

She slipped the bag from his arm, allowing her

fingers to trail over his wrist, and peered inside. "Yummo! Peaches and cream for dessert, Nirupam."

Tom snapped back to the present. She had a cheek. Inviting him over under false pretences then acting all innocent—overtly friendly and covertly seductive at the same time. Playing on his weakness for her. He glanced at Danny. How was she going to broach the subject? This would be interesting to say the least. Together he and Danny had a fighting chance against her gangbuster technique. He'd gladly give advice and he had plenty of ideas but Danny had to ask. Freely. From the look on his face right now Primrose was in for a tough evening and Tom wasn't about to make it any easier for her.

"Sit down, Tom," said Nirupam.

He pulled out a chair next to her. There was a platter with cracker biscuits, carrot and capsicum slices surrounding a bowl of dip, on the table. Some of the white roses from out front were in a glass vase as centrepiece. Four places were neatly set. He glanced about the kitchen curiously. Tidier and cleaner than he'd ever seen it.

"Rosie made this. It's delicious," Nirupam said. "Try it."

He obediently selected a cracker and scooped up the pale brown paste, tasted it. "Mmm. Good," he mumbled through a tastebud exploding mouthful.

"It's Greek," said Primrose from the stove where she was stirring something. The movement jiggled her bottom beneath the thin fabric of her dress. He licked his lips.

"Have some more," said Nirupam. His response was instant, but fortunately not spoken aloud—*I would if I could*. Startled, he looked across to see her watching him watching Primrose. Her mouth had a slight curve. Was she a mind reader? Was her remark deliberately ambiguous? No, not the Nirupam he knew. One track mind. His own lustful thoughts. She consumed him. His Rose. He reached for a carrot stick.

"What names are you thinking of for the baby?"

"Rupert," interjected Primrose.

Nirupam giggled.

"I wouldn't do that to a kid," Danny said, suddenly joining the conversation from the end of the table.

"I had to put up with Primrose Pretty. Can you imagine what that was like?" Primrose flicked a switch on the stove and turned to face them with her arms folded.

"I don't remember you ever saying anything." Danny's voice. Completely different—softer, caring, almost puzzled.

Primrose looked at him, the unspoken understanding palpable between them. Whatever their differences now, they had something together no-one else could understand or share however strong a more recent bond may be.

"Because of your father?" asked Nirupam gently.

Primrose swallowed, nodded. "His mother was Primrose. Mum wanted to call me Katrina but Dad registered me while she was still in hospital. He didn't ever listen to anyone else's opinion. He..." She stopped abruptly.

Danny thrust his chair back and went to the fridge for another beer. Tom shook his head at his silent query for a second.

"At school I knew a kid called Clement," he said into the awkward pause. "He used his middle name.

William. We called him Will."

She tossed him a tiny smile. "Everyone called me Rosie. I don't think it's much better, really. Specially now you've told me about your draughthorse."

"We had a big chestnut draughthorse called Rosie when I was a kid," Tom explained to Nirupam.

Danny snorted into his beer. "Sure it wasn't a mule?" he murmured but it wasn't said viciously.

Primrose ignored him, apart from a little twitch of a smile. "I don't have a middle name."

"Why didn't you change it later to something you liked? To Katrina?" Nirupam asked.

"Used to it, I suppose." Primrose shrugged. "What doesn't kill you makes you stronger."

"Like that Johnny Cash song," said Danny. "A Boy Named Sue."

"Exactly."

Tom studied her as she continued with the dinner, taking a saucepan off the heat and running the contents through a sieve. Rice. Steam rose in a white cloud enveloping her. She rubbed her wrist across her forehead, dumped the rice in a serving bowl.

She'd had it doubly tough. Drunken father, ineffective mother, teased about her name, constantly on the move and having to continually re-establish herself. Far from killing her it had made her resilient and independent. Tough as hardened steel. Until recently when another series of body blows had destabilised her, attacking the very heart of her. Literally. At the core she was soft and vulnerable as anyone. As he himself.

He stood up and went to her side, drawn to her, wanting to be close. "Need some help?" His bare arm brushed hers with a tingle of awareness.

She flashed him a smile. "Put this on the table, please. And this." She bent and removed a plate of flat bread from the oven. The heat enhanced her perfume, intoxicating him.

"You've been busy."

"I enjoy cooking."

Danny took small dishes from the fridge and placed them on the table. Cucumber in yoghurt, a blob of fruity brown chutney, finely chopped red chillies.

Primrose donned oven gloves and lifted the pan of fragrant curry across to the table. "Help yourselves."

So far so good. Danny was relaxed and relatively amenable to her presence and comments. Tom was a moderating influence. He fitted well into their awkward little family group—smoothing the rough angles where she and Danny grated on each other—chatting easily with Nirupam.

When to introduce the crucial topic? After they'd eaten would be best. Maybe over dessert? Both men were hearty eaters, no point disturbing their meal and risk making them cross before she could start. They'd be annoyed enough when she revealed the real reason for the invitation. Danny, in particular, would be furious. But it was in his own best interests. And Tom had nothing to lose.

"Would you like wine, Tom? Danny?" Nirupam never drank alcohol but she'd developed a recent craving for lemon cordial.

"Yes, please."

Danny shook his head. Primrose stood to fetch two glasses and the bottle of chilled Hunter Valley Verdelho. "This is a very nice white."

"Thanks." Tom lifted the glass and sniffed the contents before sipping. "Mmm This is good." He put the glass down and spooned a generous helping of rice onto his plate. "I thought about growing wine grapes once." He passed the ladle to Nirupam.

"Did you?" Primrose's ears pricked up. Maybe she wouldn't have to introduce the subject herself, Tom was about to do it for her. She hadn't considered a vineyard.

"Yes." He took the curry serving spoon, lifted his plate and dolloped big scoopfuls onto his rice. "This smells delicious. Shall I serve you Nirupam? Say when."

Nirupam pushed her plate closer. "Thanks, Tom. Not too much."

Barely able to sit still, Primrose watched him carefully serve Nirupam. Grapes, what about grapes? He passed the spoon to Danny who never stinted on food and piled on even more than Tom had.

"Pass the bread, please."

Primrose handed the plate across. Grapes, Tom. Was he going to expand on the subject or had he completely forgotten?

"So did you grow grapes?" She forced casual interest into her voice.

"Have some curry. Or is there something we should know—like why you're not eating it?" Tom grinned his lopsided grin, catching her eye so a spark flew between them. She smiled because she couldn't help it, impossible to resist the way his mouth crinkled.

Nirupam giggled and Primrose turned her attention to the food. He was doing it deliberately. Not answering on purpose, teasing her.

"Did you ever grow grapes?" asked Danny. "I don't remember seeing any vines."

"No, not interested really but the climate's good and the soil not too bad."

"Would you have made your own wine?" asked Primrose.

"I'd sell the grapes to a winemaker. It's a bit erratic, that industry. Last few seasons there's been a glut. Too many small hobby farmer type growers flooding the market. They couldn't sell their crop."

"Oh, no go then." Rows of neatly tended vines disintegrated into the dusty ground.

"I'd like to start taking out those willows on the river, Danny."

"Do they have to go?" cried Nirupam. "They're so lovely."

"They're a weed," said Tom. "They clog up the waterways."

"Fine. Give me a yell when you're ready. Know anyone who wants a couple of goats?"

Primrose looked at Danny sharply. He hadn't mentioned selling those useless animals. She chewed a mouthful of tofu and rice. Sammy the sheep should be thrown in as a bonus.

"Stick up an ad in the shop and the pub. What do you want for them?" asked Tom.

They launched into a discussion of prices. Goats, apparently, could go for as much as five hundred and fifty dollars each, or as little as twenty, depending on the breeding. That pair would have little to boast of in the way of ancestry.

"Try thirty five." Tom ripped a piece of flat bread in half. "They could give milk, you know. Just need to get them in kid again. Or there's a growing market for goat meat if you want to breed from them."

"No!" Shocked, from Nirupam.

"I suppose," said Danny. "Not the meat thing, the milk. But they're a nuisance. David and Brigid left them here last year. I don't know how to milk them and I don't want Nirupam to be over worked." He shot her such a loving glance tears welled in Primrose's eyes. Must be the wine. Or the curry was hotter than she'd thought. She sniffed. No-one looked at her that way.

"Primrose knows how to milk." Tom didn't laugh, just shoved a big forkful of curry into his mouth.

"Do you?" asked Nirupam in amazement.

"Not goats. And I've only tried milking once." She bent her head over her dinner, poking with her fork to find a cashew. What was his goal? Humiliation?

"She milked Daisy for me the other day," continued Tom blandly. "Did quite well."

Primrose snorted, red cheeked. "Hardly! The cow kicked the bucket over because I was so slow and she wanted to leave."

"Takes a bit of practice. Could you play your flute first go?"

"Of course not."

"Rosie likes to be able to do everything first go," said Danny. "She hates to fail."

"Danny, that's so unfair and wrong. What do you know about me anyway?" she demanded. "You left home when I was thirteen."

"Fourteen," Danny snapped.

"Nothing wrong with wanting to be the best you can," offered Tom.

"Calm down you two," said Nirupam. "Bad vibes

make the baby upset."

"Sorry, Sweets." Danny leaned across and rubbed his hand on her upper arm. "Sorry, Rosie."

"Accepted." Primrose studied her brother. An apology? What brought that on? Guilt?

Tom said, "If you don't like goats we could look for a quiet cow."

"So I can practise?" Primrose sent him a smile.

"Won't get better at it unless you do." Tom put his fork down. He sipped his wine. "How did you come to take up the flute? I mean, with your childhood."

"I was in year seven and they offered lessons on school instruments so I pestered Mum until she agreed I could try. I loved flute right from the start." She smiled at the memory, the incredible rush of intense feeling. "It was something I could do really well, just for myself."

"So flute is part of your life." Tom met her eye and held the contact. She knew what he was trying to say— give up this idiotic pretence of being a farmer and go back to being a musician, back in the city where she belonged.

She looked away. "I haven't practised for weeks."

"You played beautifully at the funeral," said Nirupam.

"What funeral?" Tom's astonished gaze flew from one to the other. "I didn't hear about any deaths around here."

"We had a funeral for the chooks the fox killed. Rosie played for us. It was lovely."

She knew Tom glanced at her but she spooned herself more curry to avoid eye contact. He'd be laughing for sure. But it hadn't been funny.

"You showed Mojo your flute," put in Danny. "He

loved it. And so did you."

He was right. She and Mojo had had a good time together the afternoon before they all left. And holding her flute again, nestling the mouthpiece against her lips and hearing the silvery tones emerge felt right, true to her soul.

"I suppose I could take on students."

"I think an artist *has* to pursue their art," said Nirupam. "I mean we can't not, can we? I love making jewellery and I can't imagine not creating something even if I have to stop for a while because of the baby. But I won't give it away completely and you won't either, Rosie. You'll find you can't."

"Don't give up on your dream," said Danny with the annoying esoteric vagueness that had got him where he was today. Nowhere.

Primrose bit back a rude retort. "I don't know what my dream is any more. It's all very well to talk idealistically but a freelance muse's life is tough—a really erratic income and stressful work."

"Like farming," said Tom. "But if it's in your blood you're stuck with it. Pointless denying it's there." Surprised at his tone, she glanced up to find him watching her with soft eyes.

"You're living your dream, aren't you?"

He nodded. "Pretty much."

"What's missing?" Nirupam tilted her head, glanced at Danny and smiled one of those private, loving smiles—a caress—then returned her attention to Tom. "A wife? Children?"

"One day maybe." He pushed his empty plate aside and leaned back, revolving the stem of his wine glass thoughtfully. "I'd like to have an heir to pass my place on to. But that's not going to happen."

"Why?" Nirupam asked.

Tom rubbed his lips together and drank more wine. He looked at Primrose, then at Danny and Nirupam. The words slipped out. "I can't have children."

"How do you know?" asked Danny, brow furrowed.

"At Uni I volunteered for a research thing. They wanted men from farms and rural areas. They were looking at the effects of environmental toxins on male fertility. Had to donate sperm. Mine was low count." Tom drained his glass and Danny refilled it automatically. "Must have been all that crop spraying and sheep drenching when I was a kid."

"Poisons," murmured Danny.

"Yes. It's one of the reasons I'm working on developing better organic methods."

He sipped his wine. No-one said a word. Danny poured more lemon cordial for Nirupam who looked mortified.

"I'm so sorry, Tom." Nirupam rubbed his arm gently. "And here I am..." Her eyes filled with tears.

Tom kissed her cheek. "Don't be silly. That's life." His eyes bored into Primrose then away, face blank.

Primrose couldn't speak. Her mind was empty. What did he expect her to say? That it didn't matter? It *did* matter. It mattered to him even if he pretended otherwise and it mattered to any woman who might fall in love with him and want to...she bit her lip. Why didn't he tell her before? Weren't they close? Obviously not. He'd really told Nirupam and Danny, just now. She just happened to be here.

"Anyway," he said. "Plenty of people don't have

kids for all sorts of reasons. But it'd be nice to know all the work I've done doesn't ultimately amount to nothing."

Nirupam asked, "How could it amount to nothing when you're trying new things to help farmers?"

Which brought the conversation neatly to the point of the evening and away from that other hideous, shocking, and ultimately painful subject which Primrose needed time to process. Private time.

She lurched into speech. "Lots of people will benefit from what you're doing—Mike already has. And Danny could. *We* could," she added hastily. "If you'd be willing to give us some pointers."

"Sure. But I think it's Danny's call," Tom said. Warning her? Maybe, but if she didn't get this thing happening now she'd probably not get another chance this good.

"My dream," Danny interrupted softly, "Is to make a home for Nirupam and me and our baby. A place where we can be independent, a safe place where everyone's welcome and everyone contributes. Where we can be self sufficient and happy."

"And you have." Nirupam reached her hand across the table and he grasped it tightly.

"Alpacas might be worth investigating," said Tom. "You could make a fair bit of money from their wool It's becoming very popular."

Danny smiled. "We're not interested in making lots of money. Never have been."

"You might not be but you still need it to survive." Primrose stood and began clearing the dirty plates. They kept reiterating the "money is evil" thing to the point of annoyance, as if they operated on a higher spiritual plane than everyone else. She hadn't become a musician in the hope of becoming a millionaire. They didn't have a monopoly on finer, non capitalist feelings.

Was Tom positive about the result of those research tests? How long ago was it? Maybe the effects wore off with time. Could sperm regenerate itself?

She turned for the sink, hands laden with dishes. "Which is why you've had to sell so much land. What happens when you don't have any left?"

"Give it a rest, will you?" Danny, more aggressive than she'd ever heard him. Peace and love obviously had a limit even in Nirvana.

Primrose dumped the dishes on the bench and whirled around. "I'll give it a rest when you tell us what you spend all that money on. It's my money too, in case you've forgotten conveniently—in your utopian paradise."

"We needed it to pay rates and things," Nirupam said.

"But the land must have been worth far more than the rates. Wasn't it Tom?" Primrose folded her arms across her chest

He grimaced uncomfortably under her glare. Too bad Tom. He was in this up to his neck. "A fair bit more," he admitted.

"I don't know." Puzzled, bewildered, Nirupam looked at Danny. "Hon?"

"Spit it out, Danny. I thought your whole raison d'être was sharing." Primrose let her arms drop and stepped closer, staring intently at her brother. She recognised his expression from childhood. The cornered, frightened one. From when their father accused and demanded in one of his drunken rages, wanting to know where Danny's pay was, the money he'd earned at his after school supermarket job. And Danny tried to say he hadn't been paid yet. Unsuccessfully. "You're hiding something, aren't you?"

His breathing resonated in the hot, silent kitchen.

"Danny?" Doubt clouded Nirupam's previously happy face, causing Primrose a twinge of guilt. What had she blundered into? Never in a million years would she deliberately cause them pain and neither would she deliberately distress Nirupam.

Tom's chair scraped as he shoved it back and stood up. "I'd better go."

"Stay." Danny threw him a meaningful look. He sat back down without a word.

Primrose frowned. What was going on here? Danny and Tom had secrets. Big ones.

Danny took Nirupam's hand in both his. He leaned forward, searching her face. She stared back anxious, fearful. Primrose watched, breath catching in her throat. Danny really had been hiding something and it was something Nirupam knew nothing about. Something he'd decided was better left unsaid. Even from Nirupam whom he adored.

"Danny," Primrose said softly, urgently, terrified of what he might be about to say. "It doesn't matter."

His eyes swung to her, cold, hard, and angry. "You pushed and pushed for this, Rosie. You wouldn't let things be but in some ways you're right. It's time." He clung to Nirupam's fingers, fixing his eyes on hers again. "I have another child. A son."

Chapter Ten

Primrose pressed both hands to her mouth. Her eyes flew to Nirupam sitting cold and still, a marble statue, her hands imprisoned in Danny's. She disengaged them deliberately and he let her go, sitting back biting his lower lip anxiously.

"Whose child?" Nirupam's voice was almost unrecognisable, hoarse with the shock.

"Cassie Bennett."

The name meant nothing to Primrose. A commune resident?

All the life, the colour, the expression, drained from Nirupam's face. "Cassie Bennett was years ago. Before we met."

Danny nodded. "Liam's twelve."

"Twelve?" Nirupam grabbed the edge of the table in both hands and hauled herself to her feet. Now the emotion returned in a flood. "You've known about this son all the time we've been together and you never told me?" Tears poured down her cheeks. "How could you, Danny? I thought..." A gulping sob enveloped the rest of the sentence. She backed away from the table, her hands folded protectively across her belly. "Will our child mean so little to you, you won't think it important enough to tell your next woman about it?"

She turned and blundered for the door with one hand outstretched, the other pressed against her mouth.

Danny leapt to his feet but Primrose darted forward to prevent him chasing his wife. "Let her go, Danny. A son? You have a son?"

"I hope you're satisfied," he said through lips stretched thin and hard as fencing wire. He didn't look at her. He stared after Nirupam, eyes wide with desperation and regret.

Primrose shook her head. Tears pushed at her lids but she forced them to retreat. "No, I'm not, but you can't blame me for this. Why didn't you tell her?"

"He didn't know." Tom's quiet voice brought her up short.

She spun toward him. Danny slipped away before she could snatch his arm and stop him.

"Danny!" But Tom grabbed her with both hands on her shoulders as Danny disappeared toward the bedroom.

"Leave them be, Primrose. Just leave them!" She wrestled against his hold but his fingers were strong, biting into her flesh. "You've interfered enough in their lives lately, don't you think?"

The words landed like blows. Her defiance fizzled and her legs suddenly collapsed under her. Tom relaxed his grip enough to allow her to sit down.

"You call it interfering," she hissed. "I call it caring. How come you never mentioned this child to anyone?"

"To you?" One eyebrow lifted in derision. He dragged out a chair and sat facing her. "Nirupam?"

Primrose firmed her lips and looked at her fingers twisting themselves into knots in her lap. Of course he couldn't have told Nirupam. But still...

"Danny asked me not to tell anyone," he said when

she didn't comment. "I keep my word."

"When did he find out?"

"About two years ago. I don't know why the mother took so long to tell him," he said, forestalling her next question. "But he had no idea. He was really shocked. Stunned."

"Why would he tell you rather than Nirupam?"

Tom shook his head. "Maybe because he knew I wouldn't judge him or tell anyone? I don't know. I said he should tell her but I couldn't do much more than that. I'm his friend, not a counsellor."

Primrose frowned, pondering Danny's reasons. She didn't have to think for long. The answer was obvious—Danny was being Danny. Avoiding confrontation, avoiding difficult decisions and unpleasantness, hoping it would go away. But his son wouldn't be going away. Quite the reverse.

"Has he seen his son?"

Tom nodded. "Once. He met them in Canberra. Nirupam was at some art show. The boy doesn't want to live with him. Danny said he was a nice kid, happy and settled but his mother wanted help with school fees. She'd separated from her partner."

"So she decided all of a sudden Danny should be involved with the son she never told him about. How does he know Liam's his?" Indignation jerked her spine upright.

"I told him to have a DNA test. Liam is his son."

"So you got yourself involved that much," said Primrose, bitterness acid in her mouth. Men! A conspiracy of silence.

"Look." Tom stood up. "I don't need this. Danny's a mate. I helped him the best I could. I'm not his confessor by choice. I'd rather he hadn't told me any of it but seeing he did, I respected his privacy and his wishes. Why can't you understand?"

Primrose leapt to her feet, knocking the chair over in her rush. "I understand you two are exactly the same. You prefer to avoid making decisions which might upset your nice comfortable lives despite what it does to other people. Lying by omission. At least I'm honest."

"Yes, we all know what you think." Tom righted the fallen chair. "I'm leaving. Thanks for dinner. I'll see myself out." He headed for the hallway with a determined stride, back rigid, disgusted.

Primrose subsided into her chair, head sunk into her hands. What an unholy mess. Poor Nirupam. She was fragile enough as it was without this shock. What was Danny thinking? She shook her head and leaned back, thumping her palms onto the table top. And bloody Tom was no better. Men!

A door closed. Primrose froze, ears straining. Danny's voice. And Tom's. She frowned. They were murmuring—she couldn't hear what they were saying. She lifted her chair away from the table and, holding her breath, tiptoed to the doorway. Footsteps clumped toward the front door. Two pairs of feet. The door opened and closed. Silence. She sprinted to her bedroom and without turning on the light, eased the curtain away from the window with one finger.

A car door slammed. Tom's white ute gleamed in the moonlight. The engine roared, shattering the quiet. They were leaving. Both of them. Danny's motorbike engine erupted, a throaty growl. Was Danny going to Tom's or somewhere else? Headlights shone erratically as the vehicles bounced through the trees and disappeared over the ridge. Primrose let the curtain drop into place. Did Nirupam know? Had she thrown Danny out?

Primrose dragged in a shaky breath and pressed her fingers to her eyes. This was her fault. She'd broken up her brother's perfectly happy marriage. What a total bitch she was. No wonder Tom and Danny hated her. Would Nirupam? She had to see if she was all right, offer comfort and apologies. Had to take whatever was dished out to her. She deserved it.

Primrose paused outside Nirupam's bedroom, gathering courage before venturing inside. She tapped twice and eased the door open a crack. The light was off. Muffled sobs emerged from the dark. Her eyes scanned the room, found a dim shape on the bed.

"Nirupam?" Her stomach clenched in apprehension. What could she say? Sorry I busted up your marriage? Nirupam had every right to throw her out.

"Oh Ro—o—o—sieeeee." It came in a wail of despair broken midway by a hiccupping breath and followed by more heartrending sobs. "Danny's gone. He's left me."

"He'll be back." Primrose cautiously pushed the door wide with trembling fingers. The strip of yellow light from the hall illuminated Nirupam's distraught, tearstained face crushed against the pillow. No anger, just despair. She levered herself into a sitting position. Primrose rushed across to clutch her sister-in-law in her arms. "I'm so sorry. It's my fault."

Nirupam returned the embrace desperately. "Why is it your fault? It's mine," she wailed. "I said horrible things. Oh, Rosie. He's gone."

"Danny loves you. He'll come home." Of that she was positive. Danny adored his wife. Primrose eased her arms from Nirupam's shoulders. "I shouldn't have pushed Danny about the money."

"Danny should have told me about his son." Nirupam sniffed and reached for a tissue from the bedside table.

"Yes." There was nothing else to say. He should have told her. He had no excuse. Primrose moistened her lips. "Danny always hated any sort of confrontation or fighting." She paused, met waterlogged blue eyes with a confidence she felt certain was justified. "That's why he left. He hates arguments—not you. He loves you. He'll come back."

Something in her tone must have reassured Nirupam because she said softly, "I know. I know he loves me and I know he hates arguments. He told me about your father. How terrified he was growing up. We never fight. This is our first." She blew her nose, sniffed again with the tissue scrunched in her hand. "Where did he go? Did he say?"

"He went with Tom. On his bike but at the same time as Tom. Probably went home with him."

"I like Tom. It's so sad about...you know," Nirupam said vaguely. She yawned.

"Tom knew about the boy. Danny told him." Primrose couldn't prevent the anger filtering into her voice.

"Yes. But it's not Tom's fault. He's a good listener and he minds his own business. His soul is good." Nirupam shifted in preparation for heaving her bulk off the bed. "Danny knew I'd be upset. He knew he'd left it too late." Now she sounded sympathetic. Amazing.

Primrose stood up. "How do you feel about the boy?" She extended her hand. Nirupam grasped it and rose slowly to her feet.

"I haven't had much time to feel anything except shock. But it's not his fault either." She waddled toward the door. "He's a lucky kid to have Danny as a father."

"Like a cup of tea?" Primrose asked, defeated by the calm, almost bovine aura of late pregnancy.

"Yes, please. And some of Tom's peaches and cream." She stopped and turned. Smiling, a little watery and red-eyed but definitely smiling. "I'm so glad you came, Rosie. Thank you."

"But I've done nothing but cause trouble since I arrived."

Nirupam laughed. "Not for me. You've been wonderful for me."

Not for Nirupam? No, looked at that way even this blow-up was better for Nirupam in the long run. Their marriage was stronger than one fight, the way a marriage should be. Danny would come home. This was his family. He couldn't and wouldn't desert the woman he loved. He'd never walk away from the birth of the child he was so excited about.

Tom wouldn't let him for one thing. There was a strong underlying network of love and friendship here. One she didn't belong to, except peripherally. Primrose swallowed back a rush of tears. She bit her lip. She didn't belong here or anywhere despite the reassurance of Nirupam. She was the interloper peering through the window at the people inside, allowed in briefly before being sent on her way.

The trouble she'd caused had all been focussed on

the men and they weren't nearly as forgiving as her lovely pregnant sister-in-law. She'd stay until the baby was born and then leave. They'd all heave concerted sighs of relief and get back to their lives. So would she. Her holiday was over. Tomorrow she'd have to start practising again if she wanted to hold down any playing positions in the near future. The whole idea made her stomach clench in dread.

****

Primrose must have slept because Nirupam woke her. Scratchy-eyed and muzzy- headed she blinked and tried to focus on the shadowy figure leaning over her bed.

"Rosie, I think the baby's coming."

The soft words roused her instantly. She snapped on the light and sprang out of bed. "How soon?"

"I've had contractions since about two thirty. They're quite a way apart but—ooohhh." She clutched her hands to her middle and sagged on to the bed. Primrose scrabbled about for clothes, raced to the bathroom and then to Nirupam's room for the bag they'd packed in preparation. When she returned Nirupam was waiting by the door, large in her Indian cotton dress.

"Danny's not home. I want him, Rosie. I want him to be at the birth."

"We have to call Ellie. Do you want to come with me to Tom's or wait here?"

Blank faced, wide eyed, fingers twisting around each other. "I don't know. I just want Danny."

No decisions forthcoming there. Primrose yanked the door open and helped Nirupam outside. No way was this going to be a home birth. Not with just the two of them.

"I know. He'll be at Tom's. We have to go there first to call Ellie." Damn the lack of mobile coverage in the area. Front or back seat for her passenger? Primrose slung the bag on the back seat. "Do you need to lie down?"

"No." Nirupam reversed herself carefully on to the seat and swung her legs inside the car. "It's exciting, Rosie," she said as Primrose reversed out of the shed.

"Very." Five twenty five in the morning. A minimum thirty five minute drive over a rough country mountain road to the hospital. No father so far. Hope like hell Tom was at home.

Fingers of pale dawn light faltered across the sky as Primrose pulled up outside Tom's slumbering house. A few birds chortled sleepily.

"Wait here." She gave two sharp bursts on the horn before leaping out and running.

As usual the front door was unlocked. Primrose yanked it wide and ran inside calling, "Tom! Danny! Wake up!" She peeped into the spare room but the bed was empty. No Danny. "Tom?"

Phone Ellie first. She switched on the kitchen light and began dialling.

"What's going on?" Tom emerged, yawning and rumpled wearing a pair of shorts, chest bare. Primrose yanked her attention away from naked skin, the dark line of hair diving beneath the waistband of his shorts, the smooth roundness of muscled biceps, the ruffled bed hair.

"Nirupam's having the baby. Where's Danny?"

"Don't know, he rode straight on when I came in. Where's Nirupam?" Primrose waved her arm toward the front of the house as a male voice answered the phone. "Hello?"

"It's Primrose. Can I speak to Ellie, please?"

"Sorry, she's at the hospital with Maria Dooley. Is Nirupam ready to go?"

"Yes. What should I do?"

"How far along is she?"

"Contractions are about ten minutes apart."

"Take her in to the hospital. The baby shouldn't arrive for a few hours at least. Have her waters broken?"

"I don't know." What did that mean?

"Get off the phone, love, and call the doc to let him know you're on the way."

"All right. Thanks." Primrose slammed the phone down and dialled again. Tom came back in with a determined expression as she hung up.

Primrose said, "I have to take her to the hospital. Ellie's already there with someone else."

"I'll get dressed."

"Are you coming with us?"

"Of course. Wait in the car." He turned. "Take some towels from the cupboard. And a sheet. Just in case."

"Okay!" Wide-eyed, Primrose did as she was told. Thank God Tom was coming with them. Where the hell was Danny?

Nirupam's pale face shimmered a smile at her as she ran across to the car with her arms full of Tom's linen. A whole bundle, whatever had been on the shelf. She flung the lot on to the backseat and said, "Maybe you should switch to the back in case you need to lie down."

214

"All right but I need to walk a bit. Baby's really uncomfortable." Nirupam heaved herself out of the car and began slowly wandering across the still dark yard toward the sheds. Primrose stared after her, too astonished to speak. A walk? She wanted to go for a walk? The screen door slammed, Tom's quick tread sounded on the wooden steps. He glanced at Nirupam's bulky figure then questioningly at Primrose.

"She needed to walk a bit. The baby's uncomfortable."

"Going to get a damn sight more uncomfortable." He held a couple of folded plastic garbage bags.

Nirupam called, "What a lovely morning. The air's so fresh."

"Come on Nirupam, we don't want to have the baby here," said Primrose.

Nirupam did a very slow arcing turn reminiscent of a supertanker in mid ocean, "I really wanted to have this baby at home."

"I know but that was when Fern was around, and Danny." Primrose virtually hopped up and down in her exasperation. Giving up, she ran to grasp Nirupam's arm and take her under tow. "Come on!"

"Oooooooohhh." Nirupam stopped, her face screwed up, eyes closed. Tom ran across and supported her on the other side.

"Try to relax into it," he said. "When was the last one?"

"Just after we got here." She grabbed at Primrose, fingers biting into the flesh of her arm.

"We've only been here about seven or eight minutes." Primrose grimaced at Tom, horror struck. "Let's go!"

"I'll drive," he said, forestalling her objection with, "I know the road better, especially in the dark."

Pastel pink and yellow light was strengthening over to the east but Primrose wasn't about to argue. She grabbed the bundle of linen and hurled it through to the front passenger seat to make room for both of them in the back.

Nirupam said, "I think my waters just broke."

Primrose's gaze flew to the fluid running down to pool in the dust at their feet.

"Just as well you weren't in the car," said Tom. "We'd better get cracking."

"Oh, gosh." Primrose wiped clumsily at Nirupam's legs with one of the towels.

Tom spread the garbage bags across the seat, grabbed a couple of the towels and folded them. "Sit on these."

Nirupam lowered herself awkwardly into the rear. "I wish Danny was here."

Primrose clutched her hand. "Me, too."

"Me, three." Tom slammed his door. The engine burst into life and the Golf charged down the driveway.

"What if he comes home and I'm not there," Nirupam cried suddenly.

Cripes! Notes hadn't entered Primrose's head. Nothing much had, beyond packing Nirupam into the car and racing for Tom's phone. Bloody Danny. He shouldn't have stayed out all night. This was his job.

"I left a note by the phone," said Tom. "If he goes home and you're not there he'll come to my place, for sure."

"Good thinking." Primrose caught his eye in the rearview mirror. He smiled. He wasn't worried at all!

216

Maybe he was used to this isolation, the lack of telecommunication, the lack of medical facilities within easy reach, the rough roads, the distances. The do-it-yourself birth.

Tom ran through the calculations. Thirty minutes from the junction of this road with the main one. Maybe twenty five if he floored it although the Golf was labouring a bit on the hills with the extra passenger weight and they had a steep climb out of the valley. Should be at the intersection in a couple of minutes.

Nirupam's contractions were about eight minutes apart. Another one due soon. A groan sounded from the rear seat. Her waters had broken so things were happening fast. First baby—no track record.

"Time them, Rose." The intersection loomed. Tom slowed and stopped at the Stop sign. No point smashing them up in the rush to get there. If worse came to worst he'd helped deliver pups and calves and once, a foal. Not much to do unless something went wrong. A baby wouldn't be very different.

He eased on to the wider highway and stomped on the accelerator. The sun peeked through the lower trees now, slanting golden rays into his eyes.

"Five minutes," said Primrose.

The road swung left toward the river, crossed over then sharp right and into the climb. Tall gumtrees crowded the roadside. The sun hadn't reached this side of the mountains yet and morning mist still hung wispy around the trunks. Cool, dark, mysterious and green with ferns. Four hairpin bends up, three down the other side.

"The last one was only two minutes. Tom stop the car. We have to...oh my goodness."

Nirupam screamed. He changed down to low gear for the first twist. "I don't think we should stop."

"Stop the car," shrieked Primrose.

"There's no point."

"Rosie, I think the baby's coming."

"Not yet, it won't be coming yet. Hang on Nirupam." Tom wrenched the Golf around the next hairpin. The engine complained, struggled and picked up speed along the straight. Round a wider curve. Up. The third hairpin. A steep straight climb. Leaning forward, urging it on.

"How long until we get there?" asked Primrose.

"Fifteen minutes."

"I can't wait fifteen minutes," Nirupam yelled like a sergeant major.

"We have to stop, Tom." No denying the intensity in her voice.

"All right—as soon as there's a place." Far too narrow here with a sheer drop on one side albeit thickly treed, and a rocky cliff face on the other. One more hairpin and they'd be at the top where the road levelled out along the ridge.

Nirupam's laboured breathing flooded the little car. Every now and again a small whimper indicated the pain and fright. Rose murmured things Tom couldn't hear. What a champ she was, rising to the occasion this way. Surprising. Not a single complaint.

"Here." He pulled into the small lay by. Just enough space to fit one car and a very pregnant girl.

Primrose was already out by the time Tom ran around to the back door. Nirupam lay across the seat with her knees drawn up, fingers clenching and unclenching the fabric of her dress.

"Let's have a look." He pulled Primrose away firmly.

"Do you know about this?"

"From animals." He lifted the dress aside. "She looks fairly close. Can we keep going, do you think?"

"No!"

"Nirupam?"

"No," she gasped. "I want to have my baby here."

Tom straightened up. He met Primrose's gaze. "What do you think?" He drew her away from the car. Magpies warbled tunefully overhead. The bush was awake and singing. The cicadas too.

Primrose's heart thudded so hard her chest felt it would burst. "Can we manage?"

"As long as there are no complications we should be all right. And we're only fifteen minutes from hospital."

"I'll try my phone." She dived into her handbag but tossed the mobile back in with a disgusted curse.

A drawn out wail rang around the treetops. A few birds scattered from their perches nearby.

Tom knelt down to study the situation again. "Much wider dilation now."

Primrose perched awkwardly half in the door of the car at Nirupam's head, wiping her clammy forehead with a moist tissue. Thank goodness Tom had come. No way could she have dealt with this alone. He was so confident and calm. She glanced at his bent head at the other end of the seat. He looked up suddenly. Grey eyes met hers.

"Won't be long now."

Nirupam smiled. "Isn't this exciting?" Her face crumpled. Tears sprang to her lids. "I wish Danny was here."

Primrose leaned over and pressed her cheek to Nirupam's. "I'm sorry. But we'll do our best. Tom's had experience with births."

Nirupam's hand flailed in the air, groping for Primrose's. She held on firmly staring over Nirupam's vast belly and raised knees to meet Tom's gaze. He grinned then bent down to check as Nirupam let out another wild cry.

"I can see the baby's head. Just the top."

"The pains are coming all the time now," gasped Nirupam.

"Hang in there. Won't be long."

Primrose's fingers were being gripped so tightly she thought they'd fall off. What if something terrible happened? She had no idea what, but things did go wrong. This whole birth experience was so violent. Primal.

"Tom?" Her voice came out weak and shaky. "Can you do it?"

"Nirupam's doing everything. I'm just an observer." Another violent contraction caused a bellow of agony. "Good girl. Few more of those and we'll be ready to go."

"A few more?" Nirupam managed to gasp but another gut wrenching pain twisted the feeble smile from her face.

Tom gritted his teeth against the screams. He could hardly tell her to stop. She was in pain plus frightened and worried and all the rest of it. What a way to start the day. Primrose wiped the beads of perspiration away with one of her little tissues. Her face was as pale and sweaty as Nirupam's but she was doing the right things, calming, soothing, encouraging as Nirupam yelled. Her eyes locked with his every now and again, fearful but trusting in his ability. Such as it was. If there were complications they'd be in trouble, have to make a dash for the hospital. But this was no time to start doubting. The baby was determined.

The little dark head suddenly pushed further through the opening. "Push hard next time. Couple of big pushes."

Nirupam did as she was told, propping herself on her elbows, accompanying the effort with more noise than he'd ever imagined she could produce.

"Here it comes." Tom snatched the last towel to catch the tiny slippery bundle as it slid into the world. Nirupam collapsed back on to the seat. Primrose rushed around to Tom's side of the car.

"What is it?"

The baby coughed and cried. Tom cleaned the little face of blood and mucus and it cried again, eyes tight shut against the light and the shock. He wrapped the towel around it as best he could, lifting it clear of the watery, bloody afterbirth to follow. "We have to cut the cord." He looked up at her. "I don't have my pocket knife on me."

"She's beautiful." Primrose was gazing at the baby with such a wondrous look of rapture Tom gulped and blinked sudden tears. She. A girl. He hadn't noticed. He looked down at the screwed up furiously indignant face. She was beautiful. A treasure.

"It's a girl," Primrose called to Nirupam. "A beautiful little girl." Tears streamed down her face. "She's perfect."

"Can I hold her?" Nirupam asked weakly.

"Rose, do you have something to cut the cord?" More insistent. This wasn't over yet.

She frowned, screwed her face in thought. "Nail scissors?"

"They'll do, I hope."

More rummaging in the handbag. The scissors were tiny but sharp and did the job eventually. He handed the towel wrapped baby to Primrose who took her solemnly and walked around the car to lay her on Nirupam's breast. They whispered and cooed and cried together while Tom watched anxiously for the afterbirth. He thought it all appeared but the hospital could check.

"We have to go. They both need to be examined properly."

Nirupam raised her head, face shining with a mixture of joy and exhaustion. "Thank you, Tom. You were wonderful." She sank back onto the seat, clutching her baby to her chest.

"Can you hold the baby while we drive, Nirupam?"

Primrose said, "I'll get rid of these messy towels first. They can go in the back." She spread the sheet on a fresh garbage bag under Nirupam's legs then leaned over to take the baby bundle gently from her arms while Nirupam sat up and rearranged herself. The little eyes were closed, the mouth pursed like a rosebud. So sweet, adorable. Light as a feather.

Nirupam clicked her seatbelt and held out her arms for her daughter. Primrose reluctantly surrendered her treasure and climbed in beside Tom.

"No rush now." To Primrose's surprise his hand was shaking as he extended it to turn the key in the ignition. He drew a deep breath, wiped his brow with the back of the other hand. "Okay, let's go." He started the engine.

"Look it's only six," said Primrose. "Baby must have been born at about ten to. What's her name, Nirupam?"

"I want to tell Danny first," she said hoarsely.

"At least we know she won't be Rupert." Tom slid a sidelong look at Primrose who laughed, then burst into tears at the same time.

****

"You were fantastic." Primrose slumped wearily in the blue plastic chair opposite Tom in the only café open and serving breakfast in the main street. He was finishing a plate of eggs and bacon while she nibbled on toast and drank tea, half asleep, emotionally and physically drained. The clock behind the counter said eighteen past seven.

Nirupam and her baby were fast asleep in the maternity ward. Danny hadn't appeared.

"You did pretty well yourself," he said between bites.

"I would've been totally hopeless without you. I didn't have a clue."

"Neither did I, really." He put his knife and fork neatly on his plate.

"I'm glad you saved that to tell me now rather than on the mountain." She raised a laugh then fixed him with a penetrating eye. "But you did, didn't you? Know what to do?"

"Sort of. Most farmers have dealt with animals giving birth."

"Not much different?" Her smile was cut short by a gigantic yawn.

He shook his head. "Tired?"

"Exhausted and I didn't do anything. Nirupam must be completely wrecked."

"They don't call it labour for nothing."

"Ellie said it was a perfect birth." Primrose yawned again, quickly covering her mouth with both hands.

"Except for it being on the mountain in the back seat of a car." He drained his tea cup and leaned forward. "You'd really love to have a baby, wouldn't you?"

She froze then dragged in a big, shuddery breath and exhaled it slowly. Her eyes met his, swimming in unshed tears. She nodded. "I'm sorry. It's just something..."

"It's natural," he said. "No need to be sorry."

"I can't help it. I've wanted a baby for ages. I don't think I could..."

"You don't have to. I understand." He stood up. "Time to go home Aunty Primrose."

"I am an Aunty, aren't I? How fabulous." Primrose pushed her chair back. "They should make you an honorary uncle. Uncle Tom," she said with a gurgle of laughter then stopped as the thought crashed in that being an uncle was the closest Tom could get to being a father.

Chapter Eleven

The commune was eerily empty when Primrose woke at noon. She showered, dressed, stripped beds then made tea while a load of washing sloshed in the machine. Clean sheets for Nirupam when she came home tomorrow or the day after.

No word from Danny, no sign he'd returned last night or this morning while she slept. If he had he would've woken her. She hung out the washing. Soon there'd be nappies on the line.

A tingle of pleasure at the memory of Baby in her arms. So cuddlesome and sweet smelling. Very hard to hand her back. How she'd love one of her own. Definitely worth the pain and drama of childbirth, no question. Primrose wandered into the room they'd prepared. The bassinet was ready with little sheets and a soft blanket. A change table waited with wipes and powder. The stack of nappies sat on the dressing table beside an array of tiny singlets and nightgowns.

She couldn't stay after Nirupam came home—just long enough to help out until they settled down. Danny and Nirupam needed to establish their little family. Danny wouldn't want his interfering busybody sister meddling with his baby, upsetting everyone. Strangers in his house were more welcome than his sister. A tear threatened. She clamped her lips together firmly.

This had been a holiday. The break she needed

from the stress of playing long running shows back to back in difficult conditions. Plus the Martin fiasco. Losing along with him, a place to live. Everything happened at once. She'd burnt out.

Nirvana was not her home. She'd been fooling herself she could blend into the lifestyle. It wasn't the way she wanted to live, sharing everything with all and sundry. She'd been too much alone most of her life to change so drastically. Tom had seen it at once. He'd tried to tell her. He knew more about her than she did and if she hadn't been so defensive something might have developed between them. But she'd rejected him and at the time it felt right. As it transpired it *had* been right.

They didn't know each other at all when they'd tumbled into his bed so eagerly. She didn't know he couldn't father children, although *he* knew she wanted them. When would he have told her? When she'd completely fallen in love with him? When it was too late? So despite his rantings about being used he was using her that night whether he realised or not. He knew he couldn't give her the children she craved but pretended to be hurt when she cut the liaison off. Pride. Male pride.

It was too confusing, too hard. Men!

Primrose unpacked her flute. She selected a book of technical studies and her favourite Handel sonata, took her music stand and went to work in the living room in the middle of the house. Before long the familiar passion absorbed her, the desire to produce the sound she heard in her head, to execute a perfectly even succession of notes, make no mistakes in the piece she was playing, to bring out the emotion intrinsic in the piece.

After an hour she had a break. When she went to visit Nirupam this evening she'd phone her contacts in Sydney to let them know she'd be available for work. Back to the pressure, the grind. A weight settled on her heart. She loved playing her flute but orchestral playing was not her thing. The truth was, she could admit now, she wasn't good enough. Sure, she could impress the residents of Nirvana because she did play well, but playing well wasn't good enough to hold her own as a professional.

She'd have to find some other sort of work. Anything. Boring, mundane work to keep herself afloat. Teaching wouldn't bring in nearly enough, not regular enough and not fast enough. What choice was there? By forcing Danny to disband the commune she'd inadvertently done herself out of a home. Plus she'd worn out her welcome in record time.

Primrose raised her flute and began the sadly beautiful Handel slow movement. The best way she had of expressing her plight.

****

Tom heard the silvery tone of the flute before he came within sight of the house. Cindy snorted and tossed her head to clear away the flies crawling into her eyes and nose. She pricked soft black ears toward the sound as she followed the dusty track leading up between the gums from the river. Tom let the reins hang slack in his hands.

He'd never heard Primrose play before. Had no idea how good she was. No wonder she looked at him askance when he suggested she could find musical opportunities in the area. She'd go mad with frustration.

227

Like telling Pavarotti he'd be fulfilled singing in the local community choir.

She must think him a total clod. He halted Cindy in the shade near the washing line, listening to the lovely melody floating out to mingle with the cicadas. She stopped abruptly, restarted the phrase. Should he interrupt? Cindy dropped her head and began plucking at the grass around the base of a tree. Rose would want to know about Danny. He swung his leg over the saddle to dismount and looped the reins over a low branch.

He walked to the closed back door and knocked. Even the thought of her made his mouth dry and his heart thud. The flute stopped. Footsteps sounded in the kitchen. The door opened a crack. Primrose peered through the gap holding the door as a barrier.

"G'day." He removed his hat.

"Oh! Hello." She flung the door wide with a smile and stepped outside. "I didn't hear you arrive. I've been practising."

"I rode over." He swallowed. She was breathtaking. Always beautiful.

She glanced over his shoulder at Cindy. "She's lovely."

"She's okay. How are you? Had a sleep?" He turned the hat over in his hands.

"Yes." She made no move to invite him in, instead stood there looking at him expectantly, waiting for him to speak, to explain his presence. Leave.

"Practising for what?" Hadn't she had enough of music? Said she didn't want to play anymore?

"For when I go back to Sydney. I can't stay here after..." She let the sentence hang unfinished.

His lungs almost collapsed. Leaving. Of course she

was. Nothing for her here. Nothing to hold her. Not him, that was for sure. He said harshly, "Danny turned up."

Relief washed over her face followed by a frown. "At your place? He didn't come here."

"He went straight to Moruya when I told him."

She exhaled with a whoosh. "Where had he been?"

"He spent the night at a mate's place in Cobargo."

Primrose nodded but made no comment. Tom searched for something to say, found nothing. She was waiting for him to leave so she could continue practising. He stuck his hat on. "I'd better get going."

"Thanks for coming over."

"No worries." He turned and strode down the steps. "See you later."

"Would you like to come in?" Her voice was offhand, the gesture an afterthought, as though she'd suddenly realised her manners.

He paused, half turned. She was standing on the top step watching him.

"No, thanks, I won't interrupt you anymore."

She came down the steps. "I'm going in to visit Nirupam this evening. Would you like to come?"

He cocked his head, considering. "It might be better if you went in alone—being family." He had thought of driving in himself, tomorrow, to see how they were getting on. Now Danny was there he was relegated to visitor.

Suddenly she was up close, so close he could lean down and kiss her upturned face. He wanted to, frantically. His eyes fixed on her lips as she spoke.

"Nirupam would love to see you. You delivered the baby for heaven's sake! How much more familiar can you get?" Her mouth curved, the dimples danced in her cheeks. He curled his fingers into fists to stop them touching her face.

He smiled. "We did pretty well, you and I."

"Yes, we did. But I don't want to do it again."

"No." What if he kissed her? What would she do?

Her expression changed. Serious suddenly. "Thank you, Tom," she whispered. Next thing she'd pressed her lips on his for a sweet instant. She drew away but his arm was around her somehow, holding her against his body, savouring the feel of her, the scent of her sunwarmed skin, the perfume from her hair. He gazed into her eyes expecting to see annoyance, but what he saw tore the breath from his lungs.

"Rose," he murmured, swallowed, gulped. More, he wanted more of her. He leaned forward.

"I'm sorry." She frowned, placed both hands against his chest, warding him off. Mistake. Misread badly. He'd been so ecstatically sure she wanted him the way he wanted her despite her words this morning. Idiot! "Tom, I..." The tip of her tongue ran over her lower lip. She dropped her gaze to his shirt front.

He released his hold. "Sorry. See you later." He spun on his booted heel, untied Cindy and swung up into the saddle, kicked her into motion and didn't look back.

※ ※ ※ ※

An hour later Danny's motorbike roared over the hill. Primrose shaded her eyes, squinting from her position in the hail-damaged vegetable garden. She straightened slowly, clutching the basket with its measly collection of tomatoes and parsley. What kind of greeting would she get? He'd been so furious last night he couldn't speak. Her persistent nagging had driven him away, separated him from his wife at this very special time in their lives. Caused a rift between a loving, devoted couple.

Danny rode into the shed and by the time she'd walked across, heart pounding, unsure of his mood, unsure of his welcome, he was striding for the verandah steps, helmet in hand.

"Hey, Danny." He stopped, turned. Smiled.

Primrose dropped the basket at her feet and ran the few last paces into his embrace, face crumpling.

"Congratulations." A tear escaped. "She's beautiful, your daughter." She sniffed hard as he released his grip.

Danny gazed into her face, eyes intense, brow furrowed. "She is, isn't she? Thanks, Rosie. Thank you for taking care of her. Nirupam told me how you and Tom...I should have been here." He looked away over her shoulder, shook his head. "I let her down. I should have stayed with her. I wanted so much to be at the birth."

Primrose gripped his arm. "She knows. She wanted you there, too. She kept saying "I want Danny." But she'd already forgiven you before we left here. She's amazing."

Danny grinned. "I know. And so is our daughter. Did you see? She looks like me."

"She does. Same nose." Primrose picked up the basket. "What's her name?"

"Dawn Primrose."

"Really? Primrose? Poor little sweetheart." She laughed but a swell of pride made her wipe more tears from her eyes. "Dawn's appropriate." Somehow she hadn't expected such a normal sounding name but Nirupam had surprised her a lot lately.

"It's what Nirupam wants." Danny slung his arm around her shoulders as they walked up the steps to the verandah and she leaned into his side and slipped her arm around his waist. "I'm happy with it. She wanted to name her after you. Couldn't call her Tom."

Primrose opened the screen door. "Do you mind?"

"I like it."

"So do I. It's a lovely name. Are you going back in tonight? I thought I would."

"No, I told her I'd be in first thing tomorrow. They can probably come home. The local paper wants to photograph you and Tom."

"When?" Primrose headed for the kitchen.

"Don't know. Tonight, maybe?"

"Fine. Left over curry all right for dinner?"

"Yeah."

Danny opened the fridge. Primrose unloaded the vegetables from her basket.

"I'm leaving in a week or two. I'll stay until Nirupam settles in, then go."

He turned with a chilled beer in his hand, surprised. "Why?"

"I can't stay here, not after what I've said and done."

"Yes, you can. I'm not angry about having to tell Nirupam about Liam. I should have as soon as I found out myself but. . ." He grimaced.

"You didn't," supplied Primrose. Hoped the boy would go away, probably.

Danny closed the fridge. "Nirupam will be very upset if you leave."

"Will you?"

"You're my sister. I know we haven't been close and it was partly my fault. But you're here now." He gestured helplessly. "What happened when we were kids, I don't think either of us knew how to deal with it. We can't blame ourselves, or each other."

Primrose bit at her lower lip. "No. But I always felt so guilty. I couldn't help when he, you know when Dad..."

Danny's head whipped toward her wide-eyed in surprise. "You were only little, what could you do? Mum should have done something."

"I was terrified for you."

His expression changed and she suddenly thought he might cry. He said, "I always thought you thought I was weak and pathetic for not standing up to him. I thought you despised me for it."

She shook her head in violent denial, tears starting in her own eyes. "No, never. I resented that you left me and Mum but that was later, different. It was all such a mess."

"If he'd harmed you I wouldn't have left you there with them, Rosie. Believe me. But he always focussed on me."

She wiped her eyes and sighed. It was so long ago, now, the past. "I wonder why?"

"Thought I was weak and spineless? Maybe I was. Maybe I still am."

"You're not a fighter." Her lip curled. "He was a vicious, cowardly bully. I hated him."

"I wish you'd stay. We'll work it out."

"But you need to work out your own family. You and Nirupam and the baby. Don't you see? I just cause trouble for you."

He frowned and twisted the cap off the beer. The frown deepened to perplexity. "But you're part of my family, too. Nirupam feels the same. There's heaps of room. You don't *have* to leave, do you? For a different reason?"

"I'll need to earn some money fairly soon but that might not count as a reason for you." She laughed.

He acknowledged the jibe with a smile. "There must be something you can do."

"Not much for flute players round here. I can't do anything else."

"Have you looked? Stick some ads up for students." He took a long pull at the beer. "Or you could work in the pub. There's sure to be something. If you don't want to play flute, what's the problem?"

What was the problem? Danny was right. She could do anything to earn money if she really wanted to. Maybe flute *was* what she really wanted after all.

"By the way Tom said he'll be ready whenever you call in."

"Ready for what?" Tom. Again. A rush of heat started in her feet and headed north.

"Aren't you going to visit Nirupam?"

"Oh! Yes. I wasn't sure he was coming. When did you see him?" She turned so he wouldn't see the red creeping up her neck.

"Called in on the way home to thank him for what he did."

She forced a smile. "He was extraordinary. I'm so glad he was there."

"Tom's a good bloke. Why don't you marry him? You could do worse."

Primrose spun around. The idea exploded in her head. A cascade of sparkling wonderment. "Marry him?"

Danny nodded, swallowing his beer. "Nirupam thinks he needs a wife."

"Needs and wants are quite different." Just how much did Danny know? What did they talk about, those two men? Danny had certainly confided some personal secrets. Had Tom? And what about the elephant in the room? Didn't Danny think infertility was an issue? Apparently not.

He shrugged in his irritatingly vague manner and drank more beer.

"He doesn't want to marry me. He doesn't want a city girl. He needs someone who can help him milk his cow. I terrorised it." And vice versa. A hulking brown body, big clumsy hooves with a stinging swipe of a tail. Daisy, letting her know exactly what she thought of the incompetent milker.

"You can learn. We think you'd be a perfect couple."

"Who thinks that?" Hands on hips Primrose faced him square on. The flare of hope was almost impossible to hide. "You and Tom?"

"Me and Nirupam."

"You don't know anything about me and Tom."

"Maybe not." Danny smiled slyly. "But *you* interfere in lots of things you don't know anything about. Must run in the family."

How dense could he be? She dragged the elephant centre stage. "Danny, I want babies. Tom can't have children."

"You can adopt. Or there are those other ways

people manage. Sperm donors or something." He sauntered for the door. "I've been thinking. Alpacas might be a good idea. I'm going to have a shower. Give me a yell when you want to eat."

****

Primrose drove into Tom's yard shortly after seven. She sat for a moment gathering courage, calming her racing heart. The screen door banged and Tom came down the steps. He must have been watching for her. His hair was damp, slicked back from his forehead, his shirt crisp and white across those broad shoulders, neatly tucked into worn blue jeans. Utterly desirable. Utterly impossible.

"G'day," he said as he opened the passenger door.

"Hello." Barely waiting for him to close the door let alone buckle up, Primrose swung the Golf in a tight arc and accelerated down the driveway. Tom swayed against the window.

"Whoa." He grabbed for the seatbelt. "In a hurry?"

"Sorry."

She slowed for the turn on to the road. Tom's hard, jeans clad thigh was right near her fingers every time she changed gears. Should have let him drive. But it was better to have something to occupy her hands, not to mention her brain, or she'd be running her fingers up and down that tautly muscled leg. Remembering. How could she ever erase that memory? Their bodies had fitted together perfectly. His fingers knew exactly what drove her...

"Danny's happy."

She exhaled a burst of tightly held air. "Yes."

She smiled across at him. He lifted a curious eyebrow at the rush of breath but didn't comment. He

236

said, "I knew they'd get themselves sorted pretty quickly. What have they named her?"

"Dawn Primrose. Didn't Danny tell you?" Primrose shot him a sideways glance. "Didn't you ask?"

"Forgot. Danny was too busy thanking me to think of it."

"I think it's a lovely name. Even the Primrose bit."

"Dawn Primrose." He nodded. "It's all right."

"They couldn't call her Tom even though you deserve it more than I do."

"It's okay. If they'd done it the other way round she could be Rosie Dawn." He laughed. "Pretty Rosie Dawn."

Primrose grinned. "I'm surprised Nirupam came up with such a traditional name."

"Me, too."

There Tom sat, relaxed and friendly, chatting comfortably, long legs sprawled, sexy as could be. Not the slightest inkling of the emotional mess churning in the driver's seat beside him. He obviously assumed whatever awkwardness had arisen, caused by her kiss, had been defused by his departure without comment. The girl he knew would be leaving very soon. Probably thinking W*hat a relief.* Not of marriage.

The road wound up into the quiet coolness of the mountains.

"Bit different coming up here now," said Tom.

Primrose changed down a gear. Her fingers grazed his thigh. "I'll never drive this road again without remembering and I'll never forget the exact spot."

"It's surprising how quickly some memories fade." He stretched his leg out straight, away from her touch.

"Some never do, never will," Primrose said softly.

She knew Tom was looking at her, she could feel his eyes on her face in profile to him. "No, I suppose it's one that won't ever fade away," he said after a short silence.

"That's not the one I meant." Primrose kept her eyes firmly on the road. Had to or they'd be over the edge.

"You're right, it's hard to forget...some people. The ones who treat you badly."

"I'm sorry, Tom," she whispered.

He cleared his throat. "Not you. I didn't mean you." He gave a strained sounding laugh. "Hard to forget you. You're right here. I meant your fiancé."

"Right, although..."

"What?"

"I haven't thought of him at all since I arrived. Beyond a passing mention here and there. I thought I'd die of heartbreak at the time but...I guess time really does heal all wounds." She smiled briefly. "I think the real problem was everything happened at once—Martin dumping me, those tough gigs which made me question my ability, having to find somewhere to live all of a sudden. I needed a break. From everything. A holiday. I can see more clearly now. Martin wasn't right for me and vice versa. The country is really good for clearing the head."

His expression hadn't changed from polite interest "And so now you're ready to go back."

"Not really. But I have to earn some money."

"Money is the root of all evil," Tom stated like a bible thumping preacher.

Primrose smiled. "Danny and Nirupam want me to stay but I can hardly stay having made them kick everyone else out."

"But you're their family." Again the cry of indignation. Family meant a lot to Tom. His family. He wouldn't understand the loose, messy excuse for a family she and Danny had. Although wasn't a family what Danny was striving for on his commune? Hadn't she come here searching for the same thing? A family? A connection? Somewhere to belong? People to belong to?

"That's what Danny said." She paused. "He's very forgiving. They both are."

"So you've sorted out the thing about his son?"

"More or less. He's glad Nirupam knows. I don't know what they'll do financially. They have little Dawn to consider now."

"You did some good while you were here," Tom said after a while. He laughed. "In amongst the rest."

"In amongst the chaos and devastation, you mean." Primrose smiled. "Do you think so?"

"Yes."

"Are you surprised?" She looked across quickly.

"Constantly." The way he said it implied constant surprise was not a good thing.

Primrose changed gears for the last hairpin bend. When they were gaining speed again up the straight to the top of the climb she said, "We're going to be in the local paper. Danny said they wanted to photograph us."

"Hah." Tom grinned. "Our twenty minutes of fame."

Primrose laughed. But if there was a photo of Tom taken she definitely wanted a copy.

The nurse on duty in the small maternity ward confirmed their celebrity status by announcing to the three new mothers sharing the room with Nirupam that her doctors had arrived. Everyone clapped. Primrose laughed and made a stage bow.

"Tom's the real hero."

Tom shuffled his feet awkwardly, grinned, gave a little wave to his fans. Nirupam saved him by calling, "Come and see Dawn."

The baby was gorgeous. Wrapped in her soft pink sheet with her sweet little face wrinkling into a variety of expressions, she was everything Primrose had ever imagined a baby to be. She cradled the tiny bundle in her arms, cooing softly, smelling the sweet, intoxicating baby smell, reluctant to pass her to Tom, hovering by her side.

"She looks better now than when we saw her last." He touched Dawn's cheek gently with one finger. "How are you, Nirupam?"

"Tired and a bit sore but very happy. We'll never be able to thank you enough."

He bent to kiss her cheek. "Don't worry about it. That's what neighbours are for."

They shared a pleased smile. Primrose hugged Dawn tighter and the baby emitted a little squawk of protest.

Fifteen minutes later a young, round-faced reporter arrived, panting, with a camera slung around his neck, a small backpack over his shoulder, and a note pad in his hand. "Hi there. I'm Stephen Meadows, *Moruya Post.*"

He took photos of all three clustered around the baby then Tom holding her looking large and awkward, Tom and Primrose smiling at Nirupam in bed, Primrose cuddling Dawn, Dawn alone.

"Can I have some details, please? Both your names

to start then tell me what happened this morning."

He produced a small voice recorder. Tom spoke, playing down his part so it sounded as though he'd done nothing. When it was her turn Primrose gushed over Tom's heroic actions, ignoring his pained grunts of disapproval.

"Thanks," Stephen said when she finished. "Do you live in Kullanurra?"

"I'm visiting my brother and Nirupam on their property. Tom lives next door."

"Primrose is a professional flute player," Tom said. "She's anxious to get back to the city."

"Not exciting enough here for you?"

"No work here for me." Primrose sent a little frown in Tom's direction.

"Have you met the Arts Society people?"

"No, I didn't know there was one."

"Yes." Stephen's face lit up with enthusiasm. "They help run the jazz festival each year."

She offered a tiny, apologetic smile. "I'm a classical player."

"They do have chamber concerts sometimes. There are some very good musicians in the area. You may have heard of Maureen Bellows? The pianist? She moved to Narooma with her husband when he retired after his heart attack."

"Really?" That was a surprise but the woman must be at least seventy.

"Who's Maureen Bellows?" asked Tom.

"A very good concert pianist," said Primrose. "She's world famous. I had no idea she lived down here. She stopped performing years ago."

"Perhaps you should contact her," suggested

Stephen. "She knows what's happening in the region. You've heard of the Four Winds Chamber Music Festival?"

"Yes."

"She's on the committee. She also teaches privately. Call me and I'll give you her details." He handed Primrose a business card.

"Thanks." She slipped the card into her purse. What good would it do to ring Maureen Bellows? Although if she knew everyone...No, at most they'd have a chat and she'd find herself roped into being on some committee. She needed an income, a reliable, steady one. But most importantly she needed a home.

****

As they walked to the car Primrose pulled out her mobile phone. "I need to make some calls while I'm in range. Excuse me for a minute?"

"Of course." Tom hesitated. Took the plunge. "Want to have a drink before we head back?" Would she remember what happened the last time they'd had a drink? He did. And the aftermath. The words he wished he could take back, spoken in the chill of the morning and the heat of disappointment at waking alone after a night of fantasies fulfilled. Words he'd regret for the rest of his life. If he'd reacted differently would anything have changed?

Primrose gave no indication she remembered anything. "I shouldn't, I'm driving."

"Coffee?"

"No, thanks." She hesitated, fingered the phone, glanced at him then away. "I'm very tired. I'd like an early night." She pressed buttons on her phone and held it to her ear.

Tom stuck his hands in his pockets and leaned against the car while Primrose made her calls. She had her back turned but he could hear enough to know she was ringing someone about being available to play again.

She finished and dialled again. Her voice came clearly.

"Hi, Belinda. Primrose. Yes. Fine. How are you?" She half-turned and smiled quickly. One of those "sorry I'll just be a minute" smiles from people who were busy and preoccupied with more important things. "I wanted to let you know I'll be coming back. Could I stay a few days again, please?" Silence. "No, it didn't work out." Laughed. "Yes, I know. Miles from anywhere."

He'd lost her. Tom knew it with a sagging heaviness in the chest. He'd lost her and couldn't figure out how to keep her here. Didn't know what to offer. He had nothing she wanted—except sex but that was no basis for a lasting relationship. As far as she was concerned he was a nonstarter. No children, no go.

And they had nowhere near enough in common for a lifetime together. Especially on the land. To survive all the hardships farming threw at you there had to be a deep commitment. Like that of Danny and Nirupam.

He bit his lip and kicked at the ground with the toe of his boot. All true. He knew it. Sensible and right. But love wasn't sensible and often wasn't right. The inescapable fact was he loved Primrose. But the last thing he was going to do was lay his heart on the line to be stomped on. She'd be gentle because she genuinely liked him. But she didn't love him or at least not enough and no matter how soft and tactful she was that fact remained like a kick in the head.

Chapter Twelve

Primrose didn't wait for Tom to reach the door to his house before heading down the drive as fast as she could safely go without crashing off the track into a tree. She could barely see as it was what with the sudden onrush of tears. Everything swam past, blurry. She drove on automatic.

He couldn't wait to get out of the car. As soon as she pulled on the brake he had the door open and one denim clad leg out, tossing "Thanks" over his shoulder. And that one word was pretty much all he'd come out with the whole way home. Nothing to say to her. Sitting in the passenger seat staring into the darkness.

He was sick of her and she was love sick with him. She wouldn't start anything with him—he understood why, he said so—but did that mean they couldn't be friends?

Enough. Enough.

Primrose sniffed hard and released one tense hand from the wheel to wipe her eyes. He'd fade from her thoughts when she was back in the city, the way Martin had when she came here. Tom was the rebound love. Everyone had one of those and they were usually a disaster. A big mistake. Tom was a mistake.

The headlights splayed over the derelict Nirvana sign as she swung into the driveway. Nearly home. Primrose yawned. Big, big day. A cup of tea with

Danny then bed. Another giant yawned attacked her. Over the rise and down to the house.

She frowned. The headlights sprayed over a strange minivan parked by the shed. Another unfamiliar van occupied her usual space. A couple of motorbikes. Two van loads of people?

Music. They were playing very loud rock music. Laughter rang out. Perhaps Danny had invited some people over to celebrate the birth. But he would have included Tom. Primrose parked and strode for the house.

Inside, the noise was deafening. The living room was full of bodies. People sprawled on the floor, the couch and overflowed into the kitchen. The hot air was thick with screaming guitars, pounding drums. Primrose threaded her way through the crush, stepping over hairy, tanned legs in khaki shorts, Indian cotton tie-dyed skirts and sequinned harem pants whose wild, tangle-haired owners smiled beatifically up at her from faces studded with silver jewellery in odd, painful looking places.

"Where's Danny?" she yelled into the ear of a very long-haired blonde girl holding a stubby of beer.

She gestured toward the kitchen. "Cool news, ay?" A Kiwi.

Primrose nodded. The music was marginally less ear splitting in the kitchen, but a wall provided minimal shelter from the shockwaves. Her bedroom wasn't much further away. Already her head was thudding and the bass pounded deep inside her chest like a pacemaker. Except she suspected it was out of sync with her own heart beat. What did that do to a body?

Danny was leaning against the laundry door,

laughing crazily at something his companions were saying. Arms waved, drinks slopped on the floor, the beat went on.

He saw her and beckoned. "Hey Rosie," he shouted into a sudden lull in the music. Primrose smiled at the faces turned toward her. "How are my g..." But the rest was drowned out by a bellow from the lead singer on the next track.

Primrose leaned close and yelled, "They're great. Dawn's a beautiful baby." She grabbed his arm and dragged him out the back door into the relative quiet of the darkened back yard. Her ears were ringing already.

"I didn't know you were having a party."

"Neither did I." Danny grinned happily. "Word gets around."

"How long will it last?"

He shrugged. "Don't know. Few days maybe."

"What?" Primrose shrieked. "But Nirupam is coming home tomorrow."

"Yeah, I know. It'll be great. Everyone will get to meet Dawn."

"Does Nirupam know?"

"She won't mind. These people are all our friends."

"But Danny. . ." Where to start?

"What?"

Primrose licked her lips. She looked up into his face and saw nothing but joy. "Nirupam's tired. She won't want a noisy party going on."

"Give me a break, Rosie. We won't be playing this stuff when the baby comes home."

"No. Of course not." Primrose reached up to kiss his cheek. "I'm tired, too. I'm going to bed."

"Okay. Good night."

Rather than fight her way through the crowd Primrose walked around the verandah and slipped in through the front door again. She'd never sleep. The whole house was shuddering. Maybe the old weatherboard structure wouldn't cope and the joints would fall apart from the vibrations. The nails might drop out. Tom could probably hear the racket from his place. He'd laugh. Loonies, he'd think.

The toilet was occupied and someone was in the bathroom. Primrose hovered outside the door for a few minutes then gave up and went to her room. They'd have to come out eventually. The toilet flushed so she peeped into the hallway ready to pounce. An overweight girl came out and thumped on the bathroom door. "Get a move on," she yelled.

Primrose made her dash to the loo. No paper left! Just the empty cardboard tube, dammit. She had tissues in her pocket luckily. The spare rolls were in the bathroom cabinet.

When she emerged the girl was still there, oozing tattooed flesh out of a black tank top and tight black short skirt. She rolled her eyes at Primrose. Music thundered along the passage.

"Who's in there?"

"Jen's having a bath."

"What? Now?"

"Exactly."

"Does she realise we don't have a lot of water?" demanded Primrose. She banged on the door. "Get out of there now! And don't let the water out. We recycle it on the garden."

The girl's casual indifference disappeared in an instant. "Hey, cool it. You don't have to be rude."

Primrose felt her lips tighten into a thin line. "I'm not being rude, I live here and we have to be careful of our water." Who was this person who calmly supposed it was acceptable to have a bath at a party in someone else's house? Didn't she have her own bathroom at home? Most people washed *before* they went out. She'd bet they hadn't asked Danny. Not that he'd say no. And whose towel was she using? Since Kurt's departure she'd begun hanging her blue towel in the bathroom.

The door opened. The woman who emerged pushed past with barely a glance at Primrose. The big girl charged in and washed her hands in the bath water. "Happy?" she asked, straightening with a grunt at the effort.

"Fine," said Primrose. "You might mention the water situation to your friends." She sounded exactly like Kurt. Fancy that.

When she returned to her room she jammed the chair she'd gained in the rearrangement of Mojo's room against the door. No telling where those people would sleep tonight. It certainly wouldn't be in her room. If they ever went to sleep. The music was still blasting into the night. Primrose stuffed torn tissue scraps into her ears and jammed her head under the pillow. She lay curled up in the dark wishing she was curled up in the quiet of Tom's big bed with his calm, sleeping body beside her.

By four a.m. the best she could say was she'd rested her body although that was arguable as every nerve ending was screaming and every muscle tense as a violin string. No door to sleep opened or appeared likely to. Even after the music stopped around two, her brain was firing. Everything churned in her head. Fury at the thoughtlessness of those partying hippies, anger at Danny for allowing them an open-ended invitation, more anger at Danny for completely disregarding the effect these people would have on his wife and baby. Total fury at the image of poor Nirupam coming home to a house full of freeloaders when she was expecting a quiet reunion with her husband, bonding and settling time with her baby.

Then there was the outrageous volume of the music. Deafness inducing. Her ears weren't just ringing, they were clanging. It was totally ridiculous.

And Tom. Interwoven through the whole mess was Tom with his lazy lopsided smile, his quiet sense of humour, his calmness, his ability to cope with everything from a stroppy cow to childbirth without raising a sweat or his voice. Plus he was smart and efficient, had drive and vision and was extremely sexy. Put plainly he was wonderful.

The thing was did she have the courage to forego children of her own? And did he feel the way Danny assumed he did? How could she tell?

Ask him. Primrose sat up straight, legs tensed ready to spring out of bed. At four thirty in the morning? He'd think she'd gone mad. She must look horrendous—one of Macbeth's witches—a *black and midnight hag*.

And the truth was, she wasn't sure enough of her own heart nor brave enough to lay her soul before him, swear she loved him enough to be childless, risk his polite "no, thank you."

She lay down again. Back where she started.

****

Voices, heavy footfalls and a slamming door woke

her. Primrose groped for her bedside clock, squinting in the brightness, mouth furry, brain clogged. A sliver of hot sunlight cut across the far wall through the crack between the curtains. Ten twenty. She collapsed back onto the pillow. Her head ached, a dull band of pain behind the eyes stretching to each temple. Dehydration. She swallowed. Tasted like sand.

How many people had stayed overnight? Primrose clambered out of bed to peer out the window and count cars. But she dropped the curtain into place swiftly. Someone was sitting right outside. The top of a thickly thatched head of dreads braided with red bands was level with the sill. Looked like a pile of old rope.

She sat on her bed for a moment gathering her scattered, throbbing wits, pressing her palms flat against the sides of her head to stop the pain. A cool shower might help. If she could get into the bathroom and if they'd left any water. She collected clean clothes, removed her chair barricade and ventured out. The toilet was mercifully empty and someone had even renewed the paper supply. The bathroom was vacant, but showed plenty of signs of use with damp towels hanging about, someone's underwear and puddles scattered about the floor, a soggy lump of soap in the holder.

Primrose showered in her recently acquired economical style. By the time she returned to her room the headache had subsided to a low level ache. Bearable. Plus she hadn't spied a single hippy intruder except the one on the verandah. Maybe they'd all left early this morning.

They hadn't. Five of them were asleep on the living room floor. Primrose stood in the doorway studying the sprawl of comatose bodies. An obstacle course to the kitchen and a cup of tea. A total blockade on flute practice unless she went to one of the sheds. Presumably others were occupying the spare rooms. In sudden panic she turned. They wouldn't. Danny wouldn't let them. She'd murder him! Primrose flung open the door to baby Dawn's newly renovated nursery, sagged in relief against the doorframe. Empty. Untouched. Just as Nirupam had left it. Except a pile of baby wrapped gifts sat on the change table.

"Lovely, isn't it?" Primrose turned. The blonde Kiwi girl smiled. Blue eyes and crooked teeth in a tanned face. "It's so exciting. I love babies, don't you?"

"Yes. Where's Danny?"

"He's gone to pick up Nirupam and Dawn."

"Oh! I was..." Primrose stopped. Of course Danny and Nirupam should bring their baby home alone. A sister wasn't needed for that. The girl waited expectantly, a little smile hovering. "Never mind. How long are you staying?"

"Tony and I are leaving this afternoon. We want to see the baby first. He's gone down to the river to meditate."

"Right. Fine. What about the others?" Primrose gestured at the sleeping carpet in the living room. One large very hairy body in the centre resembled some sort of snoring comatose animal. The room smelled like a lion cage at the zoo.

The blonde shrugged, similar fashion to Danny. "I'm Zoë."

"Primrose."

The eyes lit up. "Danny's sister."

Primrose nodded. And what else went with that

251

remark? It implied a "the one with the bad vibe who cleared the house" continuation. But Zoë only said, "Want some tea?"

She led the way to the kitchen, deftly avoiding stepping on hands or legs or hair. Once there Zoë filled the kettle and took the teapot outside to empty it before Primrose could organise her thoughts to reach her limbs. Communal living. She still didn't have it right. Everyone else knew the protocol. Treat every home as your own. Everyone was therefore automatically welcome wherever they went. Or so it appeared. They just moved right on in.

Primrose opened the fridge in the vain hope some food had been left untouched by last night's marauders. To her surprise it was fuller than it had ever been. In amongst covered plates and bowls a tub of fresh fruit salad looked tempting, and that could only be home made yoghurt in another container. A large pot of honey had appeared from somewhere, too. Primrose helped herself. Zoë made the tea and sat at the table while Primrose ate.

"Danny said you're a flute player," she said.

"Yes."

"Tony and I are musicians. We have a band. I sing and play bass and Tony plays guitar and sings. He writes stuff too. It's kind of world music, I suppose. All sorts of influences. African, jazz, blues. We're The Buttercups. Do you play with anyone?"

Primrose shook her head. "I'm a freelance classical player. I haven't done much improvised playing but I enjoyed what I did. Where do you live?"

"Bermagui. We travel a lot to festivals. And we play the club dates up and down the coast. Tony has some students."

"Sounds fun." It did sound fun. Freelance but in control of your own music. Making your own music, no external imposition in the form of notes on a page or a conductor. Teaching people who wanted to learn.

"We love it. I'll give you a CD."

"Thanks. Do you live off it?"

"Pretty much. We're not going to be millionaires but who wants to be a millionaire?" The blue eyes sparkled.

"True. I'd settle for a steady income."

"We manage that." Zoë laughed and stood up. "I'll get the CD."

"I'll buy it from you."

"If you insist. You should come and sit in with us sometime."

Primrose smiled. "I'd love to but I'm going back to Sydney soon."

Zoë tilted her head. "I thought you lived here, now."

"Not really."

The blue eyes studied her carefully. Primrose ate a chunk of juicy mango.

"You'll stay," said Zoë suddenly, with a bright smile.

"Will I?"

"Of course." She almost danced out the door.

Primrose drained her tea. Was Zoë psychic like Fern? She seemed like such a nice girl. Or perhaps she assumed Primrose was like the rest of them. They all ended up here. Like a swarm of locusts.

Primrose kept well clear of the house by collecting the eggs, checking the goats and Sammy had water, watering and unnecessarily poking about with a hoe in the veggie garden. Gradually bodies emerged. She took surreptitious peeks at them as they wandered around or lazed on the verandah. Those seedy looking ones probably had hangovers, certainly their ears would be ringing. One had a guitar but it wasn't Tony. He and Zoë were examining a piece of their motorbike in the shade of a large gum tree. Interesting invitation to play with their band. If she stayed. Maybe there were opportunities here. Maybe she could find a part-time job in Moruya or some other little nearby coastal town, to get herself started.

A couple of the interlopers were attacked by Sammy, large rude girl included. He was having the time of his life. Victims had been in short supply since Primrose had his measure.

When Danny's van appeared over the rise she straightened and waved. With his new family aboard he drove uncharacteristically slowly, avoiding the largest potholes with care. All the visitors materialised in the yard as though by magic. By the time Primrose reached the van they were three deep. Short of pushing and shoving her way through the milling fans she had no chance of greeting her family. She stood back while everyone oohed and aahed and hugged Nirupam and Danny.

The throng surged toward the house in a flurry of excited chatter. Someone's blue cattle dog appeared from nowhere and bounced around barking. Nirupam said, "Where's Rosie?"

"Here." Primrose stepped forward and kissed the cheek smelling sweetly of baby powder and hospital soap. "Everything's ready for you."

Danny clutched the baby capsule as though it held the Holy Grail. It did. Dawn was barely visible, just a few wisps of dark hair poked out of the tightly wrapped pink and white bundle. Like a big cocoon.

"It's so good to be home." Nirupam smiled around at everyone. "And to see you all. It's a wonderful homecoming."

Absolutely sincere. No doubt about it. Where was the defiant "I want my home to myself" of a couple of days ago? Primrose sighed. Nirupam and Danny moved on up the steps with their precious little daughter and the host of followers.

She took the hoe to the shed. Everyone was inside now, the yard deserted except for the dog. He lay on the verandah ignoring her. By the time Primrose had washed the dirt from her hands and face, Nirupam had settled Dawn in her new room and sat with all the visitors round the kitchen table. A feast had materialised while Primrose had been outside attending to the chores and avoiding people.

The table groaned under an array of salads, cheese, bread and fruit with small dishes of condiments and sauces dotted amongst the plates. Zoë and the bath woman were pouring juice into glasses. Danny was handing out beers. Everyone was talking. Nirupam was beaming.

"Sit next to me Rosie," she called, budging up closer to the large hairy man who was now wide awake and telling stories about someone called Bob.

Primrose dutifully squeezed in beside her on the end of the bench.

The servers sat down. Primrose did a quick count. Thirteen.

Danny stood up with his stubby raised. "I propose a toast to my beautiful wife and daughter. I love them both." Nirupam reached to clasp his free hand. He bent and kissed her.

"To Nirupam and Dawn," roared everyone.

"I propose a toast to Rosie," said Nirupam when the noise level subsided. "She was wonderful. I'm so glad she was here."

Primrose stared at her plate while the toast was enthusiastically endorsed. Her face was bright red, she knew it. "Thanks," she murmured. "But Tom did most of it."

"To Tom," bellowed the man next to her, lifting his glass again and slopping beer on to the table. Everyone roared again.

****

After lunch, which sprawled on for several hours, Zoë and Tony climbed aboard their motorbike and left in a cloud of blue exhaust smoke and dust. One of the vans followed within a few minutes, loaded up with four passengers including hairy man, rude bath woman, large girl and the dog. Four people remained, showing no signs of imminent departure. The two men settled themselves on the verandah with Danny, drinking beer and chatting. The two women started washing clothes in the laundry.

Primrose peeped into Nirupam's room where she lay on the bed with the baby snuggled to her breast.

"Can I come in?"

"Of course." Nirupam patted the bed and Primrose sat down. Dawn was fast asleep, one tiny hand curled against her cheek.

"She's so gorgeous." She stretched a finger to

stroke the soft, dark, downy hair.

Nirupam gazed at her daughter. "I didn't know how much I'd love her. I had no idea how strong the feeling is." She looked up with shining eyes.

Primrose blinked away a tear. "I'm so envious. Seeing Dawn has made me want a baby even more."

"You will, Rosie."

Primrose nodded with a sceptical grimace. "Sure. One day."

"You will," insisted Nirupam. "Tom..."

"Tom doesn't love me and even if he did he can't have children, Nirupam. Remember?" cut in Primrose. Why did they keep on about him?

"Yes, but if you love each other you can work it out somehow. There are always ways."

"You don't understand. It's too complicated."

If she loved him? Did she? Did he love her? Such a love would have to be very, very deep and very, very strong, like Danny's and Nirupam's. Was she even capable of loving that way? Forgoing children, for the love of a man? If that man were Tom...

Nirupam firmed her mouth, but didn't say anything.

Primrose toyed with the edge of Dawn's bunny rug. "I'm leaving tomorrow."

"Tomorrow?" Nirupam looked up, startled.

"I don't think I need to be here any longer. You have all your friends. And Danny."

"Stay. There's plenty of room."

"I know. It's not that."

"They won't be here forever, Rosie." Nirupam smiled. "Shah and Christine are staying a bit but the others are leaving tomorrow, too."

"See?" Primrose swallowed tightly. "You don't need me. I was only staying to help with Dawn but if they're here," she ended harshly, "Didn't Danny tell you? I need to earn some money."

"I'm sorry, Rosie." Nirupam ran gentle, caressing fingers over the baby's sleeping body.

Primrose watched for a moment, wondering. Should she mention it? It was important. Especially now with Dawn involved. "Nirupam what about what you said? About wanting to have the house for just you and Danny and the baby."

Nirupam smiled one of her familiar, calm smiles. "I think it was being pregnant made me talk like that. Mad hormones. The commune has always been Danny's dream. We talked about it on the way home and we're making some changes. He's not going to let people stay here who don't contribute. Financially, I mean, as well as physically. You were right about a lot of things, Rosie. And he's going to make the decisions on crops. Take Tom's advice. Have a plan which people have to follow."

Dawn squawked and Nirupam lifted her to her shoulder. She began patting her back and murmuring soothing noises. Primrose slid off the bed. There was nothing to say. They had their lives. She had the fragments of hers.

"I'll head off in the morning."

"Will you see Tom before you go?"

"I suppose I should." See Tom and say what? Goodbye was all that was left. But goodbye, at very least, had to be said.

Primrose closed the door softly. So easily she slipped out of their lives. They were used to people coming and going, but she'd thought, hoped, she may have been slightly more important to them than one of those other drop-ins.

****

Tom wasn't home. Delilah wandered out to greet the car wagging her tail slowly, and followed Primrose down to the sheds which was unnecessary because the white ute wasn't there in its usual spot. And he'd locked the house which implied he was out for the day. She looked in at the chooks scratching about in the litter and muttering amongst themselves. Her attacker ignored her until she plucked some handfuls of grass and pushed them through the wire netting. Then the little flock went into a frenzy of pecking and running with pieces of the fresh greenery dropping from their beaks.

Primrose walked back to the car to stand undecided in the gathering dusk. He could be home any minute or late tonight. He may not be back until morning. She had no idea who he would visit except Mike on the peach farm. She never did go to visit Mike, hadn't tried very hard to fit in to the local community. She'd tried to change it to fit her. The part she was involved in, anyway. And failed.

She looked down at Delilah sitting patiently at her feet, ruffled her ears. "Goodbye."

The tail thumped on the ground a couple of times and a red tongue lolled as the dog grinned and panted. Primrose went home.

Everyone was in the kitchen preparing dinner when she arrived. It didn't feel like home any more. Nowhere did.

****

Tom drove over to the commune the next morning. An unfamiliar car was in the shed where Primrose's Golf should be. Out. Impossible to pretend he wasn't disappointed. She was addictive. He couldn't have her, but he still needed his fix every few days. Just a chat, a look, a smile from her. Maybe she'd nipped in to the store and would be back soon if he hung around. He'd really come over to visit the new mum and baby. Really.

Danny waved from the garden patch. Tom sauntered over to the rows of vegetables and clumps of herbs.

"G'day, Danny. How's the bub?"

"She's wonderful. How're you?"

"Not bad." He glanced around. "Garden's doing all right."

"Yeah. Rosie looked after it after Kurt left. Replanted stuff."

"Where is she?"

"Gone."

Tom's eyes jerked from the capsicums to Danny. "To Sydney? When did she go?"

"This morning."

"She coming back?"

"Don't think so. Not for a while."

"Damn." He stuck his hands on his hips and glared into the distance.

"She went over to see you yesterday afternoon." Danny offered. "To say goodbye."

"I was over at Kilgore's. Stayed for dinner."

Danny propped the hoe against a tree. "Coming in to see Nirupam and Dawn?"

Tom blinked. "Yeah, sure." That's why he'd come

over, wasn't it?

Danny gave what any other face would have been a sly smile but on him simply looked hopeful. "I'll give you Rosie's address and phone number if you like."

"Thanks."

They invited him for lunch, but Tom couldn't face a table full of commune folk, not without his Rose. Nirupam gave him a piece of paper with an address and mobile number on it. He folded it and stowed it carefully in his shirt pocket. She led him to the baby's room from whence squawks of rage were coming. Primrose had done a terrific paint job on the walls.

"Make sure you call her." Nirupam picked up the yelling baby from its bassinet and cuddled her against her shoulder. How could something so small produce such a racket? Survival was the answer, like he'd be trying to do without his Rose. "She was sorry she missed you yesterday."

She could have called in this morning he wanted to cry along with the anguished wail of the baby. Rose knew she could walk into his house any hour of the day or night and she'd be welcome. If she had he would've told her how he felt and damn the consequences. If he'd known she was leaving so soon. Why so soon?

"I thought she was staying another week," he said.

"We told her not to go but she seemed set on it."

Her voice rang in his head, the words she'd spoken on the phone outside the hospital to that person in Sydney, "It didn't work out" and "Miles from anywhere." No. She wouldn't come back.

He touched baby Dawn lightly on the cheek. "She's a beauty." The baby turned her head and blinked blue grey eyes in his direction. Her little mouth was

261

pink and soft in red cheeks, the skin still blotchy from the birth. Danny's nose. She yawned.

Nirupam said suddenly, "You know, Rosie wants kids."

She may as well have stabbed him. Had she forgotten? Surely not. And Nirupam wasn't cruel. "I thought she wanted to play her flute."

"She can do both." Nirupam gave a little laugh.

"Not out here."

"Why not?"

Enough! That wasn't the real issue and they both knew it. "*I can't give her babies, Nirupam.*" Did he have to spell it out for her again?

"Why not? If you two want to really be together you can make it work." She smiled benignly and with that slightly mysterious Madonna look she wore sometimes. "I think you love each other. That's all that really matters. The rest you can figure out. Tom, call her."

"See you later." He leaned down and kissed her cheek, touched Dawn's soft head with gentle fingers and left before some unidentifiable emotion building in his heart exploded and expressed itself in a way he would regret exposing even to someone as understanding and kind as Nirupam.

Tom climbed into the ute and drove home on automatic. "Call her," they all said. She left without bothering to say goodbye. Phones worked both ways. She could call him. Did she love him? He had no idea. He'd never asked and never told her how he felt, either.

He spent the afternoon fixing the last of the fences damaged in the flooding. Hard, hot physical work to occupy his hands and a head too full of writhing snakes to sit idle. He finished with the sun hovering red and round on the horizon, tossed the tools in the tray of the ute, whistled Delilah aboard, and headed back to the house. The empty, lonely house.

He'd never felt lonely before, always enjoyed the quiet and didn't mind the solitude. In fact he much preferred solitude to a crowd. Or had done. For some reason the hollowness of his heart spread itself to the rooms. Rose was gone. Even though she'd only spent two nights here with him she'd been just a short ride away across the river. Her larger than life presence left a gaping hole in the whole valley. Nirupam and Danny would miss her too. Not at the moment, maybe, with all those friends hanging around and the thrill of the new baby, but later. They'd miss her drive and her enthusiasm and her wild plans—some of which had actually worked.

He laughed softly as he stripped off to have his shower. Locking Kurt in the shed with a snake. How he wished he'd been there for that episode. And if she knew how desirable she was stomping furiously about in those gumboots with mud on her face after wrestling Daisy in the cowshed...Talking to the chooks—he did that too. Swore at them sometimes. Gertie was a stroppy old biddy. She'd pecked him many a time. Came very close to having her neck wrung.

Steam from the hot water wreathed the bathroom. He stepped in and closed his eyes, letting the stream pour down over his head, washing away the grime and sweat of the day. All he needed to do was grab her, kiss her silly and tell her he loved her. Take his chances. Easy now. Impossible then.

Tom stopped soaping. His eyes flew open. Was

that his problem? What if she'd been waiting for him to make a move? What if she'd been as unsure of his feelings as he was of hers? He'd been very forthright in his dismissal of her. "Find someone else" he'd shouted that morning. For all her sophistication and confidence was she as tentative as he in committing her heart? Was she prepared to compromise on babies? Adopt, for instance? Or take donor sperm? He'd swallow his pride and accept even that to make her happy, if it meant she'd accept him.

He didn't know if she would do any of those things. He'd never asked her.

"Bloody idiot!" he shouted and received a mouthful of water. She'd just been dumped almost at the altar. Who wouldn't be tentative? And he was so thick he couldn't say it—couldn't say "I love you". And so doughy he hadn't acted when he had the chance. Yesterday, when she'd kissed him. Too scared. Not waiting to hear what she wanted to say. Making assumptions. Wrong ones? What sort of man was he?

The answer wasn't pleasant.

****

Primrose had every intention of driving direct to Sydney along the coast road, but an invisible fence, a barrier protected the Moruya town limits on the far side of the river. She crossed the bridge, travelled two hundred metres and her foot lifted from the accelerator, her hands spun the wheel. The Golf slowed and turned back the way she'd come as if on automatic pilot.

What now? Couldn't go back to the commune, couldn't face her old life in Sydney. Couldn't bear to see Tom. When, on the far side of the town a sign pointing to Moruya Heads appeared, she swung left heading for the coast.

The road continued south when it reached the ocean. Primrose drove aimlessly with the vast Pacific glittering on her left and scattered beach houses nestled in the bush on her right. She stopped in the tiny settlement of Congo and walked down onto shining, soft white sand. Stopping to slip off her sandals she stood with the sun beating down on her head, staring out over the endless rolling breakers, her mind as empty as the sky.

The heat slowly began to eat into her consciousness and she returned to the car for a hat and sunscreen. She walked to a little general store and bought an ice cream and cold spring water then returned to sit on the shore on one of her towels.

People were surfing further along to the right. Groups of swimmers had set up umbrellas here and there but the beach was relatively deserted. Primrose finished her rapidly melting ice cream. She could stay here on the South Coast. Why not?

Find a part-time job somewhere. Cleaning, shop assistant. Something. Anything. Nobody said she had to make a living from music. It was a matter of pride. All in her own head. She'd spent so much time practising and studying and worked so hard to get her degree that giving up and finding other employment seemed like a betrayal, a failure. The way she'd always considered Danny as a failure because he dropped out of Uni and never finished his degree. Never finished anything. But did it matter? In the grand scheme of things who cared? The pressure and the subsequent mess in her head came from inside her mind, not from an external source.

Tom had said something along those lines soon

after they met. *Personal problems follow you around no matter where you are. And until you admit to yourself your attitude may be the cause, you're stuck with them.*

A weight seemed to lift from her shoulders. Who cared, indeed? She was free to do what she liked. She answered to no-one, there was nothing to prove to anyone. Danny had always understood that. He was happy with his life and the choices he'd made. That took a strength and courage she'd never appreciated until now. But he had Nirupam by his side. Primrose answered to no-one because there *was* no-one.

She squashed the self pity before it took hold, dug her fingers into the white gold sand and let it trickle from her grasp.

The blue Pacific stretched before her. A priceless view with sparkling clean air that refreshed and invigorated. Rents would be a fraction of the city's. Imagine living within a stone's throw of this? And close to her family. Any sort of work would do to pay the rent and she could teach flute and music theory privately. Schools might be interested. It wouldn't be easy but it was possible.

She'd played Zoë's CD in the car this morning and the music was exciting. Frighteningly good. She could try out for The Buttercups. They may not want her but she could try. Plus the retired pianist Maureen Bellows may be persuaded to do a recital with her, or know another pianist who would be interested. There were opportunities here if she made them but she was nothing if not determined and they'd be on her own terms.

Then there was Tom. There was nothing to be done about Tom. Unsuitable and unrequited love was something to be endured. Heartbreak wasn't a new experience. Her heart was used to being in pieces. A woman couldn't rely on a man to provide happiness in her life, nor vice versa, and it was unfair to expect it of Tom. This overwhelming love was her problem not his. If she stayed they would undoubtedly meet so she had to be prepared. She also had to be prepared for an eventual new partner in his life. A woman who accepted him as he was.

A tear ran down her face quite unexpectedly. She'd never be prepared for that. Never. She wiped her hand across her face. Don't cry. If she started she wouldn't stop. Mustn't mope. Time for action, a new phase of her life was about to begin. She stood up and flapped her towel to remove the sand. Back to Moruya. First, book into a motel, then buy the newspaper and start looking for a job and a cheap place to rent. If she bombed out here she'd move south and try Narooma or drive north to Bateman's Bay.

****

Her phone rang later that evening when she was contemplating pizza or Chinese for dinner. She glanced at the display. Private caller. Maybe it was Zoë returning her unsuccessful earlier call about meeting The Buttercups. Or a reply to one of the messages she'd left about accommodation.

"Hello."

"Why didn't you say goodbye?"

"Tom?" She sat down on the bed as the breath silently and abruptly left her lungs. Wasn't this part of her life over? How was she to grow a hard shell if he rang her?

"Yes. Why did you just leave like that?"

"I didn't. I tried to say goodbye yesterday. You weren't home."

"You could have called in this morning. I was home all day." He sounded hurt rather than angry. A friend who'd been slighted.

She hesitated. Had he rung just to tell her off for not calling in? "I'm sorry. I should have, I suppose." The truth was she hadn't been brave enough.

"Yes, you should have."

"I'm sorry." What more did he want her to say? "I suppose I can say it now. Goodbye. Thank you for everything."

"Rose, I wanted to see you before you left. I wanted to say...I wanted to tell you..." Silence for a heartbeat then he muttered a disgusted, "This is hopeless."

"Tell me what?" Was he about to hang-up? He couldn't. What was hopeless? "Wanted to say what?" she whispered through a throat so tight she could barely squeeze the words out.

His breath feathered into the phone then he drew in a deep breath. She couldn't speak. Her mouth wouldn't work. Her eyes blurred with sudden tears. Please don't let him hang up.

"Rose, I'm sorry." She sniffed hard and dragged in air. An apology? He wasn't the only one to blame in their fiasco of a relationship. He said, "I guess I'm too late. You won't be coming back."

"No!" Now her voice worked, the words tumbling out all in a muddle. "No, I mean I am back, I didn't go. I'm in Moruya."

"Moruya? Why?" Surprise in his voice. And delight?

She swallowed. "I couldn't leave." It came almost in a whisper. "I don't know why but I couldn't."

"Where are you?"

"The Moruya Motor Inn."

"Room?"

"Fourteen."

"I'll be there in thirty minutes. Don't go anywhere."

Primrose disconnected in a daze. Was he rushing to declare undying love? Hard to tell by his tone. Was she brave enough to tell him of hers? Why else would he be in such a hurry?

She stood immobile for several moments. Tom was coming here to this motel room. Whatever his reason, this was her last chance. Shower. Clean clothes. Hair. She sprang into action.

Thirty minutes. Barely enough time to wash the sunscreen and sand from her skin. Shampoo and dry her hair. Make-up. Iron her jeans. Was there an iron in the room? She flung open the wardrobe door. Yes.

The ute pulled into the parking lot as she was folding and jamming the ironing board back into its space. She'd know that engine sound anywhere. He must have driven like a mad thing to make it in thirty minutes. Even though he'd said he would, it was a safer forty minutes. Unless a baby was on the way.

Footsteps sounded outside. She opened the door to his knock and stepped aside, unable to look him in the eye in case she collapsed onto him. But she didn't truly know what it was he wanted to tell her. Hoped but didn't dare hope. His fresh showered scent washed over her as he brushed by her and stood at the end of the bed with his hands on his hips, glaring.

He filled the little room, used up all the air, sucked her in like a magnet. She could barely breathe for love. But she didn't know what he would say, couldn't assume. She stayed in the tiny passageway to the door and drank in the sight of him. The brown hair was damp, wetting the collar of his blue cotton shirt like yesterday when she'd picked him up. He'd prepared himself to meet her. The way she had to meet him.

"You make a habit of nicking off without saying goodbye, don't you?"

The words wouldn't come now he was here in her room so large and warm and close. All the love she had, stuck in her throat, impossible to articulate.

"Why are you still in Moruya? I thought you couldn't wait to get back to the city."

She licked dry lips with an equally dry tongue. "I'm not in a hurry. I...I couldn't...I went across to the beach this afternoon. I needed to think."

"What did you think about?" He sat down on the only chair. She moved closer, standing before him like an interviewee hoping her answers were the right ones.

"Me. My life. What to do. Flute is the only thing I can do well. I'd love to be a top flight professional but I'm not good enough to get a fulltime orchestral position. I have to stop kidding myself."

He shook his head. "I've heard you. You're fantastic."

Her voice hardened. He didn't know. He wasn't a professional musician. "No, I'm not. Believe me, I know. That's why it's so stressful for me. Sure, I can make a living as a freelance but I can't survive that way, I'd have a nervous breakdown or turn into a drunk. I have to accept the fact I'm never going to be as

270

good a player as I want to be. I've realised my limitations." But this wasn't what she wanted to talk about. Was he really that interested in her professional career?

Perturbed lines furrowed his brow. "I don't know what to say, Rose."

"There's nothing *to* say. It has nothing to do with you. It's me. Danny and I are very alike in that respect—we both want to do something we're not very good at." She laughed softly. "Coming here showed me the reality of beating your head against a brick wall."

"Danny's not doing that! He's getting along all right. Farming is a tough life for anyone. You've shown him a few realities too, you know. He'll do better from now on, I'm sure. Why not go back there, Rose?" His voice was soft and insistent. "You don't have to leave." He stood up.

"Danny had a whole lot of people there again. I couldn't stand it—even after they had that fight about having the place to themselves and agreed." She shook her head. "I don't belong there." Her throat tightened as salty tears clogged her voice. Was he leaving now? Had he come simply to say goodbye face to face?

"Where *do* you belong?" He stepped close and looked down at her. Her body ached to lean into his.

She swallowed again, eyes lowered, unable to meet his gaze, frightened even now, that what she wanted to see wouldn't be there. "I think I can find something here, get some sort of work organised, rent a flat. I might fit in. Maybe I'll belong after a while."

"You don't need to do any of that, Rose." His voice was decisive, firm. "You belong with me."

Hope flared. She looked into his eyes. "But I'm

hopeless on a farm."

He touched her cheek with gentle fingers. "I'm not talking about what you can or can't do. I'm telling you I need you with me. I can't give you babies but I can give you love. More than you can imagine or know what to do with."

A smile tugged at her lips but things had to be said. To be clear. "Tom, I don't want to be...to be...in your debt. I don't want you to think I'd move in with you because I have nowhere else to go. That I had any other reason than I want to be with you. Regardless of whether we have babies."

The fingers pressed against her mouth, stopping the flow of words. "No," he whispered. "I don't think that." The pressure released. "We can have babies. We'll find a way, somehow."

One more thing. "And I'm not a very good flute player."

"I love you. I'll cope." He grinned the lopsided grin she loved so much. "You'll learn about farming if you want to. And you're the best flute player for miles in any direction, I can guarantee. You'll find something musical to do. We'll manage. We're a good team."

He bent his head slowly, tantalising, waiting for her to move away, giving her time she didn't want. She raised her face and his lips landed on hers light as a feather, paused drew back.

"Oh," she breathed, bereft. Her hand fluttered against his warm chest then dropped to her side. "Tom?" Unsure again. Was he teasing? He'd said he loved her.

"Do you really want to be with me?" he whispered, mouth close to hers. "Regardless?"

No trouble telling him now. "Yes, I do. I love you." And she completed the distance between them, clung with both arms round his neck, fell into his kiss with all her heart.

This was the right place, this was where she belonged. Nirvana.

A word about the author...

Elisabeth Rose lives in Australia's capital, Canberra. She completed a performance degree on clarinet, travelled Europe with her musician husband, and returned to Canberra to raise two children.

She teaches classes in Tai Chi as well as teaching and playing clarinet. Reading has been a lifelong love, writing romance a more recent delight.

Elizabeth has eight other releases as well as two so far with The Wild Rose Press, Inc.

Thank you for purchasing
this publication of The Wild Rose Press, Inc.
For other wonderful stories of romance,
please visit our on-line bookstore at
www.thewildrosepress.com.

For questions or more information
contact us at
info@thewildrosepress.com.

The Wild Rose Press, Inc.
www.thewildrosepress.com

To visit with authors of
The Wild Rose Press, Inc.
join our yahoo loop at
http://groups.yahoo.com/group/thewildrosepress/

www.ingramcontent.com/pod-product-compliance
Lightning Source LLC
Chambersburg PA
CBHW070319260626
47160CB00003B/891